SU-LIN'S
Super Awesome
CASUAL
Dating Plan

Cover Design by Melissa Williams Design

Lights: Adobestock

Shoes: Freepik/Adobe Stock

Dress: Minimole Studio/Adobe Stock

Hanger: Dece/Adobe Stock

Published by Garden Ninja Books

ExtraSeriesBooks.com

First Edition: September 2020

0 9 8 7 6 5 4 3 2 1

SU-LIN'S *Super Awesome* CASUAL *Dating Plan*

THE EXTRA SERIES *Book 10*

MEGAN WALKER & JANCI PATTERSON

For Anh Ly,
a Super Awesome friend

ONE

Su-Lin

At my sister Mei-Ling's wedding reception, the hotel ballroom is draped in twinkling crystal and shades of cream and blush, with red accents at every table and double happiness symbols etched in gold on the napkin rings. All perfectly chic. Well, perfect if you're Mei-Ling and you want a wedding that looks like it emerged fully formed from some "Modern Chinese-American Weddings" Pinterest page.

I think it could use a little character, personally. A little fun. But the first thing my sister did after asking me to be her maid of honor was to hand me a list of things I am not to do at her wedding. Number one on this list: "Anything that fits Su-Lin's definition of fun."

I should be insulted; after all, I was the one who introduced Mei-Ling to her now-husband, Wes Chen. I practically made this wedding happen. If I want to perform the maid of honor speech with my Ruby Van Raspberry sock puppet and cap it off with a mic drop, I should be allowed to. *Begged* to, even.

Numbers two, three, and four on the list:

2. No sock puppets.

3. No speaking in accents from your YouTube show or anywhere else.

4. No mic drops.

My sister knows me all too well.

But I'm not insulted. I know her pretty well, too, and it's not that she doesn't love me or my "definition of fun." She's just kind of anal about things sometimes, and her wedding being *Modern Bride*-pristine is one of those things. I can support that.

And so far, so good. The outdoor wedding ceremony went perfectly—not a single drop of rain despite Mei-Ling's panic last night that LA would somehow be deluged in a Biblical-level rainstorm. The tea ceremony was traditional and sweet and kind of boring, which is pretty much what my sister wanted. My sock puppet (and accent and mic drop)-lacking speech seemed to hit the right notes of saccharine and snooze, and the audience ate it right up.

Not that I actually spent much of the day mentally present for any of this (speech included). An actual transcript of my brain today would look something like this:

Su-Lin's Brain at the wedding ceremony: Wow, Brendan looks super hot in a suit.

Su-Lin's Brain at the tea ceremony: Yep, still hot in that suit.

Su-Lin's Brain while giving her big speech: How does he look even hotter now than earlier today, wearing that same suit? Ha, I could make a birthday suit joke in this speech. Auntie's head would explode. And maybe Mei-Ling's. I shouldn't do that to my sister on her wedding day.

Su-Lin's Brain during speech, part two: It's too bad I couldn't make that joke. Brendan would have thought it was both super cheesy and hilarious. Also, I bet Brendan looks even hotter in his birthday suit.

Su-Lin's Brain, right now: I probably shouldn't spend so much time thinking about my best friend naked, even if he is my wedding date.

In an effort to take my brain's advice, I decide to peel my gaze away from said best friend, who is currently standing at the edge of the ballroom, looking at something my little sister Lan is showing him on her phone. (Lan also got a list, and number one on hers was "No cell phone." Lan's fifteen, though, and probably needs an actual phone-from-hand detachment surgery before she could comply with that.)

Before I manage to turn away, Brendan looks up and meets my eyes. He smiles that incredible smile of his, and I flush all over. Is it just in my head, or does that smile seem to contain a little something *extra* today?

I smile back and give him a little wave. His grin widens, and he runs a hand through his bright pink hair—not a look that all guys can pull off, but he sure as hell can. I finally listen to my brain and walk over to Mei-Ling before my best friend can read in my expression all the thoughts I've had today about him pulling off all sorts of things.

Like my clothes, for instance.

Okay, that's enough, Su-Lin. You've only had two glasses of champagne. Keep it together.

Mei-Ling gives me a big hug when I reach her. She smells amazing, like lilies and citrus. "Thank you for the speech," she says. "And for everything. I would have panicked today without you. You're the best sister ever."

"Don't tell Lan."

She rolls her eyes. "Do you honestly think Lan would stop looking at her phone long enough to hear anything I said?"

I laugh. "Good point. Anyway, I accept your Best Sister Award—"

"—I didn't say anything about an award, there's no actual—"

"—I accept it," I continue, breezing over her, "and any cash prizes that may come with it, because I clearly made the world's most perfect match." I tip my champagne glass toward Wes, who also looks quite handsome in his suit, though not Brendan-level hot. Probably Mei-Ling would disagree with that last bit. It wouldn't be the first time she was wrong.

Mei-Ling smiles over at her husband, her cheeks blushing a lovely pink. We both have our dad's blue-black hair, but

Mei-Ling's skin resembles a porcelain doll, while mine is what my aunt Alice calls a "peasant tan." Even though she's only an inch taller than me, Mei-Ling has always had this classic, statuesque beauty. An elegant sense of grace that I lack, apparently, if I listen to Auntie Alice, or, you know, consult a mirror.

"It is a wonderful match," Mei-Ling agrees. "Though perhaps the world's most perfect might apply to you and a certain friend of yours who hasn't been able to take his eyes off you all day."

I feel a tingle of happiness all the way to my toes, despite the fact that my toes have lost sensation hours ago in these ridiculous heels.

"Really? You think so?" It takes everything in me not to turn around and see if he's looking at me right now.

"I know so. I practically had to vault over the sexual tension between you two on the way to the altar. Why is it again that you two keep pretending you're just friends?"

"We're not pretending," I say sadly, the intrusion of reality popping the bubble of my daydreamy bliss. (List items number five and six: No bubbles. No balloons—this is not a children's party.) "And you know why."

As do I, all too well. Brendan's panic disorder is a real thing, a mental health issue he's struggled with since he was a kid. And it's not like four months of hanging out with me have erased the fallout from the totally shitty, emotionally damaging marriage to his high school girlfriend, now ex-wife. Being twenty-five and already having gone through a divorce is enough to mess anyone up, but someone with Brendan's issues . . . He starts to hyperventilate just thinking about dating again.

Mei-Ling squeezes my arm and smiles. "If things end up changing between the two of you, then I think I win the Best Sister Award for picking out that dress you're in."

She's not wrong. The advantage of having a sister who embodies elegance and class is that my bridesmaid dress isn't some hideous, Goodwill-bound mess of tulle. (Though, admittedly, I thought it might be fun to wear the most tacky bridesmaid dress ever.) My knee-length satin dress is burgundy and form-fitting and somehow makes my form actually look like something that deserves to be shown off.

If I could walk in these heels like a normal human woman, I might even approach "sexy." For a girl whose primary descriptor is "cute" or maybe "goofy," that's a pretty awesome leap.

"Look at my beautiful girls," my dad says, walking up to us with an Old Fashioned in hand. That drink—or the fact that it's, like, his third—may be the only reason he's up and walking around. Dad claims his knees are bad, but he can walk just fine. He just prefers sitting down, and when he's home, which is most of the time, he stays attached to his old, ragged armchair like Lan does to her phone. (Dad's list number one: The armchair stays home.)

I don't remember it being that way before Mom left.

"Hi, Daddy," Mei-Ling says. "I know you didn't like the idea of the jazz quartet for the reception, but aren't they fantastic?"

"You are right, as usual," Dad says. I make a face at him that Mei-Ling can't see, and he tries not to laugh. Dad agrees with me that things are more fun when they're actually, you know, *fun*. He suggested it be a karaoke reception—Dad loves singing karaoke, particularly anything by Sinatra or Coolio.

When he got his list with rule number two, no karaoke, I could tell he was a little sad. I was too. Dad's actually a great performer, even from the confines of his armchair. I assured him that whenever I get married, Dad can belt out "Gangsta's Paradise" to his heart's content.

"They were actually Wes's choice," Mei-Ling says, beaming over at her husband, who's being talked to by my adorable-but-senile grandma.

"Ah," Dad says, nodding. "Well, he is a wise and discerning fellow with excellent taste, that Wes. Especially in picking a bride."

Dad's laying it on a bit thick—he likes Wes well enough but finds him too strait-laced and serious. Which makes him a great fit for Mei-Ling, in my opinion. But what Dad really loves about Wes is that he's Chinese. Dad's big on his girls dating, and thus eventually marrying, Chinese guys.

Brendan is definitely not Chinese. Dad loves Brendan, but as my best friend and business partner. I'm not sure what he'd think about me dating him—if that ever happened.

Brendan didn't say he would definitely never date again. Just that he wasn't sure if he'd ever be ready to or when. He also never actually said that he'd want to date *me*, so it might be a moot point.

My palms feel sweaty.

Dad asks Mei-Ling to dance, and I take that moment to head toward Brendan, who is no longer talking with Lan and looks like he's wishing he could disappear into the wallpaper. He's also got social anxiety, and I worried that spending a whole day with my family and their friends would be stressful for him, but he's done really well. Now, though, I can see it wearing on him.

He smiles when he sees me approaching, which does nothing to make my palms less sweaty, but does make me feel all warm and happy inside.

"How're you holding up?" I ask.

"Pretty good now," he says.

"Because Lan has given up making you look through some celebrity Instagram feed, or because I'm here?"

His blue eyes get a little sparkle in them. "I'm going with both. I don't know why Lan thinks I need to see thirty pictures of Khloe Kardashian's lunch. I'm one kale salad and cocktail pic away from an existential crisis."

I laugh, and his smile widens.

"But," he continues, toying with the glass in his hand, "you being here is always the best."

A blush creeps up my cheeks. Brendan and I flirt with each other all the time; that's always been part of our friendship. Something's felt different the last couple days, though. I'm not sure if there's been some actual shift, or if I'm hallucinating it after four months of longing.

I open my mouth, possibly to outright ask him—sometimes I'm not sure what I'm going to say until the words tumble out—but a woman's voice from behind me cuts in. "Su-Lin, have you seen Derek?"

I turn to find my grandma standing there, a tiny woman who has shrunk several inches in the last few years. She's been looking for Derek all night.

"No, remember, Grandma?" I say. "He couldn't make it."

Her face falls, and her eyes flick to Brendan, which is the exact moment when I realize I forgot to warn Brendan about—

"That's too bad," Grandma says. "I was just thinking I'd introduce him to your friend. What was your name again, dear?"

"Brendan," he says, his eyes widening like a deer in headlights. Or a Brendan who's being talked at by someone he doesn't know. Same difference. Not nearly as wide, though, as the first time we met, when I babbled at him about his highly recommended video editing skills for about three minutes straight, and he stared at me like I materialized out of thin air for the express purpose of giving him a heart attack.

I realize too late that I've gotten sidetracked when I should have been heading off what Grandma's about to say next. "Derek is such a nice boy," she continues. "He's a homosexual, you know."

I smile, and Brendan looks confused. "I—I don't think I've met—"

Okay, now I'm not interrupting Grandma because I think this is funny.

"A lot of the kids are, nowadays," Grandma says. "But I think you two would get along."

Brendan finally gets what's happening and opens his mouth, but nothing comes out.

"I think a lot of people have always been gay, Grandma," I say. "And Derek's married, remember?"

"Also, I'm not gay." Brendan gives me a little mock-glare

for not sparing him from the Grandma matchmaking ambush.

"Oh, dear," she says. "I do wish Derek would call. I never know what's happening in his life."

I know for a fact that Derek calls her once a week, and yet she'd probably try to set him up with his own husband at this very wedding, if the two of them weren't off on some "spiritual journey" in Australia that seems to involve lots of scuba diving and high-end shopping.

Grandma spots some other cousin and shuffles off, and Brendan shakes his head at me. "You knew what she was going to say."

Brendan gets mistaken for being gay a lot, because of the pink hair. He'd never admit it, but I'm pretty sure he encourages it so that he doesn't get hit on by girls and sent into panic attacks.

"I did. But I'm incapable of saving you from social embarrassment when it happens to amuse me."

Brendan smiles. He knows I'd never set him up for something he couldn't handle, and after four months of being more or less joined at the hip, I have a pretty good sense of where that line is.

His blue eyes hold mine for an extra long moment. I wet my lips, which suddenly feel too dry. Maybe I should get another drink.

"You know," he says, his gaze dropping to his shoes. "I still haven't gotten that dance you promised me. We need to show off those new moves of yours." He looks back up. Is that a hint of nervousness in his expression?

He's never nervous around me, not since that very first day. Something is definitely different.

My pulse feels thready, remembering how it felt to be in his arms a couple days ago in our attic studio, when I told him I was worried about having to dance at the wedding. He offered to show me how to dance—a skill I've never possessed.

But with Brendan as a teacher . . . The memory makes me a little breathless.

"The world should definitely not be denied these new moves of mine." I take his hand as he leads me to the dance floor, just as the jazz band starts in on Etta James's "At Last."

I see Mei-Ling grinning at me triumphantly, as if she was somehow involved with timing.

Brendan's arm is around my waist, one hand at my lower back, his other hand clasped with mine. He guides me through the steps, as I try not to count out loud or step on his toes or bob my head like a chicken. Brendan's good at leading, though, and doesn't criticize, and it's not long before I don't have to try. We're just dancing, and I fit perfectly against him. (One advantage of these awful torture-heels is the extra three inches of height they give me—which now makes him three inches *less* than a full foot taller than me.)

God, this feels so good.

The thing about Brendan is, he's not only my best friend, he's my Desert Island Person—you know, like if I had to pick one person to be marooned with on a desert island for the rest of my life. My DIP. (Did I make that up? Should I trademark it?)

That's saying something, because I've actually been on a desert island when I was on *Starving with the Stars*—so I know the helpfulness of being able to construct decent shelter out of, like, sticks and rat guts or starting a fire with nothing but sand and soggy kelp. I'm pretty sure Brendan would suck at all that as much as I did, but I'd pick him anyway, even over my main celebrity crush Daveed Diggs. Who I also think would probably suck at harpooning dinner eel, but could entertain me by performing all of *Hamilton* in his Lafayette accent while wearing a coconut bra.

Come to think of it, I bet Brendan could do that, too. The thought makes me giggle to myself. Or maybe not so much to myself, because Brendan raises an eyebrow.

"I wonder why the coconut bra is a thing," I muse.

He groans. "Are you thinking about Daveed Diggs again? Why *is* he always wearing a coconut bra in your head?"

"No, I don't mean why it's a thing for *me*." Though that's

probably a good question in and of itself. "I mean, like, in general. It would be super scratchy. And I can't imagine it provides much in the way of support."

"Hmm. Probably not." He reflects on this. "Maybe it's the equivalent of a boob job. Makes them seem bigger? And . . . roughly textured?"

I laugh. "Sexy, right? Who doesn't want to feel those up?" I look down at my own chest, which isn't exactly the Kansas plains but definitely not the Rockies, either. Though this dress does cling to them nicely, and the keyhole neckline actually manages to show them off, such as they are. I'd be lying if I said I didn't hope Brendan would notice. "Bigger, though . . . I could use *that*."

His gaze drops to my chest, then quickly away. "Come on. Your coconuts are great the way they are." He gives me a side-eye smile, and a flush of heat goes through me.

Is this still just our normal flirting? My heart is racing, and as badly as this conversation could turn out, I have to know if I have any chance, or if I should be burying these feelings along with my angst about my absentee mom and the memory of the love poem I wrote in high school and immediately sent to Chris Pine (who would also look good in a coconut bra).

There's only one way to find out. I steel myself, something that's somehow easier with his arm around me and the weight of his hand in mind. "So, I probably shouldn't be asking this so soon after talking about my boobs . . ."

Seriously, Su-Lin? Is that the way to start this conversation?

Now both his eyebrows are raised.

Too late now. Full speed ahead.

"But, um," I continue, "just in the interest of checking in on things . . ."

"If there's something you want to ask me, you can just say it," he says, though he knows full well my need to preface potentially uncomfortable questions in super awkward ways.

"Right. Okay." I let out a breath. "I just wondered if you're feeling like you might be ready to date. In general, I mean."

He blinks a little rapidly and his shoulder tenses up, and I'm pretty sure I'm about to get rejected again, like that first time we went to lunch to talk about the business. I called it a date, and he had to break it to me that he never ever dates and maybe never will.

But then he lets out his own breath and smiles hesitantly.

"Yeah," he says, so softly I have to strain to hear it. "Yeah, I'm definitely getting there."

I chew on the inside of my cheek, trying to keep from breaking out into a full-on victory cheer. After all, him feeling like he might be able to date doesn't *necessarily* help me.

"Are you thinking about asking out anyone in particular?" I ask cautiously.

"Well, there is this one really awesome girl," he says, and the flirtatious spark in his eyes makes my heart flutter. "She's beautiful and funny and crazy, and I know she was into me when we first met. I was thinking about seeing if that's still a possibility."

I feel like I'm floating, higher and higher with every word. He does like me as more than a friend. He does want to date me.

"She sounds pretty great." I'm trying to keep my tone all coy and nonchalant, but I'm excitedly bouncing on the balls of my feet again, which isn't great for nonchalant or dancing.

"Yeah." The look he gives me is both soft and full of heat. "She is."

My breath catches, and for a horrible second, I'm sure this is too good to be true. "It's me, right? Is it me?"

Brendan laughs and pulls me closer, guiding me in circles. "Yes, it's you. You're the only one who could make me want to date again. But . . ."

But? My floating pauses, my stomach lurching a bit.

There's some sadness in his smile. "Wanting to and being able to jump into something without my chest feeling like an alien is about to burst out of it are two very different things."

I rest my head on his shoulder. I still feel like bouncing just knowing he *wants* to be with me.

"I'm sorry," he says. "The idea of a—a *relationship*, it's . . ." I look back up at him, and he seems paler at even having said that word. "I can't leap into anything serious like that, I just . . ."

I can see that he's frustrated—with himself, with his panic disorder. Hopefully also with his horrible ex-wife who must still have some hold on him despite cheating on him for years and generally being awful to him.

"I want to," he says, and I can tell he means it. "I really want to. But I don't know if I can."

"Okay," I say, and we dance in silence for a bit, while my brain tries to pull together what this means and what to do about it. This moment feels tenuous, like if I say the wrong thing, I'll be friend-zoned forever. Or worse, lose him entirely. "What if we dated . . . casually?"

Brendan's head tilts. "You and me," he says skeptically. "*Casual.*"

I hope he means it like I think he does—that anything that happened between us would be heavy and serious. People usually assume I'm not capable of being serious about anything, but Brendan knows otherwise.

If it's that or nothing, though . . . "Yes! Casual. We can date other people." I really don't love this aspect, but this would make things between us seem less serious (no matter how serious I—and him too, right?—want to be). But a plan is forming in my mind as I speak. "That way, you don't have to worry about the pressure of a relationship. It's just fun. Baby steps. A warm up."

His brow furrows. "Dating other people? I don't know, Su-Lin, I don't love *talking* to other people as a general rule, let alone trying to *date* them."

"Look." I squeeze his hand, the one he's guiding me around the dance floor with. "We've got this convention in a couple days." We're premiering our new sock-puppet show at YouCon, a convention for YouTubers over the next week. Getting ready for that and Mei-Ling's wedding days apart has been a whirlwind.

"It's the perfect place to meet new people, and I'll be there to hold your hand through it—metaphorically speaking, mostly, but you know, if we're dating too, then sometimes literally. Though probably not when you're on a date with some other girl—" I shake my head, trying to get back on track. "If you can get comfortable with casual dating, then maybe all the relationship stuff won't seem so . . . scary."

He hesitates, but he looks like he's considering it. "Okay," he says slowly. "But I don't want to lead a bunch of girls on."

"People aren't looking for permanent relationships at a convention. A lot of people will be from out of town anyway. It's the most casual environment in the world. People are mostly just looking to hook up."

Brendan goes pale again, and I blurt the next bit out so fast I'm almost shouting. "Not that you need to hook up with anyone!" I really really don't want him to, though I know that if we're not seriously dating, I don't get a say. But I don't hate that he seems terrified by that idea, at least. "We can just chill with other people at the dances and go to lunch and be . . . casual."

Brendan blinks at me, and the expression on his face is almost as wide-eyed as when I first met him. His lips press together, then he squeezes my hand back. "This sounds crazy. You know that, right?" But he's starting to smile again.

I smile back at him. "Yeah, but the best Su-Lin plans usually do. And I have a strong feeling about this."

I bite my lip, worried he might dismiss the idea entirely, that it might not be worth it to him, even if it could lead to us being together. The con was already going to be tough for him—lots of socializing and networking and meet and greets. Dating is probably the last thing he wants to add to the mix.

"Okay," he says, and the smile stretches wider. He leans in so close our foreheads are almost touching. His eyes are so blue and his breath warm against my cheeks. "I'm in."

The song has stopped, and my feet are killing me, but I don't want to pull away, don't want to let go. His eyes flick down to my lips, and I think he's going to kiss me. I glance to the side just enough to see Mei-Ling beaming at us and my dad's eyebrows drawing together in a concerned expression.

"Um," I whisper. Brendan follows my gaze and winces.

I'm not ready for this moment to end, especially not in a panic attack. "Any chance you want to kiss me, but not in front of my whole family and a sizable portion of LA's Chinese population?"

His attention snaps back to me, and he sounds breathless. "Yes. To both."

"Follow me." I waggle my eyebrows in what might look suggestive or might look insane.

Right now, I don't care. Because we're walking quickly, getting out of the ballroom and away from all those eyes, and we're both laughing, and I think maybe he's feeling as happy as I am.

TWO

Brendan

Su-Lin and I stumble out of the ballroom and into the carpeted hotel hallway, and I reach for her hand. I've only had a glass of champagne, and it's not the alcohol making my thoughts swirl like I'm on one of those spinning rides at Six Flags that goes around and around and around. Like those rides, I'm at once having the time of my life and feeling vaguely nauseous, but I'm ready to ride this as long as I can, and I have no intention of getting off.

Um.

I'm just giddy enough to say that sentence out loud to Su-Lin in all of its suggestive glory—which I know will make her giggle, and I'd include a post-script about how I certainly wouldn't *mind* getting off, as it were, which I hope she'd know I mostly mean in jest . . . *mostly*—when a man's voice calls from down the hall.

"Su-Lin! My favorite cousin!"

"Tate!" Su-Lin spins around but doesn't let go of my hand. She's clinging to it like she thinks if she lets go I might run away, which I suppose is fair.

I don't feel like running now, though. The prospect of kissing her after four months of desperate wishing makes my lips tingle and my blood rush. I look over my shoulder to see her cousin Tate approaching. I've never met him, but I remember her saying he just moved back to LA from the Bay Area. He's a tall-ish guy with his hair shaved close on one side of his head and falling long over his eye on the other. But hey. I'm not in a position to judge weird hair.

Su-Lin moves to hug him, but keeps tight hold of my hand—god, how nervous is she that I'm going to bail?—so she's limited to a side-hug. "Grandma keeps asking where your brother is," she tells him.

Tate rolls his eyes but grins. "I know. I just danced with her, and Derek was all she could talk about. He's always been the favorite. Though she mentioned seeing you on *Ellen*, too, so it looks like you're gaining ground."

Su-Lin was on *Ellen* six years ago, which sounds like about the right time frame if Grandma doesn't know cousin Derek is married. I'm a little alarmed that I know who all these people are and roughly what's been going on in their lives, but I do listen to Su-Lin chatter for an average of, like, ten hours a day, and like the pathetic, lovesick fool that I am, I remember just about every word.

Su-Lin laughs. "Maybe. But I think you're still coming in second for favorite grandchild. I'm down somewhere below Mei-Ling."

"Nah," Tate says. "Not since you got her that phone with the enormous numbers so she can actually make phone calls." He sticks his hand out toward me, and Su-Lin is forced to break her grip on mine so I can shake it. "Hey, I'm Tate."

"Brendan Pike." I fidget, a nervous thing I do whenever I meet someone. Su-Lin gives me a comforting smile. She's noticed—of course she has. She's also around me for more than half of her waking hours, and she knows I'm not great with new people.

"Nice hair, man," Tate says. "What made you go with that color?"

Ah yes. The hair. Something I can talk about like a competent person. "Thanks," I say.

"Tate's done some pretty bright hair streaks in the past," Su-Lin says. "He used to date my friend Emily, and she said he was the only guy she'd ever think was hot with frosted tips."

I laugh, but it sounds awkward, especially to me. I know perfectly well that Tate and Emily—who now does our social media—used to date, so Su-Lin's not saying that for my benefit. Su-Lin has been crowing about having set up her sister with her brand-new husband, and given her question for me, she clearly has dating on the brain.

Tate looks fond at the mention of Emily, and I wonder if he realizes Su-Lin is about to pull him into one of her crazy schemes. If he goes along with it, I guess I can't blame him. Not after what I just agreed to.

My brain falls back on the concept of dating other people—which I had quickly buried under the prospect of kissing Su-Lin, *my* Su-Lin, the girl who lights my life up like a thousand-watt bulb—and stutters there.

That's when I realize that they're both staring at me, waiting for me to respond to his comment on my hair.

"Um." I cringe. So much for being competent with this subject—which is the main reason I keep my hair pink after all these years. It basically guarantees that the first topic of any new conversation will be one I've already got an answer to. Though apparently not when I'm fantasizing about putting my tongue in my best friend's mouth. "I actually lost a bet with a friend years ago. Joke's on him, though, because I liked it, so I just keep dyeing it."

Tate grins. "Sweet. You two work together, yeah? My mom says you're putting out a new show. Another season of *Real Sockwives*?"

Su-Lin's Aunt Alice is his mom, who I have met a couple times, and who I regularly want to punch for her constant droning about how great her sons are, and how much better they are at everything than everyone else in the family, and how maybe Su-Lin and her sisters could be as great as them if they'd been raised with a firmer hand. Or a mom.

Yep. Still want to punch her. But Tate seems cool enough, even if he's keeping me from kissing the girl I've been dreaming about since the day we met on the one night that the idea of making a move doesn't make me feel like I'm going into cardiac arrest.

What can I say? Dancing with her feels *so* damn good.

"Sort of," Su-Lin says, apparently better able to focus than I currently am, what with all my blood settling . . . elsewhere. "Brendan and I are doing a total revamp of the show. Some of the same characters—still sock puppets, of course—"

"Of course," Tate says, with a hint of amusement. He better not be mocking her. Maybe we should just tell him we're busy and go . . .

What? Make out in my car? Get a room in this hotel? Where the hell *were* we going to go?

"—but with sketches that parody lots of different shows. You know, *Sockton Abbey, Socks and the City. Sock and Order*, because we needed a courtroom drama—that was all Brendan, he's a genius—and we're actually premiering the first episode at YouCon in a couple days, and hey, you're in sound-mixing or something, yeah?"

Tate doesn't even blink at all of that, which tells me he knows his cousin pretty well.

"Yep," Tate says. "I actually moved back to get into doing some sound work for TV or film. It hasn't been easy. You really have to know people."

"You should join us at the con!" Su-Lin bounces with excitement, the kind she gets when she has a new Plan.

Su-Lin Plans are always insane, and they also almost always work, which does not discourage her. Or me, apparently.

God, did I really agree to *date*? People who are *not* her?

"Yeah?" Tate asks.

"Yes." Su-Lin nods firmly. "We could use some extra help at

the booth, and I can introduce you to lots of YouTubers, some of whom need a good sound guy. You could probably make decent money just with them, but it'd give you a good lead into more traditional TV or film."

Su-Lin is sounding even more Su-Lin-like than normal, and I reach for her hand again. I don't think I'm the only one who's all wound up from our dancing. We've been flirting and hanging all over each other and passing innuendos back and forth for four months, and now we've just talked about crossing over that line, the one that makes my chest tight now just thinking about it but also somehow makes my heart feel *so good*—

Tate looks impressed. "Actually, that could be awesome."

"And, you know, Emily will be at the booth, too."

I can't help but smile and shake my head at her. She smiles back and squeezes my hand, and I'm a little proud that I knew exactly what she was up to.

"Really?" Tate looks down at the floor briefly. "How's she been?"

"Great," I say. "She's our new social media maven, and she's fantastic. I'm sure she'd be happy to see you again."

"Yeah, it'd be good to see her, too." He purses his lips and then nods. "Awesome, I'm in. Thanks, Cuz, you're the best."

Su-Lin bounces up and down again. *She* certainly thinks she is, and to be fair, so do I.

"Always happy to help family," she says, grinning widely.

Then Tate turns and, blessedly, walks away toward the ballroom. *Finally.*

I pull her against me. "You really think Emily will appreciate how happy you are to help family?"

She gives me her I'm-so-innocent face, which she is most definitely not. "I'm sure I don't know what you mean, sir," she says in her haughty *Sockton Abbey* accent.

"Uh-huh," I say, wrapping an arm around her waist. "So you're going to pretend you're not helping Tate's career just so you can play matchmaker with him and Emily."

Her mouth falls open in mock offense. "You wound me."

I laugh. "I know you. Also, for all your many amazing talents, subtlety is not one of them."

She bites her lip, then breaks into a grin. "Okay, fine. You win. But look—I made all this happen." She gestures back to the ballroom. "I have a *gift*. Who am I to deny my friends love?"

My pulse races. I want to read all kinds of things into that statement—and turn it around on her and tell her I'm hoping she won't deny it to me. But I bite my tongue. Telling her how in love with her I am is the opposite of casual, and I can't give her more right now without sending myself into a full-blown coma.

"That logic seems iron-clad," I say, though her eyes flash, and I'm sure she noticed the direction my thoughts were going. "Except, didn't Emily and Tate already date once? And break up?"

"Yeah, but I don't think they gave it a real chance. I have a strong feeling about this plan, too. I think they'd be really good together. Did you see the look on his face when he asked about Emily?"

"I saw. And I should know better than to doubt your strong feelings."

"Mmmm," Su-Lin says, pulling closer. "I'm having a few of those right now."

I eye the ballroom doors, out of which Su-Lin's dad—who was definitely plotting to kill me when he saw me cozying up to his daughter on the dance floor—might burst at any moment. He's not a scary man, but he has definite opinions about his daughters dating white boys, and I have serious father issues at the best of times. I think part of it comes from not growing up with a dad at home. I don't really know how to act around them. "Is this where you had in mind?"

She breaks into a grin and pulls me by the hand. "Nope. Come with me."

My heart pounds as she pulls me down the hall, past gilded mirrors and landscape paintings in shiny gold frames, to a door. Marked "Women's Bathroom."

"No," I say. "I will pay for a room before we have our first kiss in a *bathroom*."

Su-Lin wags her finger at me. "At least see it first." She pulls me inside—

Damn. I have never seen a bathroom like this one. It's carpeted, for one, and the door opens into a sitting area with plush couches and a fuzzy rug. Along one wall runs a marble counter top covered in cosmetics and hair dryers and curling irons and other accoutrements I assume Mei-Ling was using to freshen up before the reception. Her post-reception outfit is hanging from a hook next to the mirror, which doesn't have a single spot. In fact, the whole place is pristine, from the shining counter to the gleaming doorknobs on the opposite door that I assume must lead to a room with an actual toilet.

"Does this meet your requirements, good sir?" Su-Lin asks.

"Um, yeah," I say. "Yeah, this'll do."

Su-Lin locks the door. I turn toward her and she toward me, and suddenly she's in my arms, even closer than when we were dancing. And I'm flashing back to yesterday in the studio in Su-Lin's attic, where I played slow music on my laptop and taught her how to dance—more how to follow my lead, since I had to learn to dance for my wedding five years ago—and she laid her head on my shoulder and my whole body hummed with this perfect happiness.

That's when I'd realized I was getting there. Closer to being able to make a move—though I don't hate that she beat me to it. I'd been working toward this since we met, just praying that she'd still be single and still want me when I finally worked myself up to being able to think about dating without passing out. Even though I knew I had no right to expect her to wait for me.

I thought it would take a lot longer than four months.

Su-Lin looks up at me with this expectant grin on her face, and I can't help mirroring it back. I knew she was into me when we first met. Partly because she called me "Kung Pao

Pancakes"—which is apparently my spirit dish at Fong's All-American, this awesome restaurant where she used to work—and said my hair was hot, and partly because she called our lunch business meeting a date and then looked pretty crushed when I told her I couldn't date anyone. It took me a good hour or two of that date to get the words out, crushed as I was myself about not being capable of giving this sexy, vivacious, amazing girl a chance.

The idea that she still wants me, that she's willing to put up with my nonsense and the stupid games I have to play with my own head just to be a functional human being . . . I'd been so sure that once she realized what a mess I am, she'd feel like she dodged a bullet.

But here she is.

I run my hand along her jaw and bend down to kiss her. My eyes close as our lips meet.

Even after the hundreds of times I've dreamt this moment, I'm not prepared for the rush. My head feels light and my body heavy and we both lean into it instinctively. The kiss deepens almost instantly. Our mouths are open and our hands roaming and it feels even better than I always imagined.

I push her back against the door, and we're kissing frantically, like we need to make up for lost time. Her arms snake around my waist and up underneath the back of my suitcoat, which I shrug off.

Oh, shit.

Su-Lin's hands run up my arms, and then her eyes pop open and she stares at my shirt—which happens to have no sleeves, like a combination white collared shirt and wife-beater.

"Whaaaaaat," she says.

I grin sheepishly. "So there's a story."

She grabs me by my collar and pulls me closer, speaking against my lips. "I clearly need to hear this story, but I also want to devour you."

Oh *god*. Parts of my body are standing fully at attention and poking against her, and she has to notice. For a split second,

I'm worried she's going to be disgusted. With as much as we flirt, I've been pretty careful these last months to keep her from knowing exactly how much I want her.

But instead of pulling away, she settles closer into my arms, her fingers stroking the back of my neck. "Story first," she says, grinning wickedly.

I groan and scoop her up and deposit her on the polished marble counter, narrowly missing the pile of Mei-Ling's cosmetics. Mei-Ling has the same lip-liner that Candace used to leave on the edge of the sink that I was constantly knocking off when I went to brush my teeth—and I *really* do not want to be thinking about my ex right now.

But this story unfortunately involves her.

"I'm waiting," Su-Lin says, but her voice has a breathless quality to it, and I'm pretty sure what she's waiting for is to finish teasing me before she pounces on me. She wraps her legs around me and puts on her innocent face again.

I stumble over my words a bit before bending down and kissing her neck.

Am I really going to tell her this story while shamelessly making out with her?

Apparently I am. "I got married in this suit," I say against her skin. She tenses slightly, and I straighten to look her in the eyes. "Are you sure you want to hear this? Right *now*?"

She grins at me. Not upset that I've brought up my marriage. Noted. "If it explains why you're wearing this shirt with a suit— or at *all*—then I definitely do."

"So the night before the wedding, John and Justin threw me a bachelor party."

Su-Lin's eyes narrow, like they always do when I mention those guys. I think she might hate John more than I do for sleeping with my ex throughout the entire time she and I were together. Though for some reason I've always been madder at Justin for knowing about it the whole time and never telling me. He could have saved me a lot of pain . . . except I'm not confident I would have been self-respecting enough to leave her even then.

"And Candace made them promise no strippers, which was fine by me, but they decided to ignore her."

"Nice," Su-Lin says sarcastically, though I can tell she's torn between thinking they were dicks for breaking their promise and resenting Candace enough to not want her to get her way.

"But the joke was on them," I continue, "because they accidentally ordered male strippers. So these guys bust in and start dancing and taking off their clothes—" Su-Lin snickers "—and Justin is freaking out, while John is trying to play it off like they meant it as a joke. Like I wouldn't notice that the only reason they wanted strippers was because they wanted a lap dance."

"Did they get one?"

I roll my eyes. "No. But the strippers did get down to their banana hammocks, and one of them left his shirt behind."

Her eyes light up. "No."

"Yes. And then Justin got so drunk he vomited beer and potato chips all over the shirt I was supposed to wear the next day—"

She slaps my bare arm. "Oh my god, are you serious?"

"And that is how I came to get married in a stripper's Chippendale shirt," I say triumphantly.

Su-Lin shakes her head at me. "In the two years you were married and the three years you've been divorced, you couldn't get a new suit? Or at least a new *shirt*?"

I shrug. "I don't have that much reason to need a suit."

"When we make millions on our new show, we need to get you a new one." Su-Lin wraps her arms around my neck and pulls me in close. "Does it freak you out, wearing it again? To a wedding, of all places?"

I consider that. I've been doing a lot of self-talk today to cope with the anxiety of so many people I don't know, many of whom seem to inexplicably know who *I* am. I need to get used to that, especially because once our show launches, it's possible we'll end up doing media circuits and things. Last time Su-Lin ended up on *Ellen*, after all—she's not exaggerating when she says millions. Plural.

But I'm handling it. I've been in therapy on and off since I was three for this exact issue, so I've got the tools, and I know when to bail from a situation before I start to lose it. I haven't been close to that today.

"I don't love wearing it," I say. "But the wedding didn't really bother me. Maybe because I'm here with you."

My heart races. I meant because she's my best friend and I feel so safe with her, not to imply anything about our future because oh god I can't even think about entering into that again. Even the thought makes it difficult to breathe.

But Su-Lin is smiling, her legs wrapping tighter, pulling me up against her, and my blood roars in my ears as we get caught up in each other again. The heat between us is intense, and I can feel the anxiety creeping in the back of my mind, whispering that I'm going to get burned. But her lips are on my throat, and her fingers are unbuttoning my shirt and running down my chest.

I reach for her zipper—

And she giggles. "Careful. I had to tape myself into this thing to keep my boobs in place. It may never come off."

I lean down and kiss the tops of her breasts, and she groans softly and leans back against the mirror.

My body thrums with a pressure that threatens to overwhelm me, and I kiss back up to her neck before I get too involved below. I'm not sure exactly how far she wants this to go, and I've underestimated how difficult it's going to be not to push it further. I started dating my ex at sixteen, and we were together for four years and then married for two more. I've never so much as kissed anyone else—though it occurs to me that didn't seem strange until this moment, because kissing Su-Lin is as natural as breathing, possibly because I've spent so long wanting to. But I haven't just *made out* without going further since I was a kid, and while I know Su-Lin is no saint in the physical department,

I also know she's not into casual sex.

If I could commit to her, that might be something else. I run my mouth along her ear, trying to form the words. That I want this to be as serious as it feels, that I want us to be in a relationship. That I want her to be my—

My chest seizes, and pain shoots through my upper ribcage. I can't breathe. I can't even think that word, let alone say it. Stupid as I know that it is—I *want* all those things, more than I can possibly say, and it's not like I'm actually interested in dating anyone else, so the monogamy isn't a problem. Hell, *one* woman would be more than I've dated since my divorce.

But if there's one thing I've learned in my lifetime of fighting it, it's that you can't argue logic with anxiety. I got used to this much. I can get used to more. Su-Lin's plan is crazy and scary . . . but it makes a twisted kind of sense, which is the only kind of sense my brain is capable of making.

I can do this. Just being able to say I'm ready to date her is progress. And if there's one thing I'm good at doing, it's crazy.

She's worth it to me.

I think Su-Lin can sense that I'm struggling, because she runs her hand down my cheek and pulls back to look at me. I press my forehead to hers, and though I don't want to admit it, I know she's right when she says, "We should be getting back."

I nod. It's her sister's wedding. She can't be gone long. And besides, we're supposed to be keeping this casual. That's hard enough without pushing the physical boundaries after our very first kiss.

I brush my lips against hers, needing one last taste of her before we stop. "Okay," I say. I button my shirt again—twice, because I mismatch the buttons—and Su-Lin tries to make her hair presentable again. It quickly becomes clear that it won't be going back in the immaculate bun it was in, and so we head back to the reception, not exactly full walk-of-shame style, but definitely less put together than we were before.

Mei-Ling gives us a sly look the moment we enter, and it

takes approximately two more seconds for Su-Lin's dad to get out of his chair and stride over to us, faster than a man with bad knees should be able to go. I freeze mid-step, and Su-Lin links her arm through mine, but I still must look terrified when he approaches.

"Brendan," he says. "It's good to see you."

Rationally, I know he's not a scary man. He's a sixty-something armchair-dwelling karaoke-singing dad with a soft heart and happy attitude. But rationally I also know that I'm in love with Su-Lin, and I should be able to ask her to be my word-I-can't-even-think-much-less-say.

I can't argue with anxiety, and dads have been a source of that for me since before I can remember.

"Hey, Mr. Liu," I manage to say.

My voice breaks, and he raises an eyebrow at me. "Brendan. You look . . . *flushed*."

Su-Lin glares at her dad and tightens her grip on my arm as my anxiety spikes through the roof—all twelve stories above us. My chest is tightening like a boa constrictor, and my heart feels like it must have stopped.

Time to bolt. "Excuse me," I say. I twist out of Su-Lin's grasp and retreat back into the hallway, where I sink onto one of the floral loveseats and put my head in my hands, trying to breathe. Su-Lin doesn't follow me immediately, and I'm sure this is because she's having words with her father. She's twenty-four years old and paid for the house he lives in, so it's not as if he can do anything about us seeing each other, even if I'm not Chinese.

He's not the problem. I'm the problem. I squeeze my eyes shut, trying to keep my panic locked away inside and not do something stupid like start crying right here in the hotel hallway.

I've seen a therapist off and on my entire life, and I know she'd tell me to think through what I'm afraid of, pinpoint it so I can talk myself down. This goes way beyond a simple fear of getting hurt again.

I'm afraid of being in a relationship again where all I do is hurt and be hurt.

I'm afraid of becoming the person I was again. I'm afraid that's still who I am.

And most of all, I'm afraid of hurting Su-Lin, who is brightness and joy and doesn't deserve the shit I carry with me on a daily basis.

I've spent the last three years telling myself it's better for everyone if I just never go there, but Su-Lin is everything I could ever want and more, and it's so hard to be near her and not let myself think about what might be, for better or for worse. And even if I should walk away, I don't know that I have the strength to.

I also don't have it in me to be everything she deserves, which leaves us both in an impossible place.

God, maybe I should have told her I wasn't ready and left it at that. But kissing her felt like heaven, and I can't bring myself to regret it.

Baby steps. That's what Su-Lin said. Casual. Warming up. Getting used to the idea. She knows that's exactly what I need. While it feels like I've made a giant leap today, it was really four months' worth of baby steps, building trust, getting used to the idea of ever dating again, and even more terrified by the idea of taking too long and losing her forever.

I can do this. She's worth it.

But I also know not to push myself too far, so I'm not facing her father again today.

THREE

Su-Lin

I t's the day before YouCon officially starts, but the convention center is bustling, with vendors getting their booths set up and the convention employees running around trying to put out fires (not literally—at least not that I've seen). Even with all the chaos today, it's nothing compared to how this place will be the rest of the week, when we're flooded with fans and cosplayers and newbie YouTubers looking to get a leg up. I've gone to YouCon every year since *The Real Sockwives of Los Angeles* got big, back when I was eighteen. Even the years when I wasn't making any new content, I still got invited on panels and did meet and greets, signings, that sort of thing. So I know what to expect.

Brendan claims he does, too. He's done video editing for years, and it's not like he hasn't been to conventions before. But it's different when you're one of the celebs—something he's about to be, what with all the excitement surrounding the launch of our new project, *The Real Sockwives Television Takeover*.

I'm concerned it's going to send him into a panic attack. I've been around for a few of those. He says they feel like he's being chased by a bear. They kind of look like that, too, his breath heavy and his forehead sweaty and not for the kinds of delicious reasons I've been fantasizing about non-stop. Still, if the con gets to be too much, he can escape to the hotel room. And I'll be here the whole time.

Is it bad that I kind of like that having me around seems to help him panic less?

I'm going to go with no. Not bad. I'm his best friend. It's good that my presence helps. Being around him always makes *me* feel better, after all.

Especially since the wedding.

I grin over at him as we haul the last boxes from his car. I've got four boxes stacked on the lone dolly I found in my dad's garage (we probably should have planned better and gotten another one, but too late for that) with my signature Big Gulp perched on top. (Mei-Ling's wedding rule number seven: no Big Gulps. Or soda of any kind. Which was a tragedy of non-caffeinated proportions. Yesterday I told Brendan I'm thinking of starting a new career as a wedding planner for people who want their weddings full of puppets and Big Gulps and bubbles and other fun things, and Brendan agreed that's a niche in the market that is chronically underserved.) Brendan is carrying two more boxes in his arms, around which he's straining to see.

"Just keep walking," I say. "I'll tell you if you're going to run over anyone."

"If only I trusted your word over your desire to see me walk into a concrete pillar." But he obviously does, because he stops shifting the boxes perilously to see over.

"You're probably fine until you see me pull my phone out to film you."

"Noted." He smiles at me, and I'm so caught by the way his eyes crinkle at the corners and his face brightens that I just barely grab his arm in time to keep him from plowing over a vendor setting up a floor display. My Big Gulp nearly topples, but I right it, avoiding the even worse tragedy of losing forty ounces of carefully concocted soda mix.

It's almost as good as the soda mixes Brendan makes when he picks one up for me on the way to my house.

"Thanks," Brendan says, as if it wasn't my distraction that nearly led him to crushing a cardboard stand full of comics. Brendan's smile is quickly becoming my kryptonite. How has it become even more incredible in the last few days?

Probably because I don't have to imagine anymore how good those lips might feel against mine. I know how they feel, and it's amazing. I've never had a kiss before that made my whole body burn—but I sure have a lot of experience with that now, after all the making out we've done in the two days since that wedding night.

It's a good thing we already had most of our work for the con done before the wedding. Because while we technically were in the studio most of that time, well . . .

The memory of his mouth on my neck, of his hands stroking along my breasts under my shirt, of the feel of his chest under my fingers—I'm a little breathless, and not from pulling a dolly loaded with boxes of merch. I'm also finding myself scanning the convention hall for out-of-the-way areas I can pull him into for a repeat of that memory.

I need to focus, and not on jumping Brendan in a crowded convention center.

"So I'm thinking we need a new backdrop for *Sock and Order*," I say, guiding him around the outskirts of a major gamer display—is that PewDiePie's? "We have the courtroom and the police precinct, but we've used the hell out of those. Our detectives need a change of scenery."

"We could make a morgue," he suggests. "Or some alley—like the kind where TV cops always find the dead hooker."

"Ooh! I like the alley!" I bounce in excitement. "We always talked about filming on location, you know."

"*That's* the one you want to do on location? Dead hooker alley?"

I shrug. "There are some very realistic contenders not far from my house. Needles, used condoms, rats picking through old pizza boxes—think of all the set dressing that's already done for us!"

He shakes his head, but is still smiling. "Sounds like a dream come true."

"It'd be awesome." I can already see how we might film it. The camera work is pretty much all Brendan—my initial run of *Real Sockwives* was filmed on my iPhone, which was propped up on my dresser, so clearly I'm not the tech guru here. But he's taught me a ton about lighting and camera angles and filters. Not that we do too much fancy stuff—it's still a sock puppet show, and I don't want it to lose the low-fi feel of the original—but his expertise has definitely taken things up several notches. "Can't you see Detective McGillihooligan and Captain Woodshaft out there, standing over a chalk outline in the shape of a dead sock?"

He laughs and drops into Detective McGillihooligan's atrociously thick Boston accent, like some blenderfied Wahlberg/Affleck. "We got ourselves anothah one, Captain. Yahn spilling out all over the place. Looks like Jack the Seam Rippah is back."

I giggle. Even though Brendan signed on initially for the tech parts of the show, it didn't take long before he was an equal part in the creative process—like, within days. It wasn't too long after that I convinced him to do some of the voice work.

Honestly, I have no idea how I ever did the show without him. It definitely wasn't half as much fun.

"Then," he continues, "the shot pans down, and we see the dead hooker sock. Pierced by crochet hooks."

"Ooh, horrifying *and* punny," I laugh. "Love it. You know, if *Sock and Order* turns out to be of the more popular sketches, we could do a *CSI: Criminal Sock Investigation* spin-off. Really focus on the forensic science of sock puppet murder."

We're both laughing probably more than is warranted. I'm so happy when we're like this, lost in our own world, talking and laughing about everything and anything.

This annoying thought intrudes on my happiness, though: were things ever like this between him and Candace? In between all the awful things she did to him, did she make him feel purely happy like this?

I didn't used to wonder this very much, before. He'd told me how bad his marriage was, how it contributed to his pre-existing panic disorder now being triggered by dating and relationship stuff. So I'd always thought of her as the villain, Maleficent horns sprouting from her pretty blond head (his mom showed me a picture once, and she's definitely pretty and blond. No horns, though. But his mom agreed that they were probably invisible.)

It couldn't have been all bad, though, right? He really loved her; he must have, for her betrayal to have affected him so deeply.

Does he still occasionally think back on those times and wish he could be with her?

I push those thoughts firmly away, because they don't do anyone any good, least of all me, and we banter more about the *CSI* idea. Brendan has launched back into his McGillihooligan accent, and I'm being the gruff, no-nonsense Captain Woodshaft, when we reach our booth. I tug at Brendan's shirt before he walks right into it, and then transfer my Big Gulp onto the corner of the booth table before lowering my dolly.

"Oh my god, you guys, do you ever stop?" Emily asks. In addition to being our friend and social media wizard, she's also in charge of running our booth for the week.

"Being brilliant and sexy? Never." I wink over at Brendan, who sets the boxes down and gives me a look that says maybe he wouldn't mind finding some hidden alcove in this convention hall, too. My skin tingles.

"Well at least stop bringing me more shit to set up," she says, eyeing the full dolly. She pulls her dark shoulder-length hair up into a ponytail. "I'm going to be sitting on boxes of t-shirts the whole con just to fit back here. How many did you order?"

"We had our guy make a design for each sketch, and then we had to use them all, in all the sizes. But look how fantastic they are!" I gesture at the blue and white *Socktor Who* t-shirt Brendan's wearing—with the Terrence Clarence character from *Real Sockwives* featured as the Socktor, in front of the shoebox Tardis. Then at my bright pink *Socks and the City* shirt, featuring my fave, Ruby Van Raspberry, sipping a martini through a straw (since, you know, she doesn't have any hands).

Emily rolls her eyes and groans, but she's fighting a smile. "Yeah, okay. I'll figure it out."

"The booth looks great," Brendan says, and I have to agree. Emily took care of getting us big banner displays, which look fantastic vaulted high over the booth. She's got the puppet stars themselves displayed behind her—we don't want people messing with them—flanking either side of a mounted flat screen TV that's going to be playing our show's promo reel on a constant loop that will undoubtedly make Emily want to kill us by the end of the week. On the tables in front of her, she's got stacks of DVDs of the full run of *Real Sockwives*, keychains, postcards with characters both old and new, each featuring one of their best lines. And all those finger puppets of the characters Brendan and I spent weeks making—while also learning that hot-gluing tiny crafts at three AM while not entirely sober is a *really bad idea.*

"Thanks," she says. "Just please tell me that's the last load of stuff."

"It is," I assure her. I spot Brendan eyeing the chaos around us with a bit of a hunted look and step closer to him. "I can help Emily finish up here. You want to bring our stuff up to our room, and I'll join you soon?"

He looks like he might insist on staying to help, but then nods. "Yeah, okay. I've got some editing I can work on." I'm glad he took the out. He's got four highly social days ahead of him and needs to get what down time he can.

Before he goes, I can't keep myself from tugging on his shirt to pull him right up against me. He doesn't resist; he smiles down at me with that look of desire with a touch of wonder—still!—that makes me ache all over. I get up on my tip-toes—no heels today, thank god—and kiss him, and he kisses me back, cupping my face, stroking his thumb along my jaw, making my knees all weak.

"I'll be there soon," I say, still feeling my own sense of wonder about all of this.

Brendan squeezes my hand and grins, and Emily calls out "Bye, Brendan," as he heads off.

She turns to me with a look of shock. "Are you two finally together? I mean, I thought you guys were looking at each other in an even more gooey way than usual, but—wow. That was a *kiss*."

I make an excited squealing sound. "I know, right?"

"Spill it, Liu," she orders, even as she digs into a box and starts pulling out a stack of *Sockton Abbey* shirts. Typical Emily—she's too practical to sit and gossip when there's work to be done. Though she clearly wants the gossip, too, and I'm super happy to have someone to share it with.

I knew Emily back in high school, but we didn't become friends until after. She was a quiet, studious kid who tended to get ultra-focused on whatever computer project or accelerated learning she was working on. Whereas I was a thoroughly mediocre student dealing with the angst of my mom leaving us by rebelling in the lamest ways possible—refusing to read *Beowulf* on the grounds that it promotes animal cruelty (though probably it didn't), and trying to get my fellow students to strike (they definitely didn't). Wearing a fake nose ring. Randomly deciding to join band, and then when I was told that the best instrument for someone of my size would be the piccolo or maybe the clarinet, insisting I play the tuba instead.

High school wasn't exactly my peak years.

But a couple years ago, Emily and I met up again at a party, and we got along really well. When I found out she was doing social media freelance work for various corporations and small businesses, I knew she'd be perfect to take over all the social media stuff I didn't have the attention span for—which was pretty much all of it. It's a part-time gig for her, but has eaten up a lot more hours since we've been getting ready for the re-launch.

For now, though, I just want to tell her all about how I've been making out with Brendan. So I fill her in on the wedding, and on the incredible Casual Dating Plan and how that will hopefully lead to the even more incredible Brendan Is My Boyfriend Outcome.

Emily has stopped pulling t-shirts out of boxes by the end of this and is looking at me like my old band instructor when I wobbled in under the weight of an instrument almost as big as I was. "So you guys are going to be dating other people. Both of you."

I shrug. "We need to keep it casual. He can't do the relationship thing yet—he can barely say the word without panicking. So this way, there's no pressure on him."

She nods slowly. "Because of the panic disorder he has. Because of his really bad marriage."

"Yeah, that." I pause. "It's not just the bad marriage, though. He had the disorder before that."

"Really?"

I know Brendan wouldn't mind if I told her the rest of it. He doesn't treat it as a secret; he just doesn't talk about it much. "His dad was a really bad guy," I say. "He's actually in prison now, for abuse—he's been in jail since Brendan was three."

Emily's eyes widen. "Wow. Like he beat up Brendan's mom?"

"What she turned him in for was abusing Brendan," I say, feeling the familiar anger that bubbles up every time I think of someone hurting Brendan like that. "But yeah, I'm sure he was really rough to her, too." Neither of them ever go into details, and I haven't wanted to press, because god, that would have been brutal enough to live through once. I don't want to make either of them relive it just to satisfy my curiosity.

"Wow," she says again. "Okay, yeah, I can see him having issues. So you're dating other people and each other. And making out a lot. But you're not sleeping together yet."

My heart rate picks up, and I let out a little breath. "No, it's—we're casual. And I don't do casual sex."

She raises an eyebrow. "Even with Brendan?"

"Yeah." I pick a loose thread from a *Socktor Who* shirt. "It's not like you're big on casual sex yourself, you know."

"I'm not into sex with someone I barely know," she agrees. "But you and Brendan—I don't know, I saw that kiss. You both are dying to bone."

"I didn't say I don't *want* to." I toss a shirt at her. Yeah, I want to sleep with Brendan. Way more than I've ever wanted to in my life—and that was even before we started making out. There's something Emily doesn't know, though. Neither, for that matter, does Brendan. Or anyone.

I'm a twenty-four-year-old virgin.

This probably isn't the most shocking thing in the world, once one knows the tuba and/or *Beowulf* stories. But I've built a career making sex jokes with sock puppets, and I'm good enough at it that everyone assumes I know what I'm talking about. The truth is, I like people thinking I've got some experience. I know I shouldn't be ashamed for my lack thereof—it's not like I haven't had opportunity—but I can't help but feel kind of childish when I think about it.

Also, I make a sock puppet show. Combine that with my five-foot, small frame and my propensity for wearing t-shirts with cartoon characters on them, and I've already got childish covered.

Even still, I'm a romantic. I don't want to just go out and have sex. I want it to be with someone I'm in love with, someone who's in love with me.

Those words tug at my chest. I can't even let myself think them. Brendan and I aren't there yet. I mean, Brendan can't say the word "girlfriend" without a panic attack. There's no way he can even think about being in love with me.

That is, if he's not still in love, deep down, with Candace.

I swallow past the huge lump in my throat, fidgeting with the t-shirts like I care very much about them being stacked perfectly.

"Okaaaaay," Emily says. "No sex, because it's casual."

"Right."

"But you're sharing a hotel room."

"Right. We booked the room forever ago. Separate beds. And it's not like we haven't slept in the same room before—he ends up staying late, and we crash in the studio all the time."

Yes, the studio is in the attic of my dad's house, where I live. But sometimes, at four AM, my bed feels very, very far away, especially when Brendan is crashing on the studio couch and there's a perfectly good, huge bean bag chair for me to sleep on there.

Emily looks skeptical. "Okay. But just so you know, if you two are planning on hitting on other people at this con, you probably shouldn't be kissing in public like you just did. No one is going to want to get in the middle of *that*." Her lips twist into a wry smile. "Unless they very literally want to be in the middle of that."

I laugh, but she's got a point. We can't be acting like a couple in public, not for this plan to work.

And I really, really want this plan to work. For Brendan to be able to have a relationship with me that doesn't cause him panic and stress. For us to be able to be together in all the ways I've dreamed about since we first met.

"Do you think this is a bad idea?" I ask.

She takes a moment to consider, which I appreciate, even if it makes me a little worried. "I think it's a crazy-ass idea, but I could see it working to ease him past the anxiety." She grins. "And it'll definitely make for an interesting convention."

Which reminds me . . .

I raise my eyebrow at her. "I'm not the only one who might have an interesting convention."

Emily drops the last stack of shirts like a ton of bricks. "Okay. You've been making these hints at something involving me all morning. Please tell me you're not going to get me to date Brendan. I may support your plan, but no. I have no desire to be in the figurative or literal middle of you two."

"I'm not trying to get you to date *Brendan*, no."

The coy tone in my voice makes her glare at me. "What have you done?"

I collapse one of the now-empty boxes. "So remember how much you liked Tate? And how sad you were when things ended? And how he moved away not long after, so you guys never really got a chance to see—"

She groans loudly and emphatically.

"Well, he moved back!" I say, pretending I didn't hear her. "And was asking all about you at the wedding." This is a bit of a stretch, but he definitely seemed interested when I brought her up. Even Brendan agreed with that.

"Su-Lin, it didn't work out the first time."

I know that much. He broke up with her, blaming it on the fact that they both had business trips coming up and wouldn't see each other for a month. Which is clearly not the real reason, when things were going so well.

I have my own theory as to why my cousin ended it.

"Because he knew he had to move for work, and he was already totally falling for you. It scared him."

Emily narrows her eyes. "Did he tell you that?"

"Not exactly, but I could tell he—"

She shakes her head. "I don't think it's a good idea." She turns away to mess with the flat-screen TV, probably not wanting me to see how much she hopes I'll talk her into this.

She really liked Tate. And I could tell he really liked her. They're perfect for each other; they just didn't get a real chance.

"You should have seen the look on his face when he talked about seeing you here at the convention."

"Why isn't this thing—" She pauses with the remote, then spins to look at me again. "What?"

I cringe. "I may have invited him. He could use the networking, and I thought you could use the help at the booth. But if you really can't work with him, you don't have to. You guys can work opposite shifts. But I just thought that if you guys could talk again, things might—"

"Oh my god, Su-Lin, it's a good thing I love you and you pay me well." She's shaking her head again, but her lips have a trace of a smile on them. She turns back to the electronics. "Neither the TV or DVD player is working. It must be a problem with the outlet. If I have to set up this entire fucking booth again, I'll—"

"I'll go get someone to check on it," I offer. Best to give her time to think the Tate thing over. To remember how cute she thought he was and how funny. And how great the sex was (something she told me about in wayyyyy more detail than I wanted to know about my cousin).

I manage to track down a convention center employee, who looks like she's ready to shiv someone with the pen she's furiously clicking. I take my chances anyway—how much damage could a pen do?—and she testily explains to me that yes, there is an electrical problem with the outlets on our row, and it's being addressed. Then she sees my t-shirt, and her whole demeanor changes.

"Hey! Ruby Van Raspberry!" she says. I've had people actually call me Ruby before, so I'm not sure if she recognizes me or is just excited about my shirt.

"Thanks, I—"

"*Such* a great shirt," she says right over me. "The one I want is 'Who fucked my puppet?!'" She does this imitation of me screaming the words. It's not a bad impression, actually. "Totally brilliant. I—" She stops as another person comes up for help, and groans. "There's an electrical problem! They're working on it!"

I extricate myself, giving her a smile and a wave and hurrying back to the booth. Poor Emily's going to hear all week about whether we have *that* shirt, which we don't. It's a reference to an unfortunate incident on the reality show I was on three years ago—*Starving with the Stars*. I don't begrudge the person who probably made a mint on Redbubble off of those, but I couldn't ever bring myself to monetize poor Ruby's trauma.

Stupid Chad Montgomery. I should—

I'm stopped from thinking about what kind of scathing Chad Montgomery-mocking sketch I could write, when I see my old friend Jason—ironically a friend I met while filming *Starving with the Stars*—at our booth, talking with Emily.

Not just talking. Laughing, both of them. Emily is sort of leaning forward over the booth toward him, and Jason's doing the same.

I dodge a pair of vendors lugging boxes and pop up next to the booth, catching them both off-guard.

"Hey, Jason!" I say.

"Hey, Hobbit," he says fondly—and loudly, because he always has to say everything like he's speaking to a crowd of hundreds—throwing his arm over my shoulder. I don't love this nickname he's given me, but at least it's not because I have hairy feet. He's just crazy tall, probably around 6'3", maybe another couple inches with that spiky blond hair. "I just found out that I've actually spent the last few months tweeting at your friend here, thinking she was you."

Emily grins. "I do a pretty spot-on internet Su-Lin. Lots of exclamation points."

I mock-glare at her. This isn't entirely true. Not that there's *no* exclamation points, but *lots* is—

"Well, you convinced me," Jason says, grinning back at Emily a little too widely for my comfort.

Don't get me wrong, I love this dude. He's awesome and fun and he probably saved me from third-degree burns when I (ill-advisedly) tried to kill Chad Montgomery by leaping at him across a campfire.

But Emily can't be into him, not when I know that Tate is her perfect guy. Not Jason. He's too loud and brash for her, and too distractible. Pretty much every time I see him, he's got a new girlfriend. Emily is more serious and sensible, which is much more Tate than Jason. I can't see anything happening between her and Jason in the long-term, and I know Emily is tired of wasting her time with relationships that go nowhere.

"So how's your show going?" I ask, trying to get them to stop eye-humping each other.

He looks back at me, but it's a tad reluctant. "Great! Views keep going up and up. Which gives me the opportunity to climb more unique shit."

That's pretty much his whole show—*Jason Climbs Sh!t*. He's a professional rock-climber and films himself climbing stuff all over the world. Mountains, sure, but also crazy buildings, dams, and pretty much whatever he can without getting tossed into some foreign prison for sacred shrine desecration.

It's a surprisingly addictive show.

"I was just telling Emily about how I'm going to be doing a climbing presentation here at the con on my portable rock wall." He smiles at Emily before turning back to me again. "Any chance I can get you to help out?"

I raise my eyebrow. "Help out? With a climbing presentation?"

"Right. My old *Starving with the Stars* partner, climbing by my side—you know people will freak for it. No climbing experience necessary; it'll be totally safe," he assures me quickly. "You'll have someone belaying you."

I have never climbed anything higher than a chain-link fence, and I didn't do that particularly well. But he's right, people would love seeing the two of us together again, and it could be good for both our shows.

I consider this. "Can I have my friend Brendan belay me?"

"If he can hold a rope, sure."

Emily rolls her eyes. "You just want him to do that for the innuendo, don't you?"

I grin. She's right, I have all the jokes about "Will Brendan belaying me?" ready to tell him the minute I get back to the hotel room. Then my body heats up thinking about telling him those jokes. In a hotel room. With beds.

Maybe I should make those jokes some other place. Where

it's not so tempting to rip his clothes off and turn things a lot less casual.

Stick to the plan, Su-Lin.

And keep Emily to hers.

"Okay, I'll do it," I say. "If you agree to be on our show at some point." I have no ideas for a sketch right now, but him climbing with one of our characters could be hilarious.

Jason laughs. "Sweet, will do." He looks back at Emily. "So, I—"

"We need to get the rest of this set up," I cut him off before he can chat his way into Emily thinking she should be dating him instead of my cousin. "So we'll see you around?"

He blinks, then shrugs. "Cool beans, Hobbit. See you both around." He gives us—mostly Emily—one last grin, then saunters off with his hands in the pockets of his slouchy cargo shorts.

Emily watches him go. "You know, I never thought a guy could actually sound hot saying 'cool beans,' but he makes it work."

I wrinkle my nose.

Emily laughs. "What? He's super cute."

"Yeah, sure. But he's a little on the loud side, don't you think? Like awfully yell-y."

Emily considers. "Well, yeah, but there's a lot of noise here, so we're all being loud."

"But he's like that all the time." I feel a twist of guilt for talking bad about Jason and especially bad for what I say next, because I know this is the clincher. "And he's kind of a player."

Now it's Emily wrinkling her nose. She really doesn't like players. Not that she *never* casually dates around, but she's always transparent with where she's at with a guy, and generally doesn't feel like dating is worth her time if there's not the potential for it to go somewhere serious. Technically I don't know if Jason is a player, but from what I've seen, I don't think he's the kind of guy who does serious relationships.

"Besides," I say, pulling out my phone and doing a quick Facebook search. "You've got this guy showing up tomorrow and looking forward to reconnecting." I hold up my phone, which now has a great pic of Tate making a cute mock-disgusted face in front of a bowl of Panda Express's orange chicken—which is actually his favorite food.

She laughs despite herself, and I smile. "You really think he's still into me?" she asks, pursing her lips.

"I know it. But you'll see yourself when he gets here."

Emily sighs, shaking her head. "Fine, I'll keep an open mind and see how it goes. No promises!"

I throw my arms around her. "None needed. You guys are so great together. I have full confidence it'll work out."

"Of course you do," she says with chuckle. "Because Su-Lin plans never fail." She doesn't sound sarcastic about this, though—just amusedly resigned. Then she clicks the TV, which powers on. "Oh, hey, the outlet works! Great job," she says, as if I had anything to do with it.

But I'll take it. Maybe this is just my lucky week.

FOUR

BRENDAN

It feels like Su-Lin takes forever to come up to the room, though this may be because I've barely been apart from her since her sister's wedding. We had the excuse of preparation for the con, but the truth is, we were already prepared.

And I've gotten clingy. Not that Su-Lin seems to have noticed—or minded—yet, but I sure have. I've always been happiest when we're together, and she's pretty constantly on my mind. But now I begrudge the universe every minute we're apart. If I had my way, we'd always be near each other, always be laughing, always be touching.

I look over at the second bed, where Su-Lin has left her open suitcase and her small pillow that's shaped like a puffy stick-person and covered in tufted clouds. She sleeps cuddling it—I've seen this a number of times when I've crashed at her house.

Of all the things I thought dating again might do to me, making me irrationally jealous of a freaking pillow is not one of them.

Besides, we can't share a bed. That's the opposite of casual. I'm just glad we booked this room long before we decided to casually date, or there's no way we would have been able to justify spending our nights together.

The con is local to LA, but we decided to get a hotel room so we wouldn't have to drive and park downtown everyday, and most importantly, so I would have somewhere to retreat to when I start to get overwhelmed. The quickest way to a panic attack is to leave myself no escape. While, yeah, technically I have editing I could be doing, the real reason I didn't stay at the booth is because I'm starting to get nervous about pacing myself through this thing. Besides, Emily had things well in hand, and I've gotten the impression that she prefers to do things herself so that they get done exactly the way that she wants them.

I've been to cons before—that's where Su-Lin and I met, at a con where a documentary on geek culture that I edited made its debut. But even then, I wasn't the talent. The talent gets recognized. Everywhere. I am not looking forward to this.

I keep telling myself it's like the hair. Here, when people approach me, they're going to want to talk about the show, about how I came to work with Su-Lin, about what it's like to work together. I have answers for all of that, so it's not like I'll be at a loss for things to say.

The door opens, and Su-Lin breezes in, shaking her head. "You'll never believe who was hitting on Emily down in the dealer's room."

"Tate?" I guess. Though I'm thinking she'd be happy about that, and she looks peeved.

"*No.* Jason Winslow."

I squint at her. "The guy who climbs shit?"

She nods. "I think she likes him too, which is a problem, because Jason is totally not right for her, and—what's that?"

Her eyes have caught on a box on a table across the room, wrapped in shiny silver paper with a bow on top made out of a knotted sock. I put my hands behind my head and shrug innocently. "I don't know. Maybe you have a secret admirer."

Su-Lin squeals and skips across the room to the box. Like, she literally skips. I wouldn't have imagined any girl could make that sexy, but somehow she manages it. Probably it's her smile.

Or the fact that I haven't been laid in more than three years.

Mostly her smile.

She stands over the package and beams at me. "Can I open it?"

I hold up my hands. "I'm not stopping you."

She tears open the paper to reveal a box with a coffee maker on the side. She stares at me. "A coffee maker?"

"Don't ask me! I don't know anything about it."

I do, of course, and I'm having a hard time containing my excitement about seeing her face when she figures out what's really inside the box. Su-Lin slits open the tape on the end and pulls out a toaster, the typical silver kind with two slots in the top. And a loaf of bread.

She smiles. "Nice! I do love my toast in the morning."

She does, but that's not the gift.

"Maybe you should make some now. I noticed some butter in the mini fridge. Your secret admirer is prepared."

She grins and plugs the toaster in behind the table. Then she slips in two slices of bread, depresses the lever, and bounces up and down while she waits.

I press my lips together, trying not to give anything away. Su-Lin looks super excited, which makes all the effort I went to worth it. I knew it would be.

The toast pops up with a resounding *ding!*, and Su-Lin yanks one out of the toaster, passing it from hand to hand as it burns her fingers. She sets it on the table and stares at it. I bite my lip, waiting.

"Is that . . ." She holds up the toast, now cool enough to touch. "Is that Gudetama?"

It is indeed. Su-Lin has been obsessed with the Sanrio cartoon. There's an endless product line where the lazy egg grudgingly poses as the Mona Lisa or the guy in The Scream, or is sadly eaten on various breakfast plates while having a constant existential crisis.

I'm not sure which she likes more, Gudetama himself or the strange fact that he exists. When I found out I could get a toaster that burned images of him onto pieces of toast, I knew this was made for Su-Lin.

She sets down the toast and tackles me. She's grinning, and that smile is the best thing in the world. "How did you even *find* that?"

Now that the anticipation is over, I don't feel the need to pretend it wasn't me. "The same company will print basically whatever you want. You can send them a selfie and they'll put your face on toast. Though that might be indicative of some psychological issues."

Su-Lin laughs and snuggles up against me. My body relaxes in that way it only does when she's in my arms. It's not just a Su-Lin smile, it's *my* Su-Lin smile, the bright, gleeful one that's specially for me. I'd worried lately it might be only a best friends smile, but in the last two days she's smiled it at me more beautifully and brightly than ever. I thought I wanted her before, but now the desire haunts my every moment.

This isn't helped when she scoots closer to me, cuddling up against my side. I put my arm around her and enjoy the warmth of her body against mine. I love it when she's close to me—probably an unhealthy amount, and if she knew about the thoughts that sometimes run through my mind when she touches me, I'm pretty sure she'd agree.

I want this—I want it so bad it hurts. Not casually, either, but—

My chest tightens. I can't breathe. I hate my body for doing this to me, for rebelling against the very thing I know I want. But I don't know how I'm going to handle a relationship, and if it goes like the last time—

I tell myself to relax. Time will help. My therapist would tell me to have empathy with myself, to be patient.

I don't want to be patient. I want to seize the moment while Su-Lin is still willing to put up with my shit. Which is selfish, because I'm not sure putting up with me will end up being good for her.

I run a hand through her hair, and she basically purrs.

It's okay. Casual. We can do this.

"So," I say. "If we're casually dating . . . do you want to go out with me tonight?"

Su-Lin beams up at me. "Really? Like on a real date?"

I should have done this days ago, but I've been . . . distracted. "Yeah. Like a real date."

Her face falls. "Oh. But I was talking to Emily, and she made a really good point."

My stomach drops. A good point that means she won't go out with me. I mean, yeah, this plan is crazy, and probably not fair to her, and—

"She said that if we act like a couple in public, it's going to make it hard to see other people. At the con, I mean. Because people will assume that we're, like . . ."

She doesn't say the words, but I get it.

"Okay," I say. "But we do get to date each other, too, don't we? 'Cause that's kind of the point."

"Absolutely! But maybe we should make some rules about when and where. And how much."

That makes sense and is way less bad than what I was thinking. "Yeah, sure. But the con doesn't start until tomorrow. There's no official events tonight, which is where we're going to meet people, right? So we could go out tonight, maybe somewhere away from the con?"

Su-Lin nods. "Good plan. And when we're not on official dates . . . maybe we shouldn't, like, kiss and stuff."

She doesn't sound any more thrilled about that than I am, which shouldn't make me happy, but does. "Yeah," I say reluctantly. "I guess that makes sense. So then after tonight, maybe we get, like, one more date?" I want to suggest more, but the con is only four days, and if the plan is to be casual . . .

Su-Lin nods against my chest. "That seems reasonable, yeah? I mean, we want to take advantage of the con events to see other people, right?"

"Right," I say. Except I don't. I want to spend my time cuddled up with her every night.

If only I could be sure I could do that without turning into the needy, desperate person I was with Candace. If only I could say the world "girlfriend" without having a panic attack.

If only I could be the person Su-Lin deserves.

check out a local map on the internet and find a fondue place a couple miles away.

We hold hands on our way into the restaurant and sit on the same side of the booth with her tucked up against me and our arms around each other. We laugh and cuddle and feed each other fruit dipped in chocolate and probably appear like we're a committed couple who are deeply in love.

My heart feels as heavy as a stone. *I'm* deeply in love, but I'm not sure how long she's going to want to do this casual thing, and I have no idea when I'll be able to give her anything more than this.

"So," Su-Lin says, dipping a piece of bread into a dish of cheese with a flame beneath it. "Are you looking forward to finding other girls to date?"

She says this casually, but the question feels loaded. "Um, no. That sounds miserable. Besides, I thought *you* were going to find me other girls to date."

She looks up at me. "You want *me* to pick?"

I hadn't thought much about it, but the idea of pointing out to Su-Lin exactly which girls at any given event I find the most attractive feels like the sort of thing that may backfire. It sure as hell would have with Candace.

"Yeah," I say. "I mean, I'm going to retain veto power, definitely, but I think that would be better."

"*Really*," she says.

I smile at her. "Come on. Tell me you want me to tell you which other girls I think are attractive. Because that's totally

54

something you do with people you're casually dating."

"You don't usually let them pick your other dating partners either," Su-Lin says. "But okay. If you trust me." She gives me a devilish grin. Then she waves her tongs at me. "But I'm picking my own dates. No way do I trust you with that."

That's fine by me, but I put a hand to my chest, as if she's wounded me. "You don't trust me?"

"I trust you to do things you think are hilarious. Which would include setting me up with the worst possible people, am I right?"

I laugh. She's right, out of jealousy as much as for my own amusement. I *really* hate the idea of her dating anyone else. "Touché."

Su-Lin is quiet for a moment. "We should probably tell the other people we're dating that you and I are just friends."

My heart aches. I hate that even more, and it's all my fault. "I don't want to lie about it."

"But with us working together as close as we do, if you tell girls you're also dating me, they're going to think they don't have a chance with you."

They don't have a chance with me. I'm pretty sure that was the point of doing this at a con, where people are mostly looking to have fun and not to fall in love and live happily ever after.

But she has a point. Also I'm pretty sure I can get away without any outright lies, using phrases like "it's not like that," or "I'm not in a relationship."

Su-Lin swirls a strawberry around in chocolate, creating a twisting pattern on the surface. She does this for so long that I'm sure she must be thinking about something.

I hope it's not that she's ready to move on from this plan before we've even begun. Su-Lin's ideas are both insane and amazing, but she does have a habit of jumping from one to another—

"What was your relationship with Candace like?" Su-Lin asks. "When you were first dating, I mean."

I blink at this quick change of subject. I've told her tons about my marriage to Candace, but first dating . . .

"It was intense," I say. "Really intense."

She withdraws the strawberry and stares at it. "So you were in love with her, like, right away?"

I shake my head. "Actually, I'm not sure I was ever really in love with her."

She looks up at me in surprise, and I wince. I know it makes me sound like a horrible person, but since I met Su-Lin, I've been fairly certain that what I felt for Candace, while intense and all-consuming, was obsession and not love at all.

I obviously can't tell her the details of that realization.

"You must have some happy memories of her. You guys were together so long."

I think about that for a moment. The good times have been so shrouded in pain and betrayal that it's hard for me to remember them. "Sure. I mean, she's the first girl I ever slept with. The first girl I ever *kissed*." Theoretically the first for both of us, but now I'm not sure if she was really a virgin when we first had sex. The idea that this may have been one of her many lies spoils the memory even more.

Su-Lin's voice grows quiet, and I feel like she's gathering information from this that I don't even know I'm giving her.

"What was it like, then?" she asks. "You must have been really into her."

"I was." I sigh. It's hard to describe what happened with Candace. Hard for me to understand, even. "I was lonely and desperate to feel like someone loved me. Which is stupid, because my mom always did, and I knew it."

I've never been able to totally understand why I was so needy, especially since afterward, I had no problem swearing off relationships. Quite the opposite, actually. "Anyway, when we first started dating, there was a lot of passion, I guess. But then she would get bored or annoyed or angry, and she'd brush me off or ignore me. And then I'd get clingy and chase after her.

Sometimes she'd threaten to break up with me, and I'd cry and beg her not to leave me. Then she'd come back, and we'd make up and be all over each other again. And it would start over."

It was worse than that, but I'm too embarrassed to talk about the other stuff. The things Candace used to say to me, the many ways I disappointed her, over and over again. And no matter how much she put me down, the obsessive desperation with which I used to chase after her when she left me, leaving fifty messages, sobbing into the phone, threatening to kill myself.

I'd like to think I've learned something from that. I'd like to think it wouldn't happen again. But I'm still worried that, while I can be a mostly normal best friend and a tolerable casual dating partner, once I'm in a serious relationship, all my issues are going to come bubbling to the surface again. I want to believe that I've grown and changed . . . but I'm still the same person, and I can't guarantee that I won't revert to that again.

I don't ever want to be like that with Su-Lin.

Su-Lin's face is serious—an expression other people might be surprised to see, but that I know well—and I wonder if, even without all that information, she's starting to rethink whether she wants to be involved with me.

"Do you still miss her?" Su-Lin asks.

"No," I say. "Once we broke up for good, I actually didn't miss her at all." After she left me, is how it really went, because I didn't have the self-respect to do it myself, even after I found out she'd been cheating on me the whole time. "I was hurt, obviously, but when it came to not having her around, I guess maybe I felt relief." I'd been trying so hard to hold on to her and that terrible relationship for so long, I think it was a relief to be rid of that version of myself, as much as anything.

Su-Lin is quiet for a moment, and I wonder if she's thinking I'm a total ass for not even missing my ex-wife.

"Things were just so bad between us," I say. "Not just at the end, but before we even got married. I still have the scars that she gave me, but I'm glad she's out of my life."

Su-Lin moves closer, sitting right up against me. "Me too."

I want to kick myself. I know she brought it up, but this isn't stuff I should be talking about on our first date—on *any* first date.

"The way you felt with her . . . Do you ever feel like that with me?" she asks.

My heart stops. She *is* worried I'm going to be like that with her. "No!" I say. "I mean, it's different, you know? You're like this bright beam of light that illuminates everything. And with Candace . . . it was like I was in a never-ending race, like a greyhound after a lure, chasing this high, this *zing*, that I could never permanently catch."

Her voice is still quiet. "What exactly were you chasing? Was the sex that good?"

I shake my head. Sex with Candace had some very high highs and some very low lows, and was inextricably mixed up in how bad we were together. "It wasn't sex. I think—I think it was security. I think I was running away from the idea that I'd always be alone."

Su-Lin's forehead crinkles. She pities me, which is probably deserved, but not at all how I want her to feel. It's not her fault, though. She can't help that I'm pathetic. She lays her head on my shoulder, and we sit there for a while in silence.

And I can't help but think that any date she finds at the con will be a whole lot more fun for her than this.

FIVE

Su-Lin

The thumping beat from the convention center hall makes the floor tremble as we approach. It's the night after our date, and we're going to the YouProm, the evening kick-off event that always starts YouCon. Some people dress in proper prom attire and some in geek-themed prom wear. Some of the younger set aren't even old enough to have been to their high school proms yet, but everyone always has fun.

I grin over at Brendan as we watch crowds of people swirl by us to enter. "You ready for this?"

"I have a feeling this is nothing like the prom I went to in high school," he says, fidgeting with the sleeve of his suit coat. "For one, I wasn't trying to pick up a date *at* the prom." He smiles over at me, which normally makes me all the fluttery, but there's a little twist in my stomach.

Of course he wasn't, because he was with Candace. She was his actual date and his girlfriend. Words plucked from our conversation at the restaurant echo in my head. *Really intense. Passion.*

I shouldn't be jealous. Probably I wouldn't be, if I could be his date tonight. If I could walk in holding his hand and spend the night dancing with him and kissing him and going back to our hotel room and—

Well, okay. We still wouldn't be doing everything that he and Candace did on their prom night. We'd still be just casual. But it would be something.

Better than something. Amazing.

Like our date last night, which was easily the best date of my life. Getting to be all romantic at the fondue place, then afterward going to this old nickel arcade where we played Skee-Ball and trash-talked each other through bouts of *Street Fighter*, even though neither of us actually knows how to do more than mash buttons. Then making out back in our room, curled up in each other's arms.

That's why we're doing this, going into prom and finding other people to dance with and possibly have dates with this week. So we can have last night and more.

I wonder, though, if that "more" will ever be as *really intense* for him as it would be for me.

"I don't know," I say, keeping my voice light. "There'll be people dancing really poorly and sneaking in alcohol and trying desperately to get laid. Sounds like prom to me, just on a bigger scale."

Surprisingly, given my high school experience, I did actually go to prom. My date was Eddie Yang, the super-cute younger brother of one of Mei-Ling's best friends, who went to a different school. Not surprisingly, everyone thought he was my cousin, which was probably less motivated by racism and more motivated by my peers' judgment of my dating prowess.

I was totally embarrassed, but that didn't stop me from letting Eddie get to second base in the backseat of the Ford Taurus he borrowed from his mom for the night.

Brendan laughs. "Okay, yeah." Then his expression softens. "You look so beautiful."

He might be overreaching a bit—I'm wearing a strapless black-and-white dress with a short skirt in layers of puffy tulle, lacy black fingerless gloves, and of course my signature black and white Converse sneakers I wear every day (that is not my sister's wedding). While it's a cute, fun look, beautiful is probably stretching it. But damn if I don't love hearing him say that. Not to mention the way he says it—all soft and sincere, like me in a cast-off from the eighties Madonna collection is something truly special.

That fluttery feeling is back, big time. I wish I could kiss him right here. And right there. And down there. And—

I pull my thoughts away from my best friend naked. Again. "Well, I've already told you how hot you are in that suit. It's even hotter now I know it's part stripper costume."

He smiles, and his cheeks have a pink flush to them. He opens his mouth to say something, but I hear a shout from someone standing by the exhibit hall doors. "*There* you guys are! I've been looking everywhere for you—get in here!"

It's Emily, grinning broadly as she waves for us to join her. She's in a slinky red dress that looks less prom-ready and more perfect for a trendy club. It looks incredible on her. I also know it's not the dress she originally planned on wearing.

I smile, because I have a pretty good idea why she changed.

"So," I say, having to shout over the music getting louder the closer we get to the doors. "Things with Tate went well today?"

I saw them at the booth together when I checked in after Brendan and I went to a few panels—just as audience members. Our programming doesn't start until tomorrow.

But when I went to the booth, it definitely seemed like Emily and Tate were more interested in each other. They were deep in some conversation I wisely chose not to interrupt.

Emily shrugs. "It was really nice talking with him again." There's a little smile at the edges of her lips.

"Mmm-hmmm." I nod knowingly and waggle my eyebrows at Brendan the moment Emily turns away. He laughs, and we enter the exhibit hall behind Emily. Brendan's fingers brush against mine, maybe by accident, but it takes everything in me not to fold my hand in his and never let go.

The moment we walk into the massive hall, it's obvious

Brendan was right—this is nothing like a high school prom. There are thousands of people packed in here, for one, a massive sea of heads bobbing up and down, glow sticks waving. Strobe lights in neon colors sweep the audience. The DJ raises one hand to the beat from up on the stage, wearing a big futuristic helmet like a wannabe Deadmau5, surrounded by some LA dance troupe shaking their asses in shiny silver bodysuits. Huge screens frame the hall, right now all synced to the music video for the Kylie Minogue song currently playing. Bubbles float in the air, fed into the room from suspended bubble machines, glinting in the strobe lights, popping as they hit the crowd below.

See Mei-Ling? Bubbles are *awesome*.

"Where is Tate, anyway?" I ask.

"Getting some drinks." Emily points at one of the bar stations. He's leaning against the bar, all suave in a tux vest over a fitted white shirt and black dress pants. Tate always dresses well.

All YouCon events are open to minors—teens make up the bulk of our audience—so the bars here don't serve alcohol. But they do a fun job with virgin specialty drinks and way over-charge for them, so the kids probably *feel* like they're at a real bar.

"Hey look, there's Jason," Emily says, gesturing toward the edge of the dance floor, which is ringed by puffy red couches. There, indeed, is Jason, looking like a member of the modern rat pack, in pants with suspenders and neon green wingtip shoes.

He manages to somehow make that look good, but what really catches my attention is the girl he's talking to. Or rather, the girl who is holding court, with him being one of a group of guys hanging around her like moths fluttering around a bright, sexy porch light. (Do moths think porch lights are sexy? How would we even know?)

Jane Shaw. Gorgeous, skyrocketing YouTube star, who first started off doing incredible cosplay and gaining cred in the geek world, and then, two years ago, added a comedy element to her show with—guess what—puppets.

Which, whatever. I certainly didn't invent the concept of adult puppet comedy. And we don't even go for the same audience, not really. She's a ventriloquist, for one, which is a talent I do not possess, but which admittedly seems super cool. Her show still focuses more on the geek element, and she does some sharp feminist bits on the treatment of women in the geek world. And mine—now Brendan's and mine—is more generally pop-culture based, more mainstream (when it comes to sock puppet shows, anyway).

Our shows are nothing alike, but she and I are always grouped together in the press—the YouTube "puppet girls." And while it's not her fault, it's sooo not fun to be constantly compared in side by side photos to a girl who looks like *that*.

She's currently rocking a tight black corset and tiny green booty shorts over fishnet pantyhose, with over-the-knee black stiletto-heeled boots. Her platinum blond hair is crowned with a tiara of silver twigs.

It's a cosplay of Hemlock, the comic book hero who in the movies is played by the beautiful Kim Watterson (formerly of it-couple Watterpless, before Blake Pless supposedly cheated on her with the nanny, which is bonkers because *Kim Watterson!*).

Jane holds her own, though, even in comparison to the actress. Her figure is curvy in all the right places, and she knows how to show it off to full advantage.

Every time I see her, I feel like a little girl pretending to be an adult (and not terribly well, considering both other times I saw her in person I was wearing a Super Mario Bros t-shirt).

The worst part is, she seems super nice, so I can't really dislike her and still feel even remotely good about myself.

Jane sees me and waves, jumping up and down as if to get my attention. Her boobs bounce even in the tight corset as she jumps, and the guys around her enjoy the show. I smile and wave back, looking away quickly enough that I think I can safely pretend I didn't see her beckoning me to come join her.

I really don't need the real life side-by-side comparison.

"Yep, that's Jason," I say. "Apparently making sure he gets a front-row view of Jane Shaw's rack."

This makes me feel slightly vindicated about what I told Emily earlier—it doesn't exactly prove he's a player, but it certainly doesn't disprove it.

Brendan shrugs, a grin on his face as he looks back from his own study of Jane. "Well, it *is* a nice rack."

Emily laughs like she agrees with him, and I do, too, but I feel a little sick.

Of course it's a nice rack. She's got a nice everything. She's sexy and confident and totally the type of woman—not girl— that would make a guy feel *really intense passion*.

Not like a certain virgin in a puffy dress and sneakers who is short and small-boned and barely fills a B-cup.

Maybe I should have worn something sexier. Maybe I should have brought The Dress to the con—the one that's been hanging in my closet waiting for me to have the courage (and a reason) to wear it ever since I impulsively bought it two months ago while bridesmaid dress shopping with Mei-Ling.

Emily asks Brendan about the panels we went to today, and I try to pay attention, but I start going back to our conversation last night about Candace—who looks a little like Jane, actually, at least in being blond and pretty and curvy.

He doesn't think he actually loved Candace, which was a shock to me and a huge relief. She didn't deserve to be loved by a guy like Brendan. Not with what she did to him.

But this thing he had with her—this passion, this high, this *zing*. Maybe he doesn't consider it love, and maybe he's right. But I wish I made him feel a little like that. Not in the ways that hurt him—god, I never, never want to hurt him. When he said he didn't feel that way with me, I think he mostly meant the bad aspects of their relationship. But it sounds like those bad aspects and that passion were all tied up in one, and if he doesn't feel the passion part of that with me at all . . .

Shouldn't *zing* be part of a good relationship? Even if only a little bit?

Because I know I sure feel it.

"Drinks for all!" Tate shouts, interrupting the thoughts pricking at my heart like there's a seriously annoyed pufferfish lodged in my chest. He holds up a tray of huge, brightly colored mocktails. I grab one that looks like a strawberry daiquiri, wishing there was some legit alcohol in this.

Brendan takes a tall, fizzy, bright green one. "Thanks, man."

"Of course," Tate says. "It's the least I can do, after you guys let me help out at the booth. One day in, and I already have a solid lead on a job. Not to mention," he says, bumping his shoulder against Emily, "getting to spend the day with this one."

She grins up at him, and I am happy to see that the Su-Lin Plan to Get Emily and Tate Together Again (For Good) is humming right along.

"Why don't you two go dance, and I'll guard the drinks," I say, taking the tray from him.

Emily gives me a small, disbelieving shake of her head, but she certainly doesn't seem unhappy to accept when Tate is all, "Shall we?" and leads her into the bobbing crowd. He winks at me before they go.

"That seems to be working out well," Brendan says.

"Right? I told you, I've got a gift for—" I burst into giggles as I turn to face him. He's got a thick, fizzy, bright green mustache, and it's adorable and hilarious and also I want to kiss it right off of him.

"What?" His expression is all innocence, and I immediately know he meant to do this.

"You look like Ron Swanson at a St. Patrick's Day rave."

"You don't think this is hot? You don't think this will get me all the ladies?" He steps in closer to me, and my pulse quickens.

It'd definitely get him this one. But he already has me, at least as much of me as he can take without hyperventilating. I find myself moving closer to him, moving the tray to my other hand to keep it out from between us.

Would it really matter so much if I kissed him right now?

65

How many people would be paying attention enough to see? My breath goes all shallow just thinking about it.

But no.

If I want any chance to actually be with him—and I do, more than anything—we have to stick to the plan.

"Let's rely on your usual brand of Brendan hotness for tonight's date," I say. "Speaking of which . . ." I survey the area for girls to set him up with.

There's no shortage of girls, that's for sure. "How about her over there? The one with the long red braid and the glow necklace?" I pride myself on actually picking him a cute girl, instead of someone I know he'd never go for.

Brendan wipes the mustache off with a napkin from the tray—why am I still carrying this stupid tray? Am I taking up waitressing?—and eyes the girl. He's no longer smiling, back to fidgeting nervously. "I don't know," he says after a beat. "She's got a lot of makeup on. Like caked on, you know?"

I frown. "I think she's going for a smoky eye thing. It's a trend."

"She looks like the Winter Soldier."

I laugh. "Okay. So that's a pass." I look around some more and catch a girl at the bar staring right at us. She quickly looks away when I catch her, but there's a smile on her lips. She's also pretty and doesn't appear out to assassinate any Avengers. I motion for Brendan to follow me while I set the tray with Tate and Emily's drinks down on one of the small tables lining the edge of the exhibit hall.

"All right, over at the bar. Twelve o'clock. There's a girl who's totally checking you out. She has shoulder-length brown hair and—"

"The bar's not at twelve o'clock. It's at, like, three. Have you ever *seen* a clock?"

I point right at it. "Twelve. Up top."

Brendan shakes his head. "No, you're supposed to call it for where the other person is. So for me it's"—he puts his arm out like the hour hand, hitting each point—"Twelve, one, two, three."

The girl is looking at us again and probably wondering why we're both pointing at her.

Or not wondering at all, because we're not super subtle and she's not an idiot.

"Stop stalling and just look at the girl at the bar!" I say, barely holding in a laugh. "God, I didn't think getting you to check out other girls was going to be such an issue."

It wasn't with Jane, anyway, a little thought pings in my mind, before I ignore it like a text from that second cousin who's always inviting me to her fake designer purse parties.

Brendan glances over and back. He lets out a breath. "Okay. Yeah. She's okay."

She's definitely better than okay, but I appreciate him not extolling her physical virtues to me.

"So you should go ask her to dance." Earlier today, we figured that spending the evening dancing with other people, maybe hanging out and chatting a bit, counts as a date. That's the beauty of doing this at a con—the date itself is already set up, no need to pay for fancy dinners or come up with creative plans.

He shifts, his brow furrowed, and I can tell he's super uncomfortable. And probably all the anxious.

I wish we didn't have to do this. I know how stressful this is for him. But the very fact that he's willing shows me how much he does want to get to a place where he can have a relationship. Maybe it's not crazy passion, but I know he feels *something* for me more than just friendship. Maybe he believes he can one day feel a lot more.

It means so much that he wants to be with me enough to try.

"So I just go up and ask her to dance," he says with the enthusiasm of a veterinarian about to inform the girl her dog is dead.

"Right. Introduce yourself and just straight-up ask her. No obnoxious pick-up lines—they're totally useless. Girls hate them, and even though you're cute enough to get away with it, it'll only work against you."

"Damn," he says, his lips quirking up. "I was really looking forward to being *that guy*."

I smile. Brendan would never be that guy. The only way he'd ever use an obnoxious pick-up line is as a total joke to make me laugh.

He glances down at his feet and then back up. "How about you? Who are you going to ask?"

He doesn't sound particularly thrilled about this prospect, which I have to admit makes me happy, but maybe it's still that he's dreading his own task.

"Don't worry about me," I say. "I'll find someone. Let's get you dancing first."

He gives me a dubious look, but then nods. We meet eyes for a long, lingering moment that sends a tingle down through my toes and an ache in, well, other parts of me.

Then he turns and heads over to the bar. I try not to look like I'm staring and sip more of my daiquiri, but I can't help but watch as he approaches her. The way he carries himself is tense, and I chew my lip, hoping it goes all right.

A giggle threatens to escape me at how ridiculous it is that I'm hoping the guy I'm super crazy about doesn't strike out with this random girl.

The girl smiles as he introduces himself, and they shake hands—a little awkward, but okay. She looks over at me and he says something, and she nods, her smile getting wider. She's got a nice smile and a heart-shaped face. Probably he told her we're just friends, like I told him to.

I let out a breath. That's good, right? Good.

Then she laughs about something and nods, and he guides her to where everyone's dancing.

Even better, I tell myself firmly. *Fantastic.*

I slurp at the bottom of my daiquiri. God, this would be so much better if it were alcoholic.

Now I'm trying not to creepily watch them dance. It's a fast song, so it's more like club dancing than the type we did at the wedding, but really, does she need to be so close to him? I mean it's not grinding, exactly, but—

I force myself to look away and grab Emily's drink, still not taken from the table. I'll find someone to dance with when I'm done with this one. Well, maybe after Tate's, too—no reason to waste these drinks. Then I'll probably need to pee pretty bad. So after that.

I'm more than halfway through Tate's virgin mojito and thinking maybe I need to move to the other side of the exhibit hall to keep myself from peeking over at Brendan and this girl—whose skirt is way shorter than I thought when she was sitting at the bar—when I look back and there's a guy standing right behind me.

"Hi," the guy says, smiling at me. He's good-looking, probably in his early to mid-twenties. A little shorter than Brendan, a little stockier. He's got blond hair that falls over his ears, mostly covered by a fedora, and he's wearing nice jeans and a short-sleeved button-up shirt. "I'm Warren. I was hoping I'd get a chance to talk to you."

"Oh, are you a fan of the show?" This happens a lot at cons. Usually I spend most of my time at functions like this answering questions about the *Sockwives* or whether Alec Andreas on *Starving with the Stars* is as hot in person (he is, but he's *Alec*, so that detracts a bit).

He looks confused. "What show?"

"Oh, I—sorry, I thought you wanted to ask me about my show." I laugh nervously. "Sorry, I'm not as self-involved as I sound."

He grins. "Well, now I do. But no, I just meant I noticed you when you first walked in, but I wasn't sure if you were with that guy. But since he's off dancing, I figure . . ." He gives a little shrug.

I look over to Brendan. The song has ended and a slower song has started up, and the two of them are still dancing—and it's this amazing song he loves (and introduced me to) about zombies that shouldn't be something one could slow dance to, but totally is. I want to be there with him, singing along with the lyrics and laughing.

But he's dancing with someone else. Because of the Plan, I remind myself.

It's still not easy to see his arm around her waist like it was around mine at the wedding. My throat is dry, despite the three mocktails. "Yeah, no," I say, "That's Brendan Pike. He's my business partner. He does the video editing too, which is what I first hired him for. He's great. But we're not—we're just friends."

"Okay, awesome," Warren says with a laugh. "So I know a lot about Brendan, but I haven't caught your name yet."

I cringe. When did I get so bad at this? Apparently I'm the one who needs coaching.

"God, I'm sorry. Su-Lin," I say.

"Well, Su-Lin, would you like to dance? And then I clearly need to hear all about this show."

I smile. "Yes. Clearly."

He grins again and takes my hand, putting his arm around my waist—apparently he knows how to actually dance, like Brendan, not just doing the side-to-side sway. And though I know I'm supposed to be dancing—like Brendan and this girl are, so close together—I find I don't want to, like it hurts my heart somehow.

It takes me a couple steps to identify why. It's because of how it felt dancing like this with Brendan, both in the studio and then at Mei-Ling's wedding—how it felt to be pressed up against him, trusting him to guide me, feeling his heartbeat against me.

I think of dinner last night, my head on Brendan's shoulder as he confessed the fear he'd had about always being alone, my heart breaking for him. He's Brendan, the guy who makes me laugh like no one else, who surprises me with a Gudetama toaster (seriously! A toaster! With *Gudetama*! Who else would think of doing that for me?) The guy who thinks of me as a bright beam of light and doesn't realize how much of that light is just from being around him. My DIP.

I wanted so badly to tell him that he doesn't have to be afraid of being alone, not anymore. That I want to be there for him—to be *with* him—always. That even though he's only been in my life for four months, I can't imagine my life anymore without him.

But that's the opposite of casual. God, that would probably scare off a guy who didn't have severe relationship anxiety.

"I'm sorry." I pull back, too uncomfortable to keep going. "I'm the worst at dancing."

"Really?" Warren looks surprised. "You were doing great."

"Thanks, but I—it's just super embarrassing for me. Honestly, the only dance I can do with any real confidence is the chicken dance. I rock at that."

Warren raises his eyebrows, then drops his grip on me. I think I'm about to get ditched, but he raises his hands and starts making the chicken dance motions to the beat of this slow jam, with a big smile on his face. "Show me what you've got."

Now my laugh is real. Okay, if I have to dance with someone who's not Brendan, at least this guy seems fun. "You're on," I say, and chicken dance right along with him.

SIX

BRENDAN

This girl Katrina is pretty cool. Turns out she's a fan, so as we dance, she's asking me a million questions about our show and my partnership with Su-Lin. I have answers for these things, so I'm filling her in about our new character Shuby, who is a total wannabe Ruby and drives Ruby up the wall by copying her every move. I'm kind of proud of how well I'm carrying on this conversation. I'm handling this crowd of people. I am not having an anxiety meltdown. I've got this.

Then I spot Su-Lin across the dance floor. She's not hard to spot—her fluffy black-and-white dress makes her seem like she's floating on a cloud, and just looking at her gives me that same kind of floaty feeling.

Then I plummet back to earth, because I see what she's doing.

The chicken dance.

To Jonathan Coulton's "Re: Your Brains."

With some blond guy.

Some blond guy who is not me.

I mean, I knew she was going to dance with people who were not me. But I expected normal dancing, like I'm doing with Katrina. Her arms are around my waist, but we're mostly talking about Shuby's raging crush on Ruby's main man from the original *Sockwives*, Terrence Clarence.

Um, except we're not talking now. Because I have lost control of my eyes and can't seem to stop staring at Su-Lin and have simultaneously lost all powers of conversation.

I was saying something. What was I saying?

It's then that I realize that Katrina is mid-sentence. "—dating that guy?"

I'm pretty sure she's asking about Su-Lin, but I can't be positive. "No," I say, "she's just dancing with him. Definitely not dating him."

Katrina smiles like maybe she feels sorry for me. "I'd really love to meet her. I've been a fan forever."

"Yeah, sure." I glance back over at Su-Lin. She's doing a spin, her beautiful, beaming smile all lit up. As she turns back around to face the blond guy, she throws back her head and laughs.

Shit. That's the way she laughs for *me*.

I can't take this anymore. "Want to meet her right now?"

Katrina pauses. "In the middle of the song? I don't want to interrupt—"

Oh, but I do. I grab her hand. "Come on."

I move through the crowd, which sways in tandem as JoCo sings about the poor starving zombie who just wants an opportunity to eat his office mate's brains.

I should feel bad about this—interrupting Su-Lin in the middle of her date or dance or whatever this is. But she and this blond guy are twisting down to the floor and then rising again with their little birdie hands that look just like sock puppets, and I don't feel bad.

Dancing is one thing. But this is something that she and I might have done, and I hate that I've put us in this position.

That's why she's doing the chicken dance with some other guy. Because of me.

The song ends—it's not hugely long, thankfully—and Su-Lin turns as if to look for someone and shrieks when she finds me standing right behind her.

Okay, now I'm being a little creepy. But I cover for it by pulling Katrina up beside me. "Hey!" I say, too loud for the gap between songs. The guy who was dancing with Su-Lin looks a little stunned. "This is Katrina. She's a fan. I was just telling her all about Shuby."

Su-Lin smiles, but it's a fake smile. The music picks up again, and we shuffle out of the dancing mob where we might have half a chance at a decent conversation.

Somewhere in the middle of the shuffling, the blond guy gets lost. I know I should feel bad about that, but I don't. Apparently my jealous side is kind of a dick.

Katrina beams at Su-Lin. "Oh my god, I'm *so* glad you decided to reboot your show. I've seen your first two seasons about a billion times."

Su-Lin's appreciative smile is still fake—way more than it usually is when she interacts with fans. I wonder if she's upset that I chased off the blond guy, which I should probably apologize for and free her up to go find him. I mean, if she found someone else who would do the chicken dance with her, that should be great, right? The whole point of being casual is to date other people, and it doesn't make sense to date people we don't *like*, right?

Katrina and Su-Lin are talking—mostly Katrina, at about a mile a minute—and I'm not following them, even though I only had the one drink and it was most definitely virgin. But it's getting hot in here—I think legitimately hot, and not that I'm having an anxiety attack, because I've actually been doing okay anxiety-wise, for once—and I'm looking around for the blond guy, wondering if I should just go find him, when something Katrina is saying snags my attention.

"And oh my god, that dress," she says. "I've always loved your style. I wish I could pull that off."

Katrina is wearing a shiny gold skirt with a purple lace top. It's less fancy than what Su-Lin has on, but it's not like Katrina *couldn't* wear what Su-Lin is wearing. Katrina reaches out and adjusts one of Su-Lin's straps that's sliding down her shoulder.

I stare at her hand as it lingers there.

Oh.

Ohhhhhhhhh.

I stifle a grin as Su-Lin looks at me like she's not sure what exactly has come over me.

"So," Katrina says, filling the awkward silence. "Do you want to dance?"

Su-Lin looks at me expectantly, as if I'm supposed to answer, and I tilt my head toward Katrina, who is very clearly asking Su-Lin to dance, not me. I try not to snicker as the realization dawns, and Su-Lin's face turns pink. "Oh," she says. "Um, thank you. Really. But I'm actually getting a headache. From the music! I think I'll sit this one out." And she turns and heads for the hall.

Katrina looks a bit dejected—or rejected, I suppose, which she literally just was. I want to follow Su-Lin and see if she's okay. She seemed upset about something, though I'm not sure if it's just her failure to adequately set me up with a date, or the fact that I interrupted her and her dance partner, or what.

But I think technically I'm still supposed to be dating other people, so I smile at Katrina. "You want to dance again?"

She shakes her head. "No, thanks. I think I'm going to go get another drink." She heads off across the room, and I turn to chase after Su-Lin.

I find her standing against the wall outside, holding the bridge of her nose.

"You okay?" I ask.

"Well, I just set you up with a lesbian and then it took me an embarrassingly long time to realize she was actually hitting on *me*. So there's that."

"Hey." I hold up my hands. "I'm the one who danced two songs with her in which we talked non-stop about you. Felt pretty normal to me, so I didn't even notice."

She smiles at that, like maybe she gets my meaning. I'm totally failing at this pursuing other people thing, and not because the girl I asked to dance happened to swing the other way.

Because even if she hadn't, I'd already sent about a thousand signals that I was taken, from the stuff I was talking about to the way I couldn't stop staring at Su-Lin.

"What about that guy you were dancing with?" I ask. "He seemed cool."

"Yeah, I guess," Su-Lin says. She doesn't follow that with anything, which is a dead giveaway that something's wrong. Su-Lin always has something to say. The fact that she doesn't—

"What are you two doing hiding out here?"

I look up to see Emily and Tate coming toward us, arms slung around each other. "Come on," Emily continues, "your friend Jason has decided to climb the scaffolding next to the stage, and he's got about a hundred people underneath him with their arms out, ready to catch him if he falls. I say he's going to fall and crush someone, and Tate is so sure he won't that he's going to buy the next round if Jason makes it."

I know Su-Lin was worried about the Emily and Jason situation, but Emily looks pretty happy wrapped in Tate's arms. I look over at her. "You want to join them or call it a night?"

She straightens herself up to her full height, which is barely five-one. "Jason isn't going to fall. He never falls. I say we get one more round on Tate." Her smile seems genuine again. I suppose if she was mad at me for running that guy off, she's forgiven me.

Next time, I'll do better. But for the moment, I'm just going to enjoy the company of my best friend.

Even if I know the night is not going to end before she makes me dance with at least one more woman who isn't her.

SEVEN

Su-Lin

I was worried about how Brendan would handle our first big panel, especially because it's a particularly massive one. We're far from the most famous YouTubers on this panel, which is about making old ideas fresh. While I started my show six years ago, it didn't actually run that long—only two seasons over two years. Most of the people on this panel have been keeping their shows going—consistently coming up with creative new content—for that length of time or even longer. We're the newbies when it comes to this topic.

So between that and the sea of hundreds of faces staring at us from the audience and Brendan's natural disinclination for crowds, I've been hoping he wouldn't have a full-on panic attack. But except for him being a little quiet at the very beginning, his knee jiggling under the table, he's done so well. He's been funny and charming and informative, talking about what it's like coming onto an already established show and the kinds of changes we're making. He and I toss back and forth our usual banter (okay, maybe our usual banter with slightly less sexual innuendo), and the audience is laughing and asking questions and other panelists are jumping in and taking their turns, and, well—it's actually super fun. More fun because Brendan's here to share it with me.

It's going so well, in fact, that I'm surprised when five minutes before the panel ends, a kid in the second row asks us how long we see our show going on in this iteration, and Brendan's knee starts jiggling again.

I'm amused at this kid who can't be more than thirteen being so serious and adorable and using the word "iteration," but Brendan's face has gone pale. He takes a drink of water.

I'm not sure if it's talk of the future that bothers him—is he so afraid of commitment that he can't imagine sticking with the show? Or is it just that doing the panel is starting to wear on him? There's not always a trigger for these things. At least, not that Brendan can explain.

Either way, it leaves me to answer. "We don't have a set time frame," I say. "Brendan and I have a blast coming up with new characters and concepts and sketch ideas, so I don't expect it to end anytime soon. And probably then we'll come up with something else equally awesome and fun for you all."

It's not a spectacular answer; I would love to have ended on a clever joke, but whatever. The audience is happy, our moderator brings the panel to a close, and everyone's clapping. Brendan doesn't dart out immediately, so I think he's mostly okay.

I reach for his hand under the table (which is covered by a tablecloth, so the audience won't see us holding hands), and he takes mine and squeezes.

"Great job," I say to him as everyone's standing up to leave. He smiles at me, but it looks forced.

Fortunately, the moderator—expecting that some of the better-known YouTubers would get mobbed after this—made it clear that this room was needed right away for the next panel, so everyone would clear out.

Brendan doesn't look like he's having a panic attack, but I definitely don't think he wants to be drawn into an impromptu post-panel Q&A with a small crowd of fans.

We make our own escape and enter the main exhibit hall,

which is always crowded and chaotic, making it harder for any fans following us out of the panel to mob us.

I wish I could still hold his hand. "You okay? You seemed like you got nervous there toward the end. But you really did fantastic." I bounce a little, smiling at him. "*We* did fantastic."

He just stares straight ahead and stuffs his hands in his pockets. Maybe he's wishing he could be holding mine, too. "Yeah, I don't know what happened. I was freaked out, and then I was fine, and then I got freaked out again." There's an edge of anger in his voice that I know all too well. It's that impatience he has with himself sometimes, that frustration that he can't always handle things the way he wants to.

It breaks my heart, and I wish I knew how to make him feel better. How to make him see how incredible he is, no matter how panicky crowds—or even relationships—make him.

"I don't think anyone could tell but me," I say. "And probably only because I like looking at you a lot."

Now he turns to me and gives me a small smile, and I feel like at least I helped a tiny bit. I wish it was more. I wish I could always be more.

"I don't think I slept great last night," he says with a shrug, as we pass a booth with some gamer artwork done with spray paint on huge canvases.

I know he didn't. I heard him tossing and turning throughout the night. But I'm not sure I should tell him, or if he'll feel bad that he kept me awake. And also because I might confess how desperately I wanted to crawl under the covers with him and cuddle up and feel his body relax against me.

Would that have helped?

I'm not sure. It definitely wouldn't have felt *casual*.

Before I can think of how to respond to that without giving away my near-miss at becoming his late-night bed partner, he suddenly stops.

"Do you really want to deal with dating me?" He asks this as if it's been a question plaguing him, just waiting there to burst out in the middle of this packed exhibition hall next to the live-action *Minecraft*. The crowd swirls around us as we stand frozen in the pathway.

"What do you mean?" I feel my own burst of panic. Does he want to give up the plan? I know it's stressful for him, but—

"I'm a mess." He runs a hand through his pink hair, staring down at the floor. "I'm a total mess, and even if I can get over the relationship stuff, I'm still going to have panic attacks and anxiety. It's just a part of me, and it's not going away." He swallows. "I hate to put you through all *this* and then still keep putting you through all *that*."

Now my heart really aches.

I don't care that you have panic attacks and anxiety, I want to say. *You're Brendan and my best friend and I love you, no matter what.*

But is that the wrong thing to say? Does it sound callous, like I'm saying I don't care that he's suffering? That I don't care when he hurts?

I feel like I'm on some tightrope, and I'm not sure whether there's a net below to catch me if I fall.

Maybe that's the way he feels. Maybe he doesn't know if I'll be there to catch him (Though it's a good thing we're not talking literally here, because the dude would squash me like a Kung Pao Pancake.)

"Hey." I tug at his shirt to bring him closer. I'm conscious of all the people around us, enough that I don't wrap my arms around his waist like I want to, but I don't think anyone's paying attention to us. Not when people wearing cardboard boxes on their heads are competing in a high-stakes *Minecraft* building competition fifteen feet away from us. "I've seen your panic attacks and anxiety before. I'm not afraid of it."

"But you shouldn't have to put up with it. Especially from a—" He cringes, his face flushing, and I know he was going to say "boyfriend," but couldn't. He glares at the ceiling in frustration.

I'm not sure I can talk him out of thinking that he's someone

I have to "put up with," even though that's not even remotely the case. I decide on a different tactic. "What kind of stuff—beyond the relationship, I mean—do you think will be triggery?"

"I don't know. Lots of things. New people, still. New situations." His mouth twists, and he scuffs his sneaker on the concrete floor. "My dad will be getting out of jail eventually, and I'm not sure how I'm going to deal with that."

In a stroke of spectacularly bad timing, the *Minecraft* challenge crowd around us starts cheering and whooping.

Brendan doesn't even seem to notice.

My breath catches. Brendan almost never talks about his dad, not even to me. Probably anything he needs to say about the bastard he says to his mom—Brendan and his mom are super close, and she's awesome—but I get the feeling he doesn't exactly go out of his way to talk about it with her, either.

"Do you have any idea when that'll happen?" I ask.

Brendan shrugs. "He's still got another fifteen years or so on his sentence, but he's been up for parole already, so I don't know." His lips press together tightly.

"You don't have to see him, though, right?"

"No. I mean, I definitely don't want to. But just knowing he's out there . . ." There's this haunted look in Brendan's blue eyes that chills me.

I decide I don't care who might see and reach for his hand. He looks surprised, but then smiles again—not the full, wide Brendan grin that makes my heart swell, but still a genuine smile. And his grip on my hand is as tight as mine on his.

"I want to be there for you," I say. "When that happens, and . . ." *Always. Just always.* "And anything else that you're worried about," I finish, because I'm a huge freaking chicken. Also because telling him I never want to leave his side is soooo not casual.

He stares into my eyes for a long moment. Part of me hopes he can read in them what I meant to say, and part of me is afraid he will see and run far, far away. My pulse pounds in my ears, drowning out the announcer in Ender dragon cosplay reading off the game winner's stats.

"Thanks," Brendan says. He looks away.

I feel like I let him down somehow, like I said too much or maybe not enough.

"I'm going to go back to our room and take a nap," he continues. "Rest up for tonight's big party."

I nod. There were so many times after my mom left that I felt like I couldn't ever say the right thing to help my dad, who became like a shadow of his previous self, sitting in his armchair all the time, watching reruns of *Matlock* on what must have been some weird all-Andy-Griffith cable channel.

But if I just tried to stay happy and peppy and upbeat, that seemed to make things a little better. "You should, because it's going to be a killer party," I say, trying to act way more excited about this than I actually am. "Su-Lin room parties are pretty much the talk of the con. Su-Lin *and Brendan* parties are going to be insane."

He chuckles. "I bet." Then he gives my hand a squeeze that makes me think maybe he doesn't want to let go.

He does, though, and walks into the crowd. They part and flow back around him.

My hand feels empty, and I let out a long breath.

I decide to go back to our booth and check in on Emily and Tate. There has to be some good news there. They were all over each other at the prom last night.

I make my way past more exhibits and games and booths, bummed when I see that a Monty Python t-shirt Brendan would really like is sold out in his size. I'll have to check that out online. I pause in surprise when I see that Mystique, aka "the Human Chameleon," is here, and she's actually doing live makeovers! (Should I get a makeover? How awesome would I look as the Corpse Bride?) And then I finally—sans dramatic makeover, sadly—reach our booth, where Emily is restocking.

"Hey!" she says when she sees me. "These shirts are selling

like crazy. Especially the *Socktor Who* one."

It's hard to be super stoked about merch sales when I'm still thinking about Brendan's anxiety, but I try anyway. "Nice! Maybe in my next panel I'll talk up *Starving with the Socks*, so we can get those moving, too." I sit on one of the empty chairs behind the booth. "Sooo, how'd you enjoy prom last night?"

She grins. "It was actually really fun! I still can't believe Jason climbed the scaffolding. That guy is crazy."

She's not wrong, but I didn't need to hear about that, given that I saw it, too. Also, Jason is not who I want to hear about right now.

"Yeah, but what about you and *Tate*?" I'm not even pretending to be subtle.

"I don't know, it was kind of . . . meh."

My eyes widen. That is not how it looked to me. Besides, they're Emily and Tate! They are so cute together and liked each other so much and—

Emily bursts out laughing. "I'm kidding! God, your expression. It's like I murdered one of your puppets!"

"Wait, so—"

"Tate and I had a very good time." Her brown eyes sparkle mischievously.

"Really?" I lean in. "How good, exactly?"

"The kind of good where I remember exactly how fantastic your cousin is in bed."

"Yay! I mean, ew, but also yay!" I clap my hands together. "So my plan is a success?"

"So far. How about your plan regarding your casual dating?"

My excitement is tempered quite a bit by that question. "I accidentally set him up with a girl who it turned out was a little more into me than him," I admit. I still feel dumb about that, like I failed the Plan—and him—somehow. And also dumb about how much it bothered me seeing them dancing together, before I knew she was using him as a way to get an intro to me. "But he did dance with her, then danced with two other girls before we went back to the hotel room."

"Sounds good, then." Emily says this like she doesn't actually believe it's good.

"It is," I say firmly. "If we date other people, then it both helps him with social anxiety and makes his brain not feel the pressure of being in a serious relationship with me." *Until one day it'll let him be okay with that,* I finish to myself. *Please, please, let him one day be okay with that.*

Emily nods. "Oh! If you're looking for people to set him up with, there's always Jane Shaw."

My guts constrict on themselves. "What? Why her?"

"I don't know. I mean, she's pretty, and she's actually a big fan of yours—she stopped by earlier today hoping to chat with you. She bought a few of the finger puppets."

"Wow. That's nice," I say. But I have this image in my head of Jane, in all her curvaceous glory, cuddled up against Brendan, and I feel sick. "I don't know, her and Brendan? It doesn't seem . . ." I shake my head. "I don't think so."

Emily purses her lips. "Okay, it was just a thought." She gives me a look that seems all too knowing, and my cheeks heat up. Jane's the kind of girl I've spent so much of life wishing I was, even as I would loudly proclaim how proud I was of being a goofy Chinese girl who had to rely on humor instead of big boobs—as if a girl couldn't have both. Jane certainly does.

And I can't help but think she'd make Brendan feel that zing, as well as not be a total bitch to him like Candace. He could have both.

When, selfishly, I want him to have *me.*

I realize I'm staring off into space, and Emily's still watching me. "But yeah, things are going well with our plan."

Emily does a solid job faking being impressed, and I tell her I need to get supplies for the party and head off.

So many things run through my mind as I head out to the car: the panel today, the feeling of Brendan's hand in mine, that image of him and Jane, that haunted look he got when he talked about his dad.

It was different, him bringing up his dad out of nowhere like that. He must be worried, which makes sense with what his dad did to him and how he's been in prison now for over twenty years and . . .

My thoughts snag on that in a way they never have before. Isn't twenty years—with a much longer full sentence—a long time for domestic abuse? I mean, not that him beating his wife and his child doesn't make him a total monster, but it occurs to me that I've never heard of someone going away for that long on that charge. But that's definitely what Brendan said he went away for, though I guess there might have been other things he was charged with as well.

I pause in one of the hallways of the convention center and pull out my phone, ducking behind a big column so I don't get interrupted. I stare at the screen of my phone—a pic of Ruby and Terrence sharing a sweet kiss—my heart somewhere up my throat. I know I should be asking Brendan about this and not looking it up on the internet, but I don't want to upset him.

I Google Brendan's dad's name.

An article from a local paper twenty-one years ago pops up, with a pic of a guy who looks a lot like Brendan—the same jaw-line, the same slim nose. But he doesn't have the light Brendan carries with him. It's like some wrong version of my best friend. Below it is this sentence: *Pike was sentenced to forty years on sixty counts of criminal sexual assault of a minor.*

I think my heart stops; I sink down to the floor, leaning against the wall.

Sexual assault. I try to think back on what Brendan said. That his father abused him, definitely, and that his mother had him put away. I scan down the article, but there's no other charges listed, just that this charge had several victims. It doesn't name Brendan, but if what Brendan said is true, then . . .

Brendan was sexually abused by his own father.

I just assumed all along that it was domestic abuse, that he'd hit both Brendan and his mom. Maybe lots of times. Which is horrific enough, but this—

This feels worse.

All those years of therapy growing up, all his anxiety and trust issues and panic—it all makes even more horrible sense now.

I want to throw my arms around Brendan and cry and tell him how sorry I am this happened to him. But there must be a reason he didn't tell me. I'm hoping it's not because he thought I couldn't handle it.

It doesn't really matter what his reason is, though. He didn't want me to know, and now I feel super guilty that I pried like this. As much as I want to tell him I'm willing to listen if he ever wants to talk about it, I don't want to bring it up and risk making him relive it.

I won't do that to him. I can't. Not until he wants to tell me himself.

But even as I make this determination, I worry about having to hide this—hide anything, really—from Brendan, who knows me better than anyone else.

I resort to my usual tactic: Be Su-Lin, always happy and perky and smiley.

It's the only way I know to make things better.

EIGHT

BRENDAN

Su-Lin hosts a room party every year, and this year is no exception. She's set up a group invitation online and invited all the professionals she knows, plus anyone who might hear about it from any of them. We turn our beds against the wall sideways for seating, push the chairs against the wall by the couch, stow our luggage and valuables in my car for safe keeping, and fill the table with pretzels, beer, and several bottles of cherry vodka and hard lemonade, plus disposable plastic wine cups. I go downstairs to get ice and return to find Su-Lin laying a Twister mat in the center of the floor.

"It's going to be packed in here, isn't it?" I ask. "Do you really think there's going to be room to play Twister?"

Su-Lin smiles mischievously. "We'll find a way."

Oh, no. Suddenly, I understand what the plan is. "You just want me stuck trying to twist around a harem of women, so you can call that a date and laugh at my expense."

Su-Lin's jaw drops in mock-surprise. "Little old me?" she says in Ruby's southern drawl. "Sugar, would *I* do something like that? It's positively *devious*."

"Exactly."

Su-Lin drops the accent. "But seriously, it won't just be you.

I need to get Tate and Emily in there, too."

I raise my eyebrows at her. "I'm pretty sure they spent the night together. Isn't your devious plan complete?"

She rolls her eyes. "They messed it up last time. I can't leave them to their own devices. Not yet, at least."

I put the ice bucket on the table and look around the room. We're pretty much set, and I'm starting to have the pre-party jitters. How many people are going to be in here, anyway? It's decently big for a double room, but it's still not a full suite. It'll heat up fast with too many bodies.

I crank up the air conditioning as far as it will go.

Emily and Tate show up first, helping themselves to some cherry vodka and settling on the edge of Su-Lin's bed. I'm trying to decide if I should join them or if that would make me an awkward third wheel, when a whole bunch of other people start filtering in, including that girl Jason was talking to last night—what was her name? She's wearing a Faye Valentine outfit, complete with suspenders and yellow booty shorts, and she definitely has the figure to fill it out.

Su-Lin steals the spot I was eyeing next to Emily and Tate, and I get the message. This is not our date night. I'm supposed to talk to other women. Ones who aren't being set up with Su-Lin's cousin.

I steel myself and try to smile. "Hey!" I say, walking over to the Faye Valentine girl. I know just enough about her to start a conversation, which helps. "You're a YouTuber right? I remember Su-Lin telling me about your show."

"Jane," she says, beaming. "And you're Brendan, the new blood over at *Sockwives*, right?"

I nod. "That's me."

Jane shrugs happily, which pushes her breasts up and almost out of her collared halter top.

Yep. Definitely authentic Faye Valentine.

"Nice costume," I say. "Did you make it?"

"Yeah," she says. "That's what my show is, mostly. Costuming how-to, plus I've done some episodes about consent issues in the cosplay community. Actually, Su-Lin totally inspired me on that front. I just loved her sock puppets, so I made a puppet of my own."

She holds up her phone, and on it is a picture of her dressed in a sexy Dorothy outfit with an alien-thing popping out the top of her Toto basket. It's not a sock, but the form is basically the same.

"Oh, yeah!" I say. "I saw one of those once. You pretend to be ditzy while the puppet schools you about feminism."

"I'm glad you said 'pretend.' You wouldn't believe how many people think the puppet is the smart one."

"You're actually a ventriloquist, right? Like, you're not editing in the voice later."

"Yep. I'd always wanted to try it. It's not as easy as it looks, so I had to work at it to get it right." She grins at me. "By the way, nice hair! Not many guys can pull off pink, but you totally rock it." Jane twirls a finger through her platinum blond hair, which is dyed too, with red streaks underneath, and she has it pulled back in a yellow Faye-style headband.

I smile. "Thanks, you too." I get a lot of mixed reactions to my hair, the worst of which are people yelling "faggot" at me from passing cars. It pisses me off on behalf of gay men everywhere.

More people mill into the room, and Jane steps closer to me. It's hard for me to look at her face now without checking out her breasts, which, as I said back at the prom, are definitely worth checking out. But I don't want to do that in front of Su-Lin, and I also don't want to make Jane feel like I don't understand those cosplay consent issues we were *just* talking about.

"So do you perform in the videos?" she asks. "Or are you mostly doing technical stuff? I heard you're the video editor, but it sounds like you're pretty involved."

"I do some of the puppetry. Not as much as Su-Lin, but I've got a few characters in the first set of skits. There's this welding glove character that I came up with. The girl socks aren't fond of him."

Jane cocks her head to the side. "Why is that?"

I cringe inwardly. This joke made Su-Lin laugh when I came up with it, and we've based a whole series of sketches around it, but no one's seen those yet. It's possible it's about to completely fall flat. "Because he's so handsy."

Jane laughs so abruptly that she spits on me a little, and I laugh along with her. My face flushes with relief. I'm still a little nervous making jokes about sexual harassment, even though I'm a victim of sexual assault—even if it was before I can remember—but *I* think the way we handle it is funny. We try to always punch up and all of that. But it's still a relief to know that other people appreciate it and aren't offended.

"That's amazing," Jane says with a grin. "I am so looking forward to binging your whole season."

This is good. I'm having a conversation and not having a panic attack, even during an overwhelming convention full of strangers. I'm jittery, but I'm not having chest pain and I can breathe just fine.

I'm doing this.

I smile over at Su-Lin, but she seems to have something stuck in her nails and doesn't notice.

"Do you have any sock characters?" Jane asks.

"Yeah," I say. "I'm also playing Shuby. She's new, but you can see her at our booth in—"

"Oh my god, yes. Emily was telling me she's going after Terrence Clarence! I can't wait to see how Ruby will handle someone trying to steal her man."

Over on the bed, I hear Su-Lin mutter something. I look back at her, but she's still studying her nails. I open my mouth, then close it again.

Did I say something wrong? I was just talking about the show, which, yeah, some of those details aren't public, but I didn't think we were keeping the welding glove or the Shuby character a secret. Emily's clearly been telling people about it, which I thought was fine.

"I'm going to get a drink," Jane says and moves over to the table to pour herself a lemonade.

I sigh, more relieved now than I was when the joke went well. It went fine, didn't it? It's a sad comment on the state of my life when I'm proud I can converse with a woman. But hey, it's a step.

I move over to Su-Lin on the bed. "Hey, did I do something wrong? I thought we were talking about the new characters, but if I'm not supposed to—"

Su-Lin smiles at me, but it's fake again. "No, it's fine. Were you enjoying talking to Jane?"

Enjoying might be overstating it. "Did you see me? Not bad, huh?"

"Yeah, I saw." She sounds happy, but there's an undertone to it.

I lower my voice. "Are you okay?" I know watching her dance with that other guy made me a little crazy, and I imagine that cuts both ways, even if, ultimately, Su-Lin thinks this is a good idea. "Because I don't have to talk to her again—"

"No!" Su-Lin says. "No, it's fine." She puts her hand on my arm, and I want to just wrap my arms around her and tell her that I hate this, that we should figure out some other way to be together.

Except there isn't another way, is there? I have no right to ask her for monogamy, and she shouldn't give it to me, not when I can't even say . . . that word. Not when I'm still not sure if I'm going to be able to handle this without turning into someone she doesn't even recognize.

The room is filling up, and several more enthusiastic con-goers bounce up to Su-Lin and congratulate her on the debut of the new series. Su-Lin introduces me to a couple dozen people, none of whose names I remember. It's another hour before I get a chance to talk to Su-Lin again without other people actively listening.

I know she's not the one I'm supposed to be spending time

alone with, but my clinginess gets the best of me. I bring her a drink—she's been playing hostess too well to get her own—and stand close to her. "We okay?" I ask.

Su-Lin waves a finger in the air. "We are fine. You, however, are not doing your part in finding another girl to hang out with."

I look around. Jane is still here, but she's across the room sitting on Jason's lap while he tells some loud story about climbing suspension bridge cables, possibly illegally. I catch sight of Emily giving them a look that I could swear is jealousy, but she and Tate are cuddled up on the other bed, their backs propped against the wall and their legs extended and twined together.

Jason glances over at them, and his expression darkens, just for a second. I hope Su-Lin hasn't seen this, because she will not be pleased.

"Did you have anyone in mind?" I ask.

Su-Lin is glaring daggers at Jason—okay, so she noticed. But she tears her eyes away from him and casts about the room, finally coming to rest on a girl in the corner, nibbling on pretzels. "What about Maren?" she asks. "I just met her tonight, but she seems nice."

I consider while trying not to look like I'm checking her out. She's cute, I guess, but in a quiet way. I decide I could honestly express interest in having a conversation with her, which is all I'm expected to do.

Right?

"Yeah, sure," I say. "What should I say to her?"

"Nothing." Su-Lin grins wickedly and then commands the attention of the room. "Okay, everybody!" she says to the nearly three dozen people who are standing around or lounging on the beds or couch. "We're going to play Twister, so clear the floor."

Some people promptly vacate the room, and I want to flee along with them. "Who wants in?" Su-Lin asks, grabbing the spinner in both hands. "Emily, Tate, you guys are in, right?"

Tate gives Su-Lin a skeptical look, and Emily shrugs. "I'll

play," she says.

"Awesome," Su-Lin says. "So we've got Tate, Emily, and Brendan—"

Jason raises a long arm in the air. "I'm in!" Jane sets down her drink and declares the same.

"Okay." Su-Lin pretends to scan the room. Those who have neither fled nor volunteered look at their drinks, at the floor, anywhere but at Su-Lin. "Maren!" she says. "How about you?"

Maren pauses with a pretzel halfway to her mouth. "Me?" She looks shocked that Su-Lin remembers her name.

"Sure," Su-Lin says. "That'll be just enough people."

"I'm out," Tate says. "I've seen the length of Jason's arms. He's got the whole board in his wingspan."

"Not to mention the size of his hands," Emily says.

Oh my god. Did she seriously just say that?

Across the room, I see Jason smile.

"Okay!" Su-Lin says, though it comes out too loud. "Places, everyone!"

Jane sidles up to Su-Lin and gestures to the board, which the crowd has managed to clear. Mostly. "Let me spin," Jane says. "It's your game. You should get to play."

I let out a breath of relief. I really don't want to end up straddling Jane in that outfit. I don't want to be a jerk, and of course women can wear whatever they want, but there are just some positions I'd rather not be in with women who I'm not sleeping with who are barely dressed, and all of them become substantially more likely on a Twister mat.

Maren approaches the mat warily, while Su-Lin tries to gently suggest that she doesn't want to deprive Jane of the honor of playing. I'm not sure if she's just hoping having two possible girls I could get in a compromising position with is better than one, but I do gesture to Maren to come stand by me. We each put our feet on two of the dots on one of the smaller edges of the mat.

"I'm not drunk enough for this," Maren says.

I smile. "Me neither."

93

Su-Lin's "no-really" arguments are getting increasingly high-pitched, and Jane increasingly (and insistently) benevolent as she says that she'd really, *really* like to let Su-Lin play. My guess is she wisely decided she doesn't want to play Twister in her Faye Valentine outfit.

"Come on, Su-Lin," I say. "Play with us."

Su-Lin shoots me a death glare. I'm sure I'm going to hear all about this betrayal later, but I really want to get this over with. Playing with Su-Lin has its own compromising-position risks—though she's relatively covered up in jeans and a tank top—but she's set on getting me all tangled up with somebody else, so she'll be avoiding me as much as possible.

Jason and Emily have taken the two pairs of dots on the side opposite Maren and me, while everyone else in the room is grabbing more drinks and settling in to watch. Su-Lin grudgingly takes up position on the dots around the corner from Jason. She's smiling, and probably no one else will notice, but I can see how tense she is. I'm pretty sure the plan was for her to cheat, calling out limbs and colors that would get me appropriately tangled up with Maren.

I can't say I'm sad if that part of the plan is a bust.

Jane calls out left hand blue, then right hand green, and we maneuver around the mat, trying to get our limbs on the appropriate spots without either falling or groping each other inappropriately. This becomes harder than it sounds when Su-Lin is forced to stretch across the mat in my direction to reach a blue dot with her left foot, and then I have to reach over her to get a yellow dot with my left hand. She ends up mostly underneath me, so that I'm basically mounting her doggie-style on the Twister mat. In front of everyone.

Yep, this was the risk. And oh my god, I'm glad I'm wearing tight jeans.

"Right foot blue!" Jane calls.

"Our right feet are on blue," Su-Lin grumbles back.

I look down at the back of her head. My achilles tendon is

cramping up, and I look back to see Maren perched on four dots in the corner, not tangling with anyone. She has clearly made better limb placement choices than I have.

"Right hand red!" Jane calls, and I groan and reach for the nearest red dot that won't cause me to topple forward onto Su-Lin and squash her flat. That one gets taken immediately by Jason—who I note is mostly on top of Emily, though she's doing a crab-walk position, so they look like they're ready to start dry humping right there on the mat.

By the intense way they're staring into each others' eyes, I think they just might.

I groan again and reach for the next red dot, glad that Su-Lin can't see Emily and Jason staring at each other. Tate is on the other side of the room talking to some girl in a red cocktail dress, so I'm pretty sure he hasn't even noticed.

I get my hand on the red dot—but damn, Emily is right about the size of Jason's hands. The dot he stole from me is almost entirely concealed. To stretch this far, my body sinks a bit onto Su-Lin's.

Now I'm pressed against her ass, and I know she can feel exactly the reaction my body is having to being on top of her.

"Hey," I say in her ear.

"Hey," she says back.

I'm surprised to find her as breathless as I am.

Now we're the ones about to start grinding on each other.

"Left foot green!" Jane shouts, and as I try to slide it over, Su-Lin gives a little gasp beneath me. I feel lightheaded—just for a second, but it's enough. I lose my balance, rolling to the side to avoid Su-Lin, and take out one of Jason's arms, causing him to fall on top of Emily. Emily screams, and I think she may have been crushed by the falling giant, but then both she and Jason are laughing. Su-Lin fell over as well—probably I took her out with a flailing limb as I tried to keep my balance—and we all sit on the mat and look at Maren.

"Maren is the winner!" Jane announces. "Want to go again?"

"I'm good!" I say, in tandem with Su-Lin. I'm more interested in sitting down somewhere I can cross my legs and put an arm across my lap and not advertise to the entire room that I have a hard-on for my best friend who I am definitely not supposed to be dating tonight. I pour myself a cherry vodka and wedge myself into a corner, which still isn't as far out of the way as I'd like to be.

The room is hot. Roasting, in fact, and I'm pretty sure my face is hardcore flushed. Su-Lin is across the room talking to Tate and Emily, and from the way she's gripping Emily's arm, I think she might have dragged her there, which I'm sorry I missed. But the room seems smaller now than it did before, and a new group of people just arrived and the Twister board is covered in talking people again. Someone whoops loudly, and all the chatter is turning to static, and I'm wondering if we have enough oxygen in this room because I'm pretty sure I can't breathe.

Shit.

This is about the time I would bow out and escape back to my room for an hour, but this *is* my room. I didn't think about that when I agreed to the room party, but now I see that was a huge oversight. I can go out in the hall, but there are people milling around out there, too. This entire hotel is teeming with fans and professionals, many of whom might recognize me from the events we've been doing, and all of whom will assume I'm here to socialize.

Because I'm at a damn convention, and a normal person would be.

My chest is starting to develop an ache that is angling toward swimmer's cramp, and my head goes light again. The room spins.

I have to get out of here.

Stumbling toward the door while trying not to bump into or make eye contact with anyone is far more difficult than I would like, especially when I can't breathe or see straight. Su-Lin shoots me a worried glance, but I wave for her to stay—it's her party, after all, and our room, so we can't *both* leave.

I finally reach the door and stride out into the hall at top speed, past several more room parties on the con block and toward the elevator.

Thankfully there's nobody in it. I collapse into the corner and try to catch my breath. The elevator is small and enclosed, but I'm alone, and I find myself hoping it gets stuck between floors. Just for an hour, maybe two.

Just long enough for me to feel like I can stand to see people again without passing out.

NINE

Su-Lin

'm all flushed from Twister, which didn't go at all how I intended—none of this party has gone how I intended—when I see Brendan flee the room, sweat beading on his forehead. He catches my eye and waves at me to stay, but I recognize that look on his face. He's about to have a full-blown panic attack.

I want to follow him, to make sure he's all right. But Emily's clutching my arm now, leaning in by my ear. In a vodka-scented voice I think she means to be a whisper but is in fact much louder, she says, "Do you think Jason's into that Jane girl?"

I flinch, but Tate doesn't seem to have heard. He's focused on his phone, glaring at it and muttering about how "all anyone wants anymore is this John Williams knock-off tympani shit." I glance over to where Jason is laughing with Maren, the one who was supposed to be twisted with Brendan instead of me.

Maybe I pushed the whole Twister thing a bit much, trying to prove to both Brendan and myself how much faith I have in the Plan.

But none of that felt particularly good, at least until it was him and I all twisted together—and then it felt *way* too good to be doing in public.

Is that what triggered this attack? Did he notice how into that

I was, how I could barely breathe with him pressed against me? Stop. Focus.

"I don't know if he's into her," I say to Emily, though my eyes keep drifting back to the door where Brendan left. "Jason flirts with everyone. I told you he's a player."

Emily frowns, but brightens when Tate comes over and slings his arm around her. "Hey, you want to listen to the sample I'm sending the doc people?"

I have no idea what he's talking about—is he doing sound for a documentary? A medical show? Something nautical? Whatever. Emily is eagerly sharing ear buds with him and hopefully forgetting her Twister grind session with Jason.

My grind session, however, is still making me very inconveniently achy. And guilty.

I mean, he knows I'm super into him. We've made out a lot now. But his anxiety doesn't always make sense, and something random like that could totally lead his thoughts into "oh my god serious relationship" territory.

Probably, though, it was just the social stress of the party. So many people. So much chaos. He often has to leave things like this, go back to his room, or—

Shit shit shit.

We are *in* his room. He didn't have anywhere to calm down, to get away. I didn't think about that, and I pressed him into having this party . . .

Now my guilt is even worse. And my worry. Because this whole floor is filled with con people having parties, and the hallways will be crowded and—

"Hey Su-Lin!"

—And suddenly Jane Shaw's boobs are in my face.

Okay, I'm not actually *that* short. But really, that's what it feels like. I have no idea what cosplay she's doing right now, but I'm sure it's super accurate, right down to every single inch of her body being thrust upward or hanging outward.

That jealousy flares again, thinking of her flirting with

Brendan. Was he into that? He seemed to enjoy it. And who wouldn't? She's Jane freaking Shaw and god, even *I* can't tear my eyes away from her body.

"Hi Jane," I say, feeling myself shrinking a little. Why did I think jeans and a Pusheen tank top made for good party-wear? Was I trying to cosplay as myself at twelve? I mean, I love this shirt, and Pusheen as a sushi roll makes me laugh, but—

Jane smiles, tossing her platinum hair over her shoulder. "Great party!"

"Thanks." I don't have time for this. I need to make sure Brendan's okay.

"Hey, where did your friend run off to?"

My throat goes dry. It's pretty clear she's not referring to Emily. "I—uh, I think he needed to get some more food."

She looks disappointed, and my stomach is tying itself into little knots on top of knots, even as a guy who looks like the forgotten Hemsworth brother starts chatting her up.

Jane is totally into Brendan. And I know Brendan wants to be with me, but if given the choice between me and *Jane Shaw*, any guy would—

No. I can't worry about this right now. I need to check on Brendan, see if he found a good, quiet space to hole up. I look around the room frantically, making sure I can take off. People are laughing and drinking and eating and starting another game of Twister. It's mostly under control, and we've stashed our stuff in Brendan's car.

I run over to Emily and ask her to keep an eye on the party for me, and she nods, but she's clearly a little wasted.

I grab my Gudetama toaster on the way out, which prompts several disappointed groans from toast-munching party-goers. But no way in hell am I risking this getting stolen.

The halls are crowded and loud when I get out, and there's no sign of Brendan, which is probably good. I head to the elevators, tucking the toaster under my arm. I'm in the elevator before it occurs to me how ridiculous this is.

Brendan has had panic attacks practically his whole life. He doesn't need me to get through them. I'm not even sure I wouldn't make it worse, especially if the attack was triggered by something about our relationship.

But he's said before that it helps having me there. And I want to be there for him, to help in any way I can. To just be with him through it, if nothing else.

People in the elevator eye me and my toaster strangely, but I ignore them, bouncing nervously from foot to foot. I probably look like I need to pee and make toast and am trying to find a bathroom in which I can do both. They shift away from me, and I don't blame them.

The elevator opens into the hotel lobby near the bar, which is also on the crowded side. I scan quickly, but it's doubtful Brendan would be here. Did he go to sit in his car? I make my way past the reception desk and concierge, past the typical over-priced gift shop—hey, Twizzlers are on sale for only, like, *half* a million dollars a bag!—and am about to the exit to the parking lot when I catch the sight of a very familiar shade of bright pink.

Brendan, half-hidden behind a big potted plant, sitting on a loveseat in a sort of removed nook over by the hotel "business center." This business center consists of a computer and a printer/fax machine, neither of which have likely been used for at least a decade, since everyone and their five-year-old got a smartphone.

He's got his head in his hands and his elbows on his knees as he sits nearly bent double.

My chest aches. I walk over and put the toaster down on the little side table by the small couch and settle in next to him. He looks up, startled at first, then sees it's me and relaxes.

Relatively speaking, anyway. He's clearly still struggling to breathe, his eyes squinching shut in pain, sweat beaded up along his hairline.

I wrap my arms around him and hold him tight, resting my head on his shoulder. Maybe it's just wishful thinking, but I think he leans into me.

No, he definitely leans into me. I feel his cheek against the top of my head.

We sit like that for a few minutes, until his breathing is steady again.

"I'm sorry," he says, and the sadness in his voice almost brings tears to my eyes. "You didn't have to leave the party."

"I know. I wanted to," I say, and he gives me a skeptical look. I just smile. "I'd always rather hang out with you, anyway."

For a moment I think even that might be too much—I say that kind of thing to him all the time, even before we added making out to our time spent together, but maybe now that he's stressed about things becoming too serious . . .

But his lips quirk up at the edges, and he puts his arm around me, pulling me closer. Which feels soooo good, I don't care right now if anyone sees us through the big potted plant fronds.

His brow furrows as he looks past me. "Are you planning on making me toast?"

The look of confusion on his face makes me giggle. "I will, if you want. Except I didn't bring the bread."

His smile broadens, but he shakes his head and lets out a breath. "I'm okay." I think he means more than that he doesn't need Gudetama toast. He looks around as if taking in his surroundings for the first time.

He's probably thinking that we're way too cuddled up for this public of a place—I'm all but in his lap—and maybe that those fronds hiding us aren't as big as he wishes they were. I let my arms drop down so I'm not a Su-Lin barnacle clinging tenaciously to him (To his hull? Is there a sexy metaphor possibility involving barnacles? Probably not, unless you're a pirate.) He drops his arm, too, sadly. But I can't bring myself to scoot away.

"Are you? Okay, I mean?"

He nods. "Yeah. I just needed to get away. Too many people, and just . . ."

"Too much," I finish.

"Right, too much."

"Well, you've got yourself a calming, scenic view here." I indicate the ancient computer under the bland motivational poster of a sunset over the ocean.

He lets out a little laugh. "The ocean's not bad, but I think I'd prefer the real thing. Maybe through a big picture window." He looks back over at me, his smile soft. A happy glow warms me, because I know what he's thinking about.

A couple months ago, we were hanging out in the studio, when he asked me where I would live if I could pick anywhere in the world.

I didn't need to think long. "Honestly, not far from here. I'd get a house on the beach, but not one of those generic mansions, just, like—"

"A place with character!" He jumped in excitedly. "Maybe a fixer-upper." Brendan's actually super handy—he lived in some pretty crappy places with his mom as he grew up, and he started taking on all the home improvement stuff himself.

This is actually a huge part of the reason my dad—who can barely change a lightbulb—thinks so highly of him. Not a month after we met, Brendan fixed our dishwasher, which had been broken for two years. All it took was some tools and a good YouTube tutorial, but my dad looked at him like the second coming of Bob Vila.

So that day in the studio, we started talking about the ideal house on the beach—on which, as it turns out, we are in total agreement. We decided that the perfect master bedroom would have a huge picture window facing the ocean, taking up the whole wall.

"And a big skylight open to the night sky," he added, and all I could think of was curling up with him in bed in that perfect bedroom in that perfect little house on a perfect slice of beach, with the stars above us and the ocean right there.

Of course, what we'd actually decided was that we needed to find two beach houses side by side, so we could be neighbors (though Brendan would clearly be doing all the work on *both* houses), but in my dreams—my very favorite ones—we only need one and its *ours*.

I've never mentioned that fantasy, though, and I'm not about to now. I don't need to send him into another panic attack when he's barely recovered from this one.

"And a skylight with a night sky full of stars," I say, smiling back at him.

He closes his eyes like he's picturing it. "I love it," he murmurs.

I'm back to picturing us curled up together in that bed, and I couldn't agree more. "Seriously, we need to make all the money so we can make these epic beach houses happen."

He opens his eyes again and stares down at his hands, which are knotted together in his lap. "It would be nice to feel like a place was *home*, you know? I mean, I've always felt like home was with my mom, but we moved around so much, it was never tied to a place."

I want to ask if he'd ever felt like the apartment he and Candace lived in together was home, but I can't bring myself to form the words, and I don't want him to have to think about the bad stuff that happened there with her.

I do think I know how he feels, though. "My house hasn't really felt like home since my mom left," I say quietly.

He looks up in surprise. I guess I don't talk about my mom a lot. I try not to think about her much, which is kind of jerky, probably. But she's the one who left.

"Really?" he asks. "Even with your dad and sisters still there?" There's no judgment, just curiosity.

I shrug. "I don't know why. I was always so much closer with my dad—I think because I'm more like him." I pause, and my throat feels like it's made of sandpaper. "She always said that, you know. That I was just like him—like I didn't take things seriously enough, and I'm too silly and loud and—"

It's stupid, because she left years ago, but I'm suddenly feeling all choked up and embarrassed. Then I feel the warmth of his fingers linking with mine, and my breath catches.

"You don't hear from her much," he says. It's not a question, because he knows the answer. He'd have heard all about it if I'd talked to my mom in the last four months.

"Not really. She calls a couple times a year, but even then she really only talks to Mei-Ling. She was closest to her. Lan and I might as well not exist."

I'm about to make a joke, because I know I'm supposed to be bright and cheery, that that's how I'm helpful to my family and to him and to everyone. But he's squeezing my hand and comforting me even though he just went through a panic attack—and I find the words tumbling out.

"I think I'm the reason she left us," I say.

Brendan's eyes widen. "What? What do you mean?"

I blink, trying to hold back the tears burning at the corners of my eyes. This is why I don't talk about this, why I don't even let myself think about it. "I mean, I know it's not my fault. I was only, like, thirteen. But—" I take a steadying breath. "At some point she must have loved my dad, but all I remember is that she couldn't stand him, for all those ways in which she says I'm like him. And it's like she could handle it when it was just him, and Mei-Ling was always more serious and calm like her. And even Lan was a pretty calm baby. But I was this super energetic kid, and it just got worse and worse. I think one day she realized she just couldn't do it anymore. That I'm too much."

I realize I'm echoing what I said to him before. That with all those people, it was just too much.

Am I that way for him, too? Maybe not always—obviously not always—but sometimes?

Brendan just gapes, horrified. "Has she said that to you?"

"No, not in those words. But I—I think it's true. She's never known what to do with me. I think she just couldn't take trying anymore, with both me and my dad."

Brendan turns so he's fully facing me, and now both my hands are folded in his. "Su-Lin," he says softly, and I look up

105

to meet his eyes, which are so clear and blue. "If that's true, it's her loss. You know that, right?"

I swallow past all that sandpaper. "Yeah, maybe."

"No," he says firmly. "Not maybe. You are the most incredible, beautiful person I could ever—" He stops, blinks. "You are Su-Lin, and you are amazing. Anyone who is lucky enough to have you in their life and doesn't appreciate you is an idiot."

"Really?" I whisper.

"Really."

The warmth of his gaze, of those words, is so heady I can barely stand it. I want to kiss him so desperately I'm burning with it.

There's this breathless moment where I think maybe I will, or he will, that we'll say screw the rules about only kissing on date night and not in public, and maybe he'll tell me that he just wants to be with me, and he thinks he can do that, that we can have a serious relationship and—

He clears his throat and looks away. "I, uh," he starts, "I get what you mean about feeling responsible, even though it's not your fault." He pulls one of his hands away from mine—only one, thankfully, because I feel like my heart might actually crack if he dropped both—and runs it through his hair, tugging on the curls. "My parents' marriage ended because of me. If I hadn't been born, then maybe . . ." He trails off.

My stomach drops. I know now about what his father did to him, and it kills me, the thought of Brendan taking any responsibility for the actions of that sick sack of shit wearing human skin.

He doesn't know that I know, and I feel like if he wanted me to, he'd have told me.

I squeeze his hand. I may not be able to go into details, but even what I knew before is enough. "It's not a bad thing your parents' marriage ended. Your father was a monster. As awful as it was for your mom to find that out"—oh god, his mom *found that out*, how horrible that must have been for her— "don't you think she's better off knowing and not staying married to him

106

all these years?"

Multiple victims, the article had said. Brendan and others. Neighborhood kids? Maybe other family?

I taste bile just thinking about it.

"Yeah, but—" He looks about as convinced as I probably did when he first said my mom leaving me was her loss. "She spent my whole life after that dealing with my issues, spending all that money and time on therapists and specialists and . . . and maybe if she didn't have to take care of me, she could have moved on. Dated, maybe gotten remarried. Had more kids. She always wanted more kids."

His voice breaks toward the end, and my heart breaks with it.

I scoot closer, even though we're smooshed nicely together on this little loveseat as is. "You know how much your mom loves you," I say, and he nods.

"I know she does, but—"

"No buts. She loves you *so much*. You guys have this awesome relationship, and she wouldn't trade that for anything, I know it."

He looks like he still might argue, but I reach out and grab his other hand. "Brendan," I say, willing him to really hear me. "You were never something your mom had to *deal with*. I really think that given what she went through with your dad, having you to take care of might have saved her."

He blinks those blue eyes, and his shoulders relax. "Really?"

I smile, thinking of how just moments ago I was the one asking him that same thing. I'm so grateful for what he told me, and that maybe I can return just a little of that comfort. "Really. And by the way, all that stuff about me being incredible and amazing?"

"Yeah?" He tugs his lower lip between his teeth.

"That's how I feel about you too. You're just—you're the best person ever."

"Ever, huh? Does this include Daveed Diggs? In a coconut bra?" He's smiling back now, and I feel lighter.

"I stand by what I said. *Ever*." I lay my head on his shoulder again and close my eyes. "Hey, maybe tomorrow night we should just stay in. No parties or dances. Just hang out and finish up whatever of that cherry vodka is left."

"Do you think there will be any left, now that we've left the party unattended? Will we even have a *room* left?"

I laugh. "Maybe not. But we do have a toaster."

He slides his arm back around me. "That's good enough for me."

TEN

BRENDAN

After last night, I decide I had better take the morning off from the con. We don't have any events, so when Su-Lin heads off to the exhibition hall, I take a walk, find a Starbucks with an outside patio, buy a coffee, and call my mom. I feel a tiny bit of guilt about this, knowing Su-Lin can't call hers. Her dad is awesome, and mine is a nightmare I'll never wake up from, but she and her dad don't talk about relationship stuff, so it isn't the same.

I hope Su-Lin is wrong about the reason her mom left them, but even if she is, it kills me that she believes that her mom left *her*, specifically. She deserves so much better than that. She deserves everything.

Mom's probably at work, but she picks up anyway. "Brendan!" she says. "How are you doing?"

"Good," I say, and I realize that's actually true. Despite last night's meltdown, I'm holding it together pretty well. Especially given everything that's been going on.

"*Good*? Is that all you're going to tell me?"

I smile. I told my mom that Su-Lin and I had decided to casually date, then promptly disappeared to make out with her in the studio and set up for the con. Mom loves Su-Lin and has basically decided that she's going to be her daughter, so it's understandable she's dying for information.

Even if she knows I'm likely to give her details she'll regret hearing.

"Still casually dating," I say. "Or trying, anyway."

"Trying? I'd think with as much time as you two spend together, it wouldn't be hard to date."

"It's not," I say. "It's the casual part that we suck at."

"*Reeeeeally.*"

I roll my eyes and take a sip of my coffee. "Yes. I'm sure it comes as a huge surprise that I'm not great at dating around, which I'm supposed to be doing. And I'm totally in love with Su-Lin, and it's kind of hard to go out with her and not *tell* her that or do anything else that would make things more than casual."

"You're still going with that seeing other people thing." She says this flatly, with the same dubious attitude she had when I told her about it the first time.

"Yeah. I mean, we're trying to at least spend time with other people."

Mom snorts. "As if you ever did that before."

I groan. "Are you going to listen to me?"

"I'm listening! It's not my fault you're trying not to be serious with the girl you've been glued to for the last four months."

I bite my lip. That's true, but it feels different from the time in my life when I was glued to Candace. Even my mom knows this is different. She must, or she wouldn't be in favor of it. To say she wasn't Candace's biggest fan is the understatement of the century.

"I know," I say. "It's my fault I can't say the stupid words and be in a relationship with her already."

Mom's voice softens. "Honey," she says. "That's not your fault."

"It feels like my fault." It's like Su-Lin and I were talking about last night. Sometimes a lot of things feel like my fault, even when I know logically they aren't. "I'm in love with her, so I should be able to call her my—" My throat tightens. "That g-word."

"That's closer to saying it than I've heard you before."

"Right. And when saying the first letter of a word counts as progress, that's when you know you're really pathetic."

"Brendan," Mom says, "did you call me just to tell me how awful you are?"

I slump back in my chair like a sulky teenager. I'm pretty sure that's exactly why I called her. Half because I need someone to talk to about the mess that I'm making and half because I want to hear her tell me that I'm wrong. "Is that a problem?"

"No," Mom says. "But honey, are you happy with the way things are going?"

I think about that. "Yes and no. I mean, I love that I can finally admit I have feelings for her, you know? And the making out is amazing."

"You can spare me the details of that," Mom says. "But you're not sleeping together yet?"

I don't usually spare my mom the details, largely because I don't have anyone else to talk to. "Like, early second base. Clothes on, hands under."

"No details!" Mom says, and I smile, twisting my coffee cup around on the bistro table.

"Oh my god, Mom. Like you don't know what constitutes second base."

"I'll remind you I have been to all the bases. I just don't want to hear about my son's escapades, though I'm glad you're having them now. It's been long enough."

I take another sip of coffee and look up at the sky through the leaves of a short palm tree. "You're one to talk." My mom hasn't dated anyone since my father, and the divorce was two decades ago.

"It hasn't been all that long," Mom says.

I raise my eyebrows. This is news to me. Not that I go inquiring about my mom's sex life, but I just assumed. "Really?"

"Yes, I ran into your orthodontist a couple months ago. He was such a nice man."

I blink, sure I can't be following this conversation. "You had sex with my orthodontist? Isn't he married?"

"Divorced," Mom says.

She didn't deny it. "Oh my god, Mom. My *orthodontist?* Do you know how many hours he's spent with his hands in my mouth? And he had bad breath."

"Well he didn't have bad breath when I saw him, I can tell you that."

I reach up and cover my ear, even though the phone is pressed to the other one, so this does me no good. "Ughhh."

"Now you know how I feel. Besides, you haven't been to the orthodontist in ten years. It was all very cordial."

I have no words for the fact that my mom describes her sexual encounters as *cordial*. "So are you *seeing* him?"

"No," Mom says. "But a woman has needs."

This I understand, but I definitely do not want to think about my orthodontist and my mom getting it on. Possibly in an orthodontists chair. Though I'm pretty sure Su-Lin and I could have a lot of fun with one of those. Yes, this is a much better train of thought; I lean into this one. I imagine Su-Lin on top of me, reclining the chair, shining one of those blinding overhead lights in my eyes and making some joke about bedside manner. Do dentists have that? Is it chairside manner?

Oh, god. I'm not supposed to be thinking about that, either. Casual. We're being casual.

"How's Su-Lin doing with everything?" Mom asks. I'm not sure if she means us seeing other people or me being a crazy person or the fact that I won't call her my . . . g-word.

"Okay, I guess. She seems stressed. We both are. I think it might help if we weren't constantly winding each other up, but I don't think she wants to have sex with me if I can't commit to her."

"Brendan," my mom says, "you are committed to her."

For a second I can't speak. My voice comes out hoarse. "Am I?"

"You can't bring yourself to see other people. You spend all your time with her. You're in love with her. What piece of commitment are you missing?"

"The part where I can call it a relationship. The part where she can tell everyone we're together. They're important, those words. That sense of definition."

Those words might not have meant much to Candace, ultimately. But they always have to me, and I hate the way my mind rebels against them now, no matter how much I want them with Su-Lin.

Mom is quiet for a minute. "Have you tried practicing saying the words when you're alone?"

That's exactly what my therapist would suggest, but I'm too scared. It's stupid. I know it's stupid. I feel things for Su-Lin that I never felt for Candace, and I was in that relationship for six *years*. "It doesn't make any sense, but when I try to use the words, I freeze."

"Do you know what it is that you're scared of?"

I shiver. Mom's being nice about it—she's been listening to my illogical thought processes since I was first self-aware enough to describe them. She doesn't judge me for them—but I judge myself.

"I'm scared of it ending," I say. "The way it did with Candace."

"Do you seriously think that Su-Lin is going to sleep with all your friends?"

As far as I know, Candace mostly slept with John, but I'm pretty sure there were others. "No, not that," I say. "Just—even if she hadn't done that, things were still bad between us."

"And you think Su-Lin would treat you like that."

"*No.*" It comes out angrier than I want it to. Even though I know Mom is just playing devil's advocate to get me to see how irrational the fears are, I don't like anyone suggesting things like that about Su-Lin. She would never say the kinds of hurtful things Candace did, just to make me feel worthless and dependent on her. Su-Lin would never toy with my emotions just

113

because she could.

But that wasn't the whole picture, either.

"Not everything that happened was Candace's fault. It was her fault that it ended, but we were both to blame for how bad it was."

Mom is quiet. She doesn't believe this, because I'm her kid, and she always wants to think the best of me. But I've never fully told her how I was with Candace, how when she'd get bored or annoyed and stop talking to me, or start making noise about wanting to break up, I'd be obsessive about holding onto her.

"I know you want it to be all her fault," I say. "But when things were bad, I used to fall apart, hard. I'd call her phone dozens of times, leave needy messages, drive by our friends' houses to see if her car was there. I've got attachment issues, and I'm not good with relationships. And I don't want to do that with Su-Lin." When things got really bad, I used to threaten to kill myself. My therapist says I was never a suicide risk, because people who are at risk have plans, they have means, they know exactly how they're going to do it, and I never did. But that means that I was being dramatic to manipulate her, which, yeah, she did to me plenty, too.

Mom's right; Su-Lin isn't like that.

But that doesn't change that I'm an emotional train wreck, and I don't want her anywhere near the tracks.

"Honey," Mom says. And I know what she's going to say. She's going to tell me that it isn't my fault, that this time will be different. But she doesn't know that, and neither do I.

"It's okay," I say, before she can respond. "I'm working on it, and I'm going to figure it out."

But all I can see is the anguished look on Su-Lin's face when she knows she has to break up with me for her own stability and mental health, because I'm dissolving into a co-dependent puddle, and then I lose everything again and don't know how I'm going to go on.

And this time, I don't get to come out the other side of that storm knowing I'm better off without her, because she's *Su-Lin*. This time, I would have to live with not only having lost the most wonderful woman in the world, but having done *that* to her.

"You'll figure it out," Mom says. "I know you will."

I believe her. But at this moment, I'm afraid what I'm going to figure out is that Su-Lin—like everyone else in the world—would be better off without me.

ELEVEN

Su-Lin

I love food trucks. This isn't exactly a popular opinion in my family—Aunt Alice calls them "salmonella wagons," and even my dad eyes them with skepticism. But I love their quirky uniqueness, their tendency to focus on making one thing really well, and especially their often hilarious, punny names, like I Dream of Weenie and Nacho Business.

The only problem is that where there is one food truck, there are usually many, and I am terrible at picking between them. I squint against the sun, Big Gulp from the corner convenience store already in hand, taking the trucks in again and trying to consult my stomach. Am I in the mood for a teriyaki bowl at Pimp My Rice? Do I desperately need some Waffle Love? Yesterday I had some amazing barbecue at the Trailer Pork Boys, which should probably count them out of the running just for variety's sake, but that sauce was sooo good. I recommended it to Brendan earlier today, and he went right there and got a plate of brisket, barely bothering to look around.

Food choices are not a source of anxiety for him.

I glance back at the table where Brendan is sitting with his lunch date, a really pretty—and very tall—Latina girl I pointed out to him after our panel. He did his part, gathered his courage, went over and introduced himself, and asked her to join him for lunch. She was all for it—of course she was, he's Brendan!—and the two of them are now chatting over their super-amazing barbecue plates.

I try not to notice how nice her smile is or how much she's showing that off—she's clearly having a great time. He doesn't seem to be overly tense, from what I can tell. He's definitely getting more comfortable with meeting new people, so that's good.

Except, what if all this plan does is make him better at dating other women? What if the only reason he wanted to date me was because he was so comfortable with me, and if he becomes comfortable with other people—

No. I shut down my stupid brain, which probably should have thought about this *before* we set the plan into motion. Too late now. Besides, the concept is still solid. If we're dating other people, we're casual. And if we're casual, then he doesn't need to freak out about jumping into a serious relationship all at once.

This reminds me. I'm not just supposed to be picking out my lunch, I'm supposed to be finding my own lunch date. Ugh.

I take a slurp of my Big Gulp—a mix of grape soda and various colas this time, heavy on the grape—and scan around. I check out the guys at the back of the lines, where I could jump in and easily start a conversation, leading to a lunch invite. This isn't exactly a problem for me. I may have had some rocky dating abilities in high school, but I'd like to think I came into my own in the years following. Guys tend to think I'm cute, and I'm generally able to tamp down the extreme spazziness of my natural personality, at least for a few minutes, so they think "She's fun!" rather than "Is she on speed?"

So it's not getting the date that's the problem. It's the fact that I've had no desire to be on a date with anyone but Brendan for well . . . about four months. And follow-through on things I have no desire to do has never been my strong point.

But I owe him. He's sticking to the plan, so I need to as well.

I suss out my options. There's a cute blond guy in a *Breaking*

Bad t-shirt waiting at Pretty Thai For a White Guy—yum, Thai—and an even cuter Black guy wearing what I think is a *Game of Thrones* costume at the end of the Burger She Wrote line.

I decide that between the two, I'm more in the mood for Thai, and head that direction, trying to think of a good *Breaking Bad*-related opening line—maybe something about wishing they had a Los Pollos Hermanos around here? But I stop short when I see Jason heading toward me across the courtyard, not looking particularly happy.

More like really, really unhappy.

"Hey Jason," I say when he gets close enough. "Is something wrong with the rock climbing thing later?"

I'm kind of hoping that there is. The closer I am to this afternoon's rock climbing shindig I stupidly agreed to, the more I remember how much I hate heights and how I have the arm strength of cooked ramen noodles.

"What is it about me that would give someone the idea I'm a player?" he asks, and my gut twists.

"Uh . . . what?" I'm not great at feigning innocence, or at least Brendan has told me so on numerous occasions, but Jason isn't really paying that much attention to me, despite having sought me out.

"I asked your friend Emily out just now, and she said she didn't think it would be a good idea." Jason glowers down at his flip-flops. "She said she's not really into *players*." He makes that last word sound like he's describing a particularly disgusting body odor, which is probably how Emily said it.

"Um, okay," I start. "Well, it's probably just that she's dating someone already and—"

He shakes his head. "She told me last night that guy Tate isn't her boyfriend."

"What?" I feel a little betrayed on behalf of my cousin. I mean, I don't think Tate and her have had the commitment talk or anything, but she's into him! And he's into her! They are perfect for each other—I practically have my maid of honor speech (complete with mic drop) written for them! So why is she trying to encourage Jason?

Except clearly, she's not, given that she turned him down.

He juts out his chin. "That's what she said. That dude left the party soon after you did—I guess he had to send some demo or something? Anyway, she and I got to talking, and after the party we hung out for a couple hours. It was awesome." He runs a hand through his spiky blond hair, somehow managing to make it spike even taller. "At least, I thought it was. But then I asked her out today and—a *player*! Why would she think that?"

I flinch, and not just because he's talking really loudly again.

I have a pretty good idea why she would think that. But I'm a little afraid to tell him the direct truth. Maybe . . . an *adjacent* truth would be okay.

"I mean, you are kind of a flirt. Like, with everyone."

"So I'm friendly, and that makes me a player?" He glares at me. Coming from such a generally good-natured guy, Jason's glare is scary. I take a little step back.

"No, not—" I pause. "Look, I mean, you do have a lot of girlfriends. It seems like every time I see you, you're dating someone new. And with guys that go through a lot of girlfriends, well, there's a tendency to think—"

"I'm not a player," he says, back to glaring at his footwear like they have something to do with this. Granted, they aren't great-looking flip-flops. "I'm usually the one who gets dumped."

This last bit has a sadness to it, a vulnerability I've never heard from Jason.

"Really?" I can't hide my surprise. It never occurred to me that Jason would have been the one getting broken up with. He's just so . . . likable.

"Yeah. Really." He grimaces. "Whatever. It doesn't matter. I'm going to go drink a bunch." He doesn't even look up at me, just turns and starts walking away.

"Is drinking a good idea right before you're about to climb?" I ask, but he holds up his hand like he hears me but can't bother to respond.

At least he didn't give me the middle finger.

Gah, maybe I deserve the middle finger. I feel awful, the guilt like a fist in my stomach. I didn't want to hurt Jason; I just didn't think he'd be good with Emily. Definitely not as good as Tate.

I sigh, wishing I could run over to Brendan and tell him how bad I feel about all this. But Brendan's on a date. With a really pretty girl—god, why do I have to actually pick attractive ones?—who is leaning toward him rather obnoxiously. Give the guy some breathing room, lady.

He's not exactly leaning in himself, but he's not leaning away, either. He's smiling at whatever she's saying, and the fist in my stomach turns and turns.

Being jealous sucks. Especially when I'm jealous because of a plan I came up with.

But if it works . . .

No, not if. *When*. When it works, it'll have been totally worth it.

Brendan looks over at me, and I give him a little wave. He smiles with this challenging expression like, *so, where's your date?*

I give him a look back, like, *hold your horses, I'm working on it.*

I try to push Jason's hurt expression from my mind—really, he and Emily are so different, they probably wouldn't make each other happy, anyway. Right? I also fight my instinct to watch and pick apart every detail of Brendan's date.

I look back at my food truck dating options. Neither of those guys are at the end of their lines anymore, and *Breaking Bad* dude's now talking to a girl.

Screw it. I'm just going to pick a place to eat first and worry about finding a date after.

Trying to put myself back into a better mood, I take another sip of my Big Gulp, then quietly sing the first thing that comes to mind—the melody from that old song that starts "Jeremiah was a bullfrog," but with the words "Su-Lin loves the food trucks."

"Do you always sing about lunch?" asks a voice right behind

me, and I jump.

"Sorry!" he says. It's that guy I danced with at the prom. (Warren, I think? Yeah, that sounds right.) He's got his hands up in this "don't shoot" kind of gesture. "I didn't mean to scare you. You waved to me before, so I thought you saw me walking over here."

"I . . . what?"

"I was standing right over there, and you waved at me and . . . oh." He's gesturing over to where Brendan is having his date, and understanding dawns on both of us at once. He winces and stuffs his hands into his pockets self-consciously. "You were waving at your friend there."

Crap. As if I didn't already feel like a jerk today.

"Yeah, sorry, I didn't see you there." I pause, trying to think of some way to not be a total ass. "But I would have waved at you if I had!" I add cheerily. Because maybe I would have? I do wave at a lot of people.

His expression relaxes. "Yeah? Good."

I blink, taking in what he's wearing for the first time. He's got on this old-timey-looking long-sleeved shirt with a double row of decorative buttons down the front, and he's got goggles on his head. I might think he's going for a steampunk look, except for the shirt is this bright yellow and the modern goggles look like they came straight from a high-school chem lab.

"I'm actually kind of surprised I didn't see you, what with . . . *this* going on," I say, indicating this odd outfit.

He laughs. "No kidding. But even cosplay tends to blend in at a place like this, I suppose. It's Dr. Malodorous," he adds, because it's probably pretty obvious I have no idea who he's dressed as. "From the Chem-Guys vids? The ones where they try out all these old theoretical formulas and really just end up blowing stuff up?"

"Oh yeah! I saw their booth earlier. I've never seen the show, though."

"It's pretty great. But I'm seriously rethinking this shirt. It

121

works well for the evil doctor, but these buttons keep making me afraid I'm about to be attacked by tiny suckling piglets."

I giggle at that image, and his smile widens.

"So do you work with one of the shows here?" I ask. We'd talked a bit at the prom, but embarrassingly, much of it had been about my show. And Brendan. Oops.

Which reminds me, I need to find a date for lunch, pronto. I glance back over and see Brendan looking this way. Probably wanting me to get a move on and just ask this dude to eat so we can get on with our double date.

This could be the universe handing me a freebie.

"Nah, just a fan," he says with a shrug. "I like the science and tech geek stuff a lot. And now I'm officially a fan of your show, too."

"Really? I didn't think you'd seen any of the episodes." I hope I'm remembering that right. I'd been a bit distracted at the time, trying to both watch and not watch Brendan's dancing with that girl.

"Well, I've had some time to educate myself." He smiles. "Your show is hilarious. I'm excited to see what you guys come up with next. The launch of the reboot is tomorrow, right?"

"Thanks! And yeah, tomorrow." I grin back. It's always really nice to hear compliments like that, especially right before the launch, when I'm starting to get nervous about whether the fans really will want more of me and my socks.

I sooooo want this to do well. Brendan and I together have made it a better show, and it deserves to have twice the audience the old one did. And part of me is a little afraid to let him down. I promised him that working with me would be this fabulous opportunity, and I want it to be everything I said and more.

I'm about to ask Warren if he wants to join me for lunch when he says, sheepishly, "I have to admit, I may have binged the whole thing. You are really, really talented."

I feel my face flush. "Thanks," I say again, more weakly this time.

Uh-oh.

I knew Warren thought I was cute, but I'm starting to get the feeling he's a bit more into me than that. It's not that I'm not flattered—I mean, Warren seems really nice. (His name *is* Warren, right?) But I'm also not available, at least not for anything more than a pseudo-date to make Brendan feel comfortable in our casualness. And while I don't have any problem flirting with a cute guy for a random lunch date, I also don't want to lead anyone on and then hurt them.

So I definitely don't want to ask him out and encourage him.

"I know you've got a lot going on with the launch tomorrow, and I heard there's a rock climbing thing today?" he says. I nod, and he continues. "But I was wondering if you might want to be my date for the masquerade tomorrow night."

I feel my palms sweat, and it takes everything in me not to look over at Brendan.

YouCon starts with a prom-type dance and always ends with an even bigger dance. This year, they're calling it the "masquerade," but it's always basically the same thing—a convention cap-off gala where the dress varies from unironic formal to jeans and t-shirts. A huge number of the female attendees treat it like Halloween—a chance to wear lingerie out in public with some cat ears and call it a costume.

Brendan and I hadn't officially talked yet about whether we would go to tomorrow's dance together. We're supposed to hang out (and stay in) tonight, but is that a date? The part of me that is dying to make out with him again (okay, that's all of me) hopes so, but I would love to walk into the masquerade on Brendan's arm, as his date.

We can't do both. Those are the rules.

Shit.

"I, um." I clear my throat. I am not good at this. "I wasn't really planning on having an official date for the masquerade."

He nods. "Okay, yeah, no problem." But his smile is so sad, like Jason's.

"But I'd definitely love to dance!" I blurt out, then try not to cringe.

What am I doing? Trying to soften my rejection, obviously. But probably just sending mixed signals.

His expression lightens, confirming that last bit. "All right," he says, this time with a more genuine smile. "Sounds great. I'll get my wings ready."

I smile as he makes a joking chicken flap with his arms, but I'm still cringing inside.

"See you later, Su-Lin," he says, and grins before he walks off.

Ugghhh. I let out a sigh.

I look back over to Brendan. The girl he's with is laughing. I wish I was the one over there with him, laughing at his jokes. Just him and me.

I'm not all that hungry anymore, even here with all the amazing food truck smells. I feel kind of sick, and I know I'm letting him down and not keeping up my end of the bargain, but I can't handle the thought of going over to hang out with Brendan and his date. I don't want to see close up how much fun they're having.

I pull out my phone and send a quick text to Brendan:

Hey, sorry, I'm bailing on lunch. But have fun! I'll see you at the rock climbing!

I add a bunch of smiley faces for good measure, and then walk back inside the convention center before he can see how unsmiley my real face is.

TWELVE

BRENDAN

I catch up to Su-Lin as she's headed to her rock wall event. I need to go, too—I'm *belaying* her, as she's told me about ten times, and so far I've managed not to make any jokes back about how I could be laying her any time she feels like she's ready for that. I don't want to put pressure on her. It's me who can't be the person she needs me to be. My balls are blue as hell, but I have no one to blame for this but my own damn self.

I walk up beside her as she's heading toward the exhibition hall to the far side where Jason has erected his enormous rock wall. "Did he bring that thing in on a semi?" I ask.

Su-Lin smiles at me, and it's bright and chipper and seems normal, which is something of a relief after I saw her laughing with that blond guy. Again. "Probably. He may call me hobbit, but he's definitely the one compensating for something."

I'm trying to figure out how to casually ask about that guy she was talking to without sounding like a jealous prick. Which I totally am. I was ignoring that perfectly nice girl I had lunch with to stare at them, so that much should be obvious.

Su-Lin, thankfully, gives me a segue.

"So how did lunch with that girl go?" she asks.

"Fine. Talking with someone who was not you successfully

125

accomplished."

"Do you think you'll see her again?"

I squint at her. I'm not sure what would give her that idea. "Nah. Second dates with other people aren't required, right?"

"Right," Su-Lin says.

"But you were talking with that guy from the prom, right? What was his name?"

"Warren," she says. "Yeah, we just ran into each other."

"You were looking for a date, weren't you? You could have brought him over to eat with us."

"Maybe." She shrugs absently. "I didn't want to interrupt you, though." She doesn't sound upset or anything, but she's not meeting my eyes.

She cuts in front of me as we thread through the busy exhibition hall, around a demo for a goat simulator video game that literally simulates being a goat. Who is, if what's on the screen is any indication, occasionally on the run from the law. I'm trying to figure out how to respond. She didn't want to interrupt me? On my pseudo-date that was supposed to be a double pseudo-date when she found someone to join us? She was supposed to be (not literally) holding my hand through this, but now she's pretending like she forgot. Besides which, I saw her laughing. I don't know what they were talking about, but that was *definitely* the same smile she gives me.

I continue to follow Su-Lin—who is walking twice as fast as is warranted, especially given that her legs are so much shorter than mine—past a vendor who is trying to explain to some tween fan's father why None Pizza with Left Beef is a thing, and toward an improbable booth set up by, of all people, the History Channel. I'm not sure what the History Channel is airing that they think would appeal to this audience—perhaps a rip-off of *Drunk History?*—but as we pass their booth, Su-Lin stops so fast that I nearly run her over. She points at a blond woman standing behind a signing table and yells "Breakup Tub!"

I look at this woman. The Breakup Tub is a dish served at

the restaurant where Su-Lin used to work—a dish I've never been brave enough to try. It's a carton of ice cream mixed with whatever candy and toppings the chef feels like dumping in at the time, and while Su-Lin does have a habit of shouting upon meeting new people what Fong's dish she thinks they're most like, the Breakup Tub does not seem like a flattering one.

The clean-cut blond man sitting behind the signing table stares at Su-Lin in alarm, but the girl she's pointing at breaks into an enormous smile. "Su-Lin!" she shouts, jumping to her feet. "Oh my god, it's been years!"

"I know!" Su-Lin says. "What have you been up to?"

"Well, I got married, for one." She gestures to the guy beside her. "This is my husband Will. He's a writer, working on a History Channel show." She nudges his shoulder with her hip, and he smiles up at her. "We officially got together at Fong's, believe it or not."

Su-Lin's eyes widen. "Are you serious? That's amazing!" She bounces excitedly, grinning back and forth between them.

"Right?" Blond Woman—Breakup Tub, I guess—grins. "You'd already left by then. I heard you're rebooting your show!"

"I am," Su-Lin says. She puts a hand on my arm. "With the help of my fabulous business partner."

The woman's eyes fall on me, and Su-Lin suddenly looks uncomfortable. "This is Brendan. I want to introduce you, but I just realized I don't remember your name."

"Gabby," the girl says. "Though Breakup Tub works too."

Gabby's husband smiles, so I'm guessing I'm the only one who doesn't know *why* that's something she might want to be called. She reaches out to shake my hand.

"Don't worry," I say. "She shouts Fong's dishes at everyone. The first time we met, she called me Kung Pao Pancakes."

Gabby laughs. "I bet she did," she says, and I wince. I'm pretty sure she's getting ideas about Su-Lin and me that we're supposed to be avoiding, especially if Su-Lin is actually interested in this Warren guy. And if she is, who can blame her? I'm guessing he doesn't have panic attacks or a pathological inability to say the g-word, and he's probably totally, like, mentally and emotionally stable.

I wonder what Fong's dish he would be. I both want to know and really, really don't.

"Hey, I've got to run," Su-Lin says. "Got to go climb the big wall. But I'll drop by later, okay? We should hang out."

Gabby looks a bit confused, but she smiles. "Sure. We'll be here the rest of the day."

I wave at them, then follow Su-Lin again, pushing through the crowds that are gathering around Jason's wall.

"Who was that?" I ask.

"This girl who used to come into Fong's a couple times a week," Su-Lin says. "She'd always order the Breakup Tub, though mostly it was for lost jobs, not failed relationships. Though there were a few of those, too. I'm so glad she's happy now. Not all the sad regulars made it out so well. There was a guy I only remember as Moo Goo Gai Pizza who I heard lost all his money investing in animal breeding on the advice of his psychic. I guess there wasn't a lot of growth potential in naked mole rat farming."

I'm still trying to puzzle that out when we reach the rock wall. Jason stands in front of it scowling at a harness which I'm guessing is for Su-Lin, based on the size.

And there, sitting in the front row, is Warren. He waves, and Su-Lin waves back.

That jealousy seems to be carving a hollow in my chest.

"You guys are getting along," I say.

Su-Lin squirms. "I don't know. We don't really know each other."

This might make me feel better, if I didn't remember exactly how into her I was the first time we met and she asked me to edit her videos. I spent the entire evening whining to my mom about how it was a really good career opportunity but I couldn't possibly work with a girl that awesome and that gorgeous because I was never ever going to date again, and I would go crazy from not being able to pursue her.

I was right on the second count, anyway. I ultimately took the job, because I couldn't pass up the chance to be near her, and also because the opportunity was truly too good to turn down. But I knew, that very first day, that she was someone I'd never be able to get enough of.

Given the way Warren is looking at her as she walks to the base of the rock wall to get harnessed—somehow she looks amazingly hot in her worn Converse sneakers and Bananya t-shirt—I'm pretty sure I'm not the only one who wants to belaying her.

THIRTEEN

Su-Lin

This wall is even more enormous now that I'm standing at the foot of it, and the "lunch" I grabbed at the vending machine—two Otis Spunkmeyer chocolate chip cookies—is congealing into a thick lump of sugar and fear in my stomach.

Also, this harness is ridiculous. It's wrapped around my waist and upper legs, and I have a terrible feeling it's going to wedge my frayed jean shorts firmly up my butt crack the moment I start climbing. Which might make for a nice view for Brendan down below, but really, can *anyone* look sexy in this contraption?

Okay, Brendan does a decent job of it. He's got the same type of harness on as me, with the rope he's holding also looped through the carabiner at his waist. Jason's producer on the show—a fellow climber named Nate who makes funny jibes at Jason or taunts him to do increasingly stupid things—is showing Brendan how to tug the rope for a sudden stop and how to hold it for a slow release.

I want to make all the jokes about Brendan's slow release.

Then I look up at the top of the rock wall, and my nerves clamp my mouth shut. Which I know is a rare event.

Why did I agree to this? For a stupid belaying joke? (No, not stupid, that joke is #worthit.)

There's no way out now. Jason has been promoting this as the *"Jason Climbs Sh!t* Quiz Show: *Starving with the Stars* Edition" since the moment I signed on, and the publicity is good for our launch tomorrow. Provided I don't die. Although that might actually be even better for publicity, if worse for our show's future.

The crowd is huge, all the seats filled and a bunch of people standing around behind them. Warren's smiling at me from the front row, which doesn't exactly make me feel better, especially after Brendan kept asking about him. I know Brendan wanted me to invite Warren to lunch, but I couldn't bring myself to tell him why I didn't. If I told Brendan I didn't want to encourage a guy who I thought might really like me, then that would inherently mean I'm not keeping things casual between Brendan and me, right? That I'm way too invested in us being serious. That I'm failing the plan.

Which I've already done enough of, between picking out a girl who turned out to be into me and what must be my super obvious jealousy of any girl he dances or talks with.

I need to be better at this.

"Here you go, Hobbit," Jason says, much louder than necessary, handing me a pair of . . . water shoes? No, they must be climbing shoes. But they have that same sporty look, with the bright neoprene and the rubber sole. Also they look like they'd fit a six-year-old.

I wrinkle my nose. "I can't wear my regular shoes?" I look longingly down at my chucks.

"You can if you want to slip off every step."

"They're tiny. I am a grown-ass—"

"Grown-ass hobbit, maybe." He shoves the shoes at me. "And they're supposed to be tight. Put 'em on."

Drinking did not improve Jason's mood. Though it did give him rosy cheeks and the breath of that homeless guy who used to hang out in front of Fong's and tell me his strong opinions on the fall fashion line's overuse of feathers. He was actually pretty nice and usually not wrong.

"Are you sure you didn't drink too much to . . ." I trail off when I see the death look Jason gives me.

Okaaaay, challenging his drunken climbing abilities is on the no-no list. Got it.

I kick off my chucks and pull on the little climbing shoes, which do stretch out enough to fit. They also have a really stiff sole, which is weird.

"You ready for this?" Brendan asks, walking over to me. His tutorial with Nate didn't take long—apparently belaying isn't a difficult skill.

I cringe. There's no point in trying to hide my nerves from Brendan. He knows heights aren't my favorite. We went on a Ferris wheel once, and he had to practically pry me off of him with a crowbar afterward (though maybe not all of that was because of fear, if I'm being totally honest.) "I've got the super attractive footwear part down," I say, showing off my shoes.

"Clearly."

"And you'll belaying me," I say with a coy smile, because I can't resist saying that yet again and because joking helps ease my nerves. "No pressure, but you'd better bring your A-game."

He grins back. "Good thing for you, I *always* bring my A-game."

God, I want to find out. Even just joking about this is making me warm all over. I take a deep breath that is shaky for a number of reasons.

Jason's producer, Nate, is working the crowd, getting them to cheer even though nothing has actually started yet. He's got two lines formed on either side behind a microphone—these would be the two teams, I suppose. This thing is a quiz show, and Nate will be asking the questions. Depending on which team gets the right answer, either Jason or I will climb up to a part of the wall marked at intervals with tape. The first of us to ring the bell at the top (oh my god, how far up is that bell?) wins, and that team gets a bunch of swag, including some *Real*

Sockwives DVDs and t-shirts we donated to the cause.

Easy-peasy. I just have to climb the thing. With any luck, my team will be terrible.

"All right, everyone, are you ready to see me climb some shit?" Jason calls out into a microphone, and the crowd goes nuts. Brendan gives me a wink and steps back. I wish he would have squeezed my hand just once.

"But as you know, it's not just me climbing shit today," Jason continues. "I know who you're really here to see—say hi to the most lovely hobbit in all the shire, the talented and ferocious Su-Lin Liu!"

The crowd laughs and whoops; Jason called me "hobbit" on *Starving with the Stars,* so they all feel like they're in on the joke. And I have to say—drinking and being in a pissy mood doesn't make Jason any less capable of working a crowd. He still sounds like Jason, just a smidge louder than usual.

I wave and grin. There's even more energy here than at a well-attended panel, and it's fun to be the recipient of all that enthusiasm. I see Emily in the front row, a few seats down from Warren. She gives me a big thumbs up.

"And don't forget to welcome the lucky guy belaying her, half of the new *Sockwives* duo, Brendan Pike!" Jason says, gesturing back to him.

Brendan looks a little startled, clearly not expecting to be called out like that. He gives a little wave, and the crowd whoops some more.

"Last and certainly least, you all know Nate. He's going to be doing what he does best. Asking stupid questions."

The crowd roars at this. Nate's a fan favorite on the show, a nice wry balance to Jason's exuberance. He's also really cute, which doesn't hurt—he looks kind of like Daveed Diggs, actually. He's got the same sepia skin and curly hair, and he even pulls it back in a ponytail like Lafayette. Which might be part of the reason I made out with him once at a party two years ago, though the follow-up date was super awkward and, honestly, kind of boring. Turns out dating a guy based on his physical similarity to my favorite celebrity might not have been the brightest idea in the world.

Jason goes on to explain the rules of the game, designating the team on the right facing the rock wall to be Team Sockwives and the team on the left to be Team Climbing Sh!t. Then he hands off the mic to Nate and clips a little wireless mic around his ear. He gives me one, and I do the same.

Fantastic. Now everyone will be able to hear if I start hyperventilating.

I position myself in the lane where I'll be climbing, which I notice has a lot more of those colorful hand and foot-holds than Jason's does. This is good. Not only am I a total newb, but his legs and arms are, like, twice as long as mine. It's possible this is the kiddie track, which I'm cool with. I bounce a bit on the padding that's set up underneath the wall. It's not as thick as I'd like, but it would be better to fall on than the concrete convention floor underneath.

Also, I notice that for all Jason's insistence that I have the proper footwear, he's just kicked off his flip-flops and is going barefoot. He's also not wearing a harness at all.

Show-off.

I shoot one last nervous look at Brendan, who gives just enough tug on the rope that I can feel it in my harness, and smiles. It's his way of saying, *I've got you.*

I can do this. It's just a stupid climbing wall, and I can't actually get hurt. Brendan's got me.

"Okay, party people," Nate starts. "Team Sockwives won the coin flip, so they start. Here's the first question. On *Starving with the Stars,* who was most likely to be found wandering the island naked?"

"Ryan Lansing," a woman says almost immediately, and her team begins cheering even before Nate hits the ceremonial *Starving with the Stars* gong (or the little replica gong he got from somewhere) to signify the correct answer.

Damn it. I knew they'd start with an easy one, but really? Ryan was almost never *not* naked.

I grip the closest hand holds and pull myself up, climbing until my fingers reach the masking tape line. I'm only a couple feet off the ground. Not bad.

Jason's team gets his first question, too, about who brought the copy of the Tori Spelling autobiography as their luxury item. (Melissa: "I, like, live my life by the principles of Hollywood's favorite daughter.")

The questions get a little tougher next round, but once again, both of our teams answer correctly, and we both move up another few feet. After the third question is asked to Team Climbing Sh!t, I'm starting to realize that the real problem may not be the height, but staying in these super uncomfortable positions on these tiny little hand and foot-holds for any length of time. Jason's team pauses before they answer, and my fingers start to cramp.

"How're you doing, Hobbit?" Jason taunts, while his team deliberates. "You're almost at normal-person height now."

"Never better," I say back. "It's okay, Jason's Team. He'll understand if you have to take your time. Jason knows all about performance anxiety."

The crowd laughs and applauds at our banter—I think they especially love any callback to our supposed on-show romance (that wasn't really anything more than a few sex jokes and some inventive editing by the producers). But damn, I'm happy when my team answers the next question quickly and I can move again—at least until I find myself in a similarly uncomfortable position, this time even higher off the ground.

Why on earth do people do this for fun?

This goes on, Jason and I moving higher up the wall with each question. My team, unfortunately, continues to do really well, even as his misses a couple questions, and I climb higher and higher, until I start to be afraid to look down. My heart is pounding against my ribcage, but the real pain is in my hands and, right now, my left leg. I'd put my foot on a hold that was higher up than I'd figured, so now I'm doing some sort of weird yoga-like position against the wall, the Bent Lotus Pose of Extreme Discomfort.

This is where I'm stuck while my team proceeds to start missing questions, and by the time Jason's up next to me, my arms are actually shaking.

"You guys are pretty high up there," Nate says, and I grit my teeth, wishing he wouldn't remind me. "How're you feeling?"

"So gooooood, man," Jason calls out. He lets go of a grip and turns to face the audience so he's only holding on by one hand—his feet aren't even on footholds! God, the dude has arm strength. The crowd cheers. He's not even breaking a sweat, though his face is flushed more than usual, which I'm guessing is from the alcohol. "I'm feeling fucking awesome. How about you, Su-Lin? You feeling fucking awesome?" He swings back so he's in a more normal climbing position.

I have made the mistake of looking over at him, which then shows me that we're way farther from the ground than I am comfortable with. My breath is getting shallow and tight, and the sight of him dangling like that—with no harness, like a gigantic drunk idiot!—didn't help things.

"Yep," I manage, but it comes out as a squeak. The audience laughs—some in sympathy, I hope. They know I'm not the real climber here.

"She's doing great, yeah, guys?" Nate says, getting cheers from the audience.

"Thanks, but maybe we could just move on with the questions?" I say. I'm not sure how much longer I can hold this position.

Brendan's got me, I tell myself. If I have to let go, he's got me.

But even knowing that—even looking up just enough to see the steel bar with the carabiner that my harness rope is hooked through, knowing all the safety equipment is in place and I've got a guy down there who wouldn't ever let me fall—my brain can't shut off the increasing, irrational panic.

Is this what it's like for Brendan?

Nate chuckles. "Okay, Su-Lin, you'll like this one. We all know it was Chad Montgomery who fucked the puppet. But who was the first one accused?"

Jason glances over at me, clearly remembering that whole terrible sequence of events and probably checking to make sure I'm okay.

"Ryan Lansing," a girl from my team announces triumphantly.

Nate hits the wrong answer buzzer. "I'm afraid Ryan was not the first one accused. Team Climbing Sh!t, the question's yours to steal!"

There's some deliberation among Jason's team, and I grit my teeth, practically willing the answer to them just to move this along: Alec Andreas. It was Alec I first accused; he hated Ruby. Though it only took the look of horrified disgust on his face to convince me it wasn't him. Alec isn't exactly great at hiding his true feelings.

"Hey," Jason says, cutting into the murmuring from the team below. I'm not sure if he's trying to get my mind off the question or what, but he lifts first one hand and then the other until he's literally gripping the wall holds *with his bare-freaking-feet*. "Look Ma, no hands!"

My already galloping heart jumps into my throat, even as the crowd goes nuts. He doesn't have a harness, and while he's usually doing stupid things, this seems worse than usual. Probably because he's drunk.

"Jason, stop it!" I hiss, past caring about witty trash-talk.

"Better hurry up, guys," Nate says. "If he dies showing off because he's bored, you're out."

Nate doesn't sound like he's freaking out, but maybe he didn't get a good whiff of Jason's breath like I did.

Jason flexes his feet, making himself bounce a little. Still not holding onto anything. He's seriously going to kill himself. Does he think he's Spiderman? Does he not see how high up we are?

I make the mistake of looking down.

137

"Jason—" I start again, gasping it out through the panic making my throat close up.

"Aww, Hobbit, don't worry. This is nothing. In fact . . ." He slowly starts to lift one leg, so now he's only standing on one foot. One bare foot, his toes gripping the wall. He wobbles—

And I instinctively reach out for his arm. I don't know if in that half-second I think I'm actually going to be able to do any-thing—I'm, like, half the dude's weight and barely buff enough to dead-lift a Burritozilla at Taco Pete's. But it doesn't matter, because in the next half-second, just as Jason rights himself, my other fingers slip.

I shriek as I drop, even though it's only a few inches before the rope catches me with a sharp, bouncy jerk, and then I shriek again as the momentum swings me to the side—and I collide hard with Jason.

There's a big collective gasp and then a loud, horrible *thwump* sound as he hits the mat below.

I hear Nate swear and people are freaking out and I'm dangling there, partially scrabbling against the wall in terror and partially straining to turn myself around enough to see Jason lying on his back on the mat, with Emily crouched down next to him on one side and Nate on the other and OH MY GOD DID I JUST KILL JASON—

"I'm not a player," I hear Jason mumble into his headset mic, and I nearly pass out in relief. He's not dead, that's for sure, and from what I can tell he doesn't seem to have any limbs jutting in odd directions. Maybe that mat was more helpful than I thought.

"He's going to be okay," Nate says, his voice picked up by Jason's mic, sounding about as relieved as I feel. "You're good, man."

That's when I realize I'm being slowly lowered, and there's Brendan, looking pale but determined, carefully letting out the rope. Tears spill onto my cheeks, and all I want to do—after making sure Jason is okay and Nate is not just delusionally hopeful—is run into his arms and stay there forever.

It's a good thing we're staying in tonight. Because I need a break from dates with other people and heights from which I nearly kill Jason. I need our leftover vodka, and my feet on the ground, and more than anything, I need my Brendan.

FOURTEEN

BReNDAN

It may not be the smartest thing to be downing shots with the girl I'm desperately in love with but only casually dating, but the hard lemonade and cherry vodka mixed with 7-Up taste so good, especially lying on the couch in our hotel room with her body so warm and just inches away.

Su-Lin waves her empty glass at me. "Top me off, my good man," she says in her *Sockton Abbey* accent. She's had fewer drinks than I have, but she's also a lot smaller, so I think we're pretty equally yoked.

I bow my head to her, and we both laugh, high pitched and giddy.

Yes, I'm buzzed. Not that we don't deserve it—what with the stress of the con and dating other people, not to mention Su-Lin's terrified climb earlier today, and Jason's brush with death, and the anticipation of the launch tomorrow. When I think of it all together like that, it's a wonder we're not both in some sort of panic-induced coma.

"Of course, my dear lady," I say, adding more 7-Up to her glass, then the vodka. That's the end of it—there wasn't a lot left after the party. "I am ever your humble vodka purvreyor." That's not right. "Purvreyor? Purv—purv . . . Damn it."

Su-Lin giggles. "My vodka perv. Yes."

Ha. I've got it. "Purveyor!" I hold up my glass and smile at her, and she grins back.

Su-Lin holds up her glass, and I clink mine against it. "To my purveyror," she says. Her nose crinkles adorably. "God, that *is* a tough word."

"Right? Vodka perv," I say, shaking my head. She laughs, and I try to just enjoy this for what it is. Two casually dating best friends, loving each other in the way we do best, by just spending time together and messing around.

Um. But not that kind. Not yet . . . Though the alcohol has quieted my anxiety to the point where I'm not really sure *why* that is.

Oh right. Because I'm messed up beyond belief and can't say the g-word without hyperventilating. I down my shot while Su-Lin cuddles against me, her hand absently resting on my knee, massaging it through my jeans. I'm pretty sure she doesn't realize she's doing it, but god, it drives me wild. I pour myself another shot of lemonade—if I drank every time I wanted to calm my stress, I'd be an alcoholic, but I do need the occasional vice. God knows I deny myself enough pleasures in life—besides my own personal sock collection, anyway.

Su-Lin giggles, and for a startled moment I think maybe she knows exactly what she's doing to me. The results are obvious, though thankfully my jeans are tight enough to hold things down somewhat, so I'm not fully standing at attention. She moves closer, her arm stretching across my waist, dangerously close to—

Wait. She's not looking at me, but across the room at . . . "Are you still giggling about the toaster?"

Her giggles intensify, and I lean in and kiss her.

We've made out a lot in the last week, but every time, I'm struck by the intensity of desire that washes over me. I slide my hand up her shirt, running my thumb across the soft skin of her back, and she moans.

I'm not the only one worked up, but Su-Lin seems to have an easier time stopping than I do. I wish I could say the words, that I could assure her I'm in love with her, that none of this is casual for me. I wish I could trust myself to do so.

"Maybe I should buy a coconut bra," I say. I've thought seriously—and usually drunkenly—about getting one at some party store and wearing it for her like women wear lingerie.

"Mmmmm," she says, her head resting against me. "You *should*."

Her voice is sultry, and I wonder if she'd really be into that. I could sneak off for a while tomorrow, and when we get back to the hotel to collapse after the launch, I could slip it on and lie back, pretending nothing was different. And then she'd—

"Mmmmm," Su-Lin says again, as if she's imagining this, too, though by this point she's probably back to mentally ogling Daveed. I look down at her and my gaze falls on her chest and gets stuck there. I'm a total breast man, shameful though it is, and I've always appreciated quality over quantity.

God, her breasts are perfect. I have a near-overpowering urge to lean down and run my tongue over the tops of them. I might have indulged, but Su-Lin snuggles closer into my side. "I hope Jason's okay," she says.

I kiss the top of her head. "They said he'd be fine. It's just a minor concussion."

She nods, but I can tell she still feels bad about what happened. She was scared enough up there on that wall, it was rough to hold onto the rope and lower her slowly, not to be able to run over to her and lift her off the wall and hold her as she trembled.

Not that I could actually have done that. If I tried to climb that wall to help her down, we'd probably both have concussions.

"Hey," I say, rolling over to face her. "It wasn't your fault."

"I know," she says, but from her tone I can tell that she doesn't.

"Trust me. I am the master at blaming myself for things I can't control."

Su-Lin smiles. "And do you have a lot of luck stopping, even when you know you should?"

"Almost none." I'm trying to think of something comforting to say, something that will make her feel better, but I realize when I get into that place, there's very little anyone can do for me. "Damn it."

Su-Lin giggles and kisses me again. She tastes like cherries and lemons and sugar and desire so hot it burns. Chills run down my spine, and she rolls until she's lying half on top of me. I run my hands up the back of her shirt to her bra catch and under, feeling the smooth skin of her back. I want her beyond reason, and I'm so scared that if I don't get it together, she's going to give up on me. She'll be gone forever.

More than anything, I want to give her something to hang on for. I kiss my way down her neck, behind her ear, and her arms around my neck feel like they never want to let go. I imagine what it would feel like to be able to give her all of me. To tell her that I love her and I want her to be my girlfriend, that I want to be with her for the rest of my life, even though I still can't think the words for what that kind of commitment is called. I want to make love to her, to whisper all these things in her ear and to feel her shudder beneath me, on top of me, all around me. My need for her is powerful, more so even than my obsession with Candace was, and it's this thought that scares me enough to finally wake me up to what I'm thinking.

I need to snap out of it. Those thoughts are dangerous. Not in the least because I've had a few drinks, and I don't know what I might say out loud. I don't want Su-Lin to know how often I have sexual fantasies about her. She might feel used or objectified, and I hate myself for that, even though virtually every fantasy I've carried through to the end resolves with us lying naked in each other's arms, confessing our undying love and loving each other desperately until we're old and wrinkled and gray.

I love her, I want her, but I can't be the person that kind of love makes me. I can't be with her, not fully, until I can be sure I can do one without the other. I stand, and Su-Lin makes this sad noise as she slumps into the space I've left beside her.

I can't make love to her, but I can make her laugh, and Su-Lin's laugh is the best sound in the world, even better than the noises I'd like to elicit.

"Just for you," I say, "since this is apparently a thing . . ." I dump the crumbs out of the pretzel bowls right there on the table and nearly shed my shirt as well, but stop myself just in time.

Too much. Too weird. Not casual. I congratulate myself on this rational thought. Definitely not as drunk as I could be.

Yet still sloshed enough to do this. I hold the bowls up to my chest like a coconut bra and rap "Guns and Ships" from *Hamilton* in a crappy French accent.

Su-Lin melts into a puddle of happy shrieks and giggles, which is pretty much my favorite. She knows I can do this song—we've both rapped it to the album in the car over and over and over again, along with the rest of the musical. But to see my solo performance with pretend-coconuts makes her so happy—my whole body is warm and buzzing and it has nothing to do with the alcohol.

I make it most of the way through the song before I stumble over the word "tacsicle," which I know isn't right, but I can't think of what is. Tasticle? Um. No. "Damn it!" I shout and slump down next to her again.

Su-Lin has laughed so hard she's about to cry, and against the better judgment I apparently lack, I pull her close again. God, just being here like this, it satiates me in a way I never thought possible.

But not completely. Never completely.

Su-Lin's forehead brushes against my jaw, and my lips burn with longing. She makes her hand like a puppet and reaches it up by my ear. "Oh, I'll keep your secret, Darlin'," Ruby says in a whisper. Ruby has no breath, of course, but my ear tingles wildly anyway. "But I can't make any promises for Su-Lin. She's . . ."

144

Su-Lin doesn't finish the sentence, but my mind does, in a million different ways. She's beautiful, perfect, the love of my life. She's everything to me, everything I want and can't have, everything I do have that makes me feel happy and safe and desperate to keep her. Just like this. Forever.

Though a large part of me screams it wants so much more.

None of this is how she intended to end the sentence. I look into her eyes, and I think I see desire there that mirrors my own.

"She's what?" I'm sure that the strain in my voice gives away all my thoughts.

And then—oh my god—Su-Lin's hand brushes against my penis, and my hormones shoot into overdrive. At first I think it was a mistake, and I try not to react, but then her hand settles right there on my jeans, her fingers brushing gently back and forth, and my libido revs to life, my whole body humming like a V8 engine.

"Unpredictable," she says.

She is nothing if not that.

FIFTEEN

Su-Lin and Brendan

Brendan's face is close to mine, so close that I can feel the brush of his evening stubble against my forehead. I can feel his surprised intake of breath, feel him hard under my hand and oh, wow, how that makes me ache. My eyelids flutter with the strength of it.

His eyes flick down to my lips; his are parted, his breathing uneven.

I'm not sure what possessed me to do this, other than this longing, this feeling for which I would use both the words "intense" and "passion," though they sting a bit, because I'm not sure if he feels the same.

God, I want to know.

I don't really know what I'm supposed to *do* with my hand, so I find myself petting his dick like it's a bunny, and his body is responding, stretching, and a little groan escapes from deep in the back of his throat.

Okay. Petting the bunny is apparently good.

"I, um," he says, wetting his lips. I lean in, and my body goes weak. I want to taste him forever, all over. "I want to make love to you. If you don't want that yet, we need to stop."

I don't take my hand away, still stroking lightly, which he

seems to like, but I don't escalate, either—wait, did it just throb? Like in a romance novel? Does it really do that?

It's not a question of whether I want to be with him—I want it so bad my body feels like it will burst if I can't have it.

But I don't want to push him too fast, which might send him over the edge into panic. And though I know I've agreed to be a kind of training girlfriend—without the label, of course—I'm starting to worry about whether I'm the one he's going to want when the training wheels come off.

Then again, maybe what he needs is a taste of more, so he won't *want* to look elsewhere.

"Are you ready?" I ask. My breath is shaky, and the words are too. "Do you think it might help you . . . progress?"

His dick flexes under my hand—I didn't know they could do that, either. Is that good? "Hell, yes," he says breathlessly. "To both. But I know you don't want it to be casual, and—"

There's an intensity to his gaze, his blue eyes so, so close to mine, and I'm glad for the happy alcohol-fueled haze that hog-ties all my doubts. I want to press even closer, my body knowing how to ease this ache.

"Does it feel casual?" I ask.

Brendan shakes his head. "Not to me."

A chill runs down my back. I shudder involuntarily, and for a moment he looks concerned. But then I rub him harder, faster on top of his jeans, and his hips shift as he responds, and I bend down and speak into his ear in what I hope is a sultry voice. "Then yes. Let's do this."

I cup Su-Lin's face in my hands and kiss her desperately. That "yes" is the sweetest, most precious thing, and it drowns out all my fear. I don't hold back anymore. My sex drive has always been strong—a fact I've cursed over the years—but it's like I've slammed on the gas with the engine in neutral, then suddenly

147

popped it into drive. My whole body is humming and roaring. Our tongues find each other, and there again is that delicious taste of cherries and lemonade and a salty flavor all her own, and I'm aware that my hands are gripping her, pulling her closer, reaching for her ass, pulling her onto my lap and rubbing her sensually against me. She moans against my mouth, and her arms are tight around my neck.

Something inside me breaks. The chains that hold back my sexual desire—forged long before I was celibate—can't hold up to this strain. She wants me, I can tell by the way her hips are grinding against me, rubbing in all the right places. I want to tear off her clothes and make love to her immediately—condom be damned—but more than that, I want to savor every second of this, draw out this moment and remember it for the rest of my life.

I stand, lifting her in my arms, and she clings to me, her legs wrapped around my waist, and god, how she turns me on. She kisses me fervently, and I open my eyes just enough to guide us to the bed, because if I bump into anything, I swear I'm going to end up fucking her against a wall.

I want this to be so much more than that, though even that kind of crass encounter would mean the world to me. She wants me, desperately, it feels like, and as I lay her on my bed, I'm struck with how beautiful she is, how singularly miraculous and perfect.

Brendan only wobbles slightly with the unbalance of holding me against him, my legs wrapped around his waist. We're kissing furiously, and I feel him carrying me to the bed, and even through the fuzzy, golden haze of passion and several shots, I have a thought that is equal parts panic and excitement.

I'm going to have sex.

With Brendan.

My whole body is on fire, and I have this strange desire to text

148

someone and brag about this. But Brendan is the one I text when something exciting happens, so . . . Sex. With Brendan. In his bed.

Of course, in his bed. Like, he's not going to do this on the table up against the toaster.

Focus, Su-Lin.

But the idea of us banging away on the table, and then toast popping up at exactly the right moment, makes me start to giggle, just as we drop down onto his bed, the soft bedding puffing up around us. He pulls back and grins at me; even though Brendan can read my mind about Daveed Diggs, there's no way he's guessing this one.

Now I'm just giggling with the pent-up thrill of this, of us. I pull him down by his shirt so he's kissing me again. Because god, I never, never want to stop.

S u-Lin bursts into giggles. I've practically finished my doctorate in Su-Lin giggles—the nervous, the uncomfortable, the mocking, the random, the joyous, the tickled, the gleeful. This is none of those—it's her rarest giggle, the one reserved for things that truly, miraculously astound her, like Actual Cannibal Shia LaBeouf.

"Ding," she says. And while I'm kind of incredulous that she's thinking of the damn toaster right now, I grin like an idiot because this, random noises and all, is the most singularly exultant moment of my entire miserable life. I've never experienced anything like this before, the heady rush of being here with her—even still fully clothed—the thick anticipation of all that might come next. Su-Lin's always had this glowing effect on me, engulfing me in her brilliant, beautiful aura and making me feel so much better than I am. Lying here with her, carrying her in my arms while she's pressed against me—it makes me feel sexy, powerful, special, safe, triumphant, *wanted* in a way I've never felt in all my life. The combination, far more than the liquor, is intoxicating.

've always thought I'd have sex for the first time with someone I was in love with—I know that's not important to everyone, and I've certainly thought about abandoning that goal a time or two.

I definitely *love* Brendan, my DIP, more than anyone else. He's the most important person in my life. And I definitely have a massive, desperate crush on him.

But *in* love with him?

I mean, sure, he's crazy hot. And that smile still makes me swoon, even after months of seeing it a lot. He makes me laugh like no one else can, and he makes me feel like I can be myself, truly me, in a way no one else does. I want to be touching him all the time, even if it's just, like, leaning against his arm, or nudging him with my shoulder. I want to be *near* him all the time, having him there, his presence like a warm, safe hug even when his arms aren't around me. And when his arms *are* around me, the way my body heats up, the way I ache for him . . .

So yeah, I'm definitely totally in love with him, but not—

Wait, what?

u-Lin grabs me by the collar and pulls me down on top of her and kisses me with such force that I'm lost to the sweet bliss of everything *her*. I forget to be self-conscious of how aggressive I can be, and my hands reach up her shirt, unhitching her bra. I almost laugh, imagining the coconuts again, but we're both pulling off our shirts fast—so fast I think she must want me as desperately as I do her, which is a feat.

I cup her breast with one hand, holding off on pressing my mouth to her chest. I like that a bit too much—as my ex told me many times—and I don't want her to think I'm some kind of perv, vodka or otherwise. Her hands are working up my back, and as good as that's felt before, this time my skin is erupting in flames. I kiss her throat, running my fingers over her nipple, feeling electric currents passing from her breast to my hand and running frantically up and down my arm.

There was an important insight there, but my thoughts are scattered apart by the sensation of his mouth working at the hollow of my throat, of the smooth skin of his back under my hands, the lean muscles of his chest pressed against mine, the glorious feeling of his thumb passing over my nipple, hand gently stroking my coconut—um, boob.

I've done this much before with a couple guys, but that's about where it stopped. And it never, never felt like this.

Now he's kissing downward, his tongue on my breasts, and that feels even better. Maybe I should be doing more than gripping his back and moaning, but I don't feel capable of much more. Until I do.

I love her so much. More than I knew it was possible for any person to love another. I finally allow myself to lower my tongue onto her breasts, and she moans, digging her fingers deliciously into my back. She likes it, god, she likes it, and I run my tongue in circles around the edges of her nipples, feeling good and free and *wanted* in a way I never have.

Then she's unbuttoning my jeans, and if I thought my engine was revving before, it's nothing compared to the body rush now. I help her take them off, shivering at the desire in her eyes as she looks me over. We both reach for her pants, and she slides her underwear off with them and then she's lying naked beneath me and the body rush intensifies even more. My cheeks are burning, and I let my eyes slide over her body, drinking her in.

Su-Lin. I'm about to make love to my Su-Lin, the girl who has a hold on my heart that not even Candace ever had claim

151

to. The woman who provides me a safe space, where I feel happy and loved, even when all I can offer her in return is laughter and friendship and the terror and panic that so often consumes me.

I can be different with her. I can be the person I want to be, love her the way she deserves to be loved. God, if it takes me the rest of my life, I'm going to learn how to do this. I only hope I can learn it before it's too late.

T he ache is so strong, so overpowering, and oh my god, there's Brendan in his underwear. And then I'm totally naked, which probably should feel super terrifying, but his cheeks are flushed a pink that nearly matches his hair, and he gives me this soft smile that melts me.

He starts kissing me again, our bodies pressed together, only this thin layer of his cotton boxers separating us—damn it, why are those still on? And his hands are wandering, and my hands are wandering, and I'm just about to reach right into those boxers, when he starts moving downward again, trailing kisses down my chest, along my stomach, and down and down and—

E very trace of panic is gone now. I press my body to hers, kissing her, hoping she feels the love and passion and commitment I feel for her, even though I can't say the words. There's only my boxers between us, and I want to be inside her—god, we'll get some Plan B tomorrow please let me be inside her—but I wrest control over myself again as I slide my mouth down her body. She tastes like salt and anticipation, and beneath her soft skin, her muscles are tensing, waiting. I work my way down past her pubic hair—she hasn't shaved, but hell if I care—and brush my tongue so softly against her.

OH. MY. GOD.

It's not like I've never played around down there myself, but neither my hands or any vibrator the internet has to offer compares to that first single flick of his tongue, which sends a jolt of pure electricity through me. I gasp and arch, and he pulls back for a second like he's checking to see if I'm okay, and I have to fight to keep from shoving his face forcibly back in my crotch.

Whatever he sees in my face must convince him, though, because he goes back in himself, his hands caressing my inner thighs, his mouth and tongue everywhere between, doing things that pull more gasps from me, make my vision spark at the edges. The electricity builds and builds, and my hands are tight in the curls of his hair, and I can't breathe around the sheer, climbing, glorious ache, and I want to say his name right now, because he's all I can think about, all I ever want to think about, and—

She lets out a gasp that startles me into looking up, afraid that I've pushed her too far. But her head is thrown back in ecstasy, her knees fallen to the sides, inviting and open. I smile and work her up with my mouth, then slide my fingers inside her, massaging the upper part of her vaginal wall. Su-Lin gasps and groans, and the sounds are so delicious I can hardly stand it—I'm fully at attention and have never been harder. Suddenly she's holding her breath, and I focus, bringing her through.

I'm blinded as the electricity, that amazing surge of bliss, peaks. My whole body shudders in his hands, my limbs suddenly robbed of all muscle, all ability to move, and I start to laugh, incredulously, with the sheer happiness of it.

She laughs—her joyous, happy laugh—as her body collapses, and I smile and watch her. She makes me feel so strong, like a man, something I can't remember ever feeling so deeply.

"That was—" she gasps. "That was—wow."

It's probably dumb of me to be so proud of that reaction, but I am. I'm aware I'm grinning stupidly at her, but I can't help it. God, even if we stop there, I'm so happy.

I don't want to stop there.

"Yeah?" I ask.

Her body writhes against the covers like she's reliving it. "Oh, yeah." She draws a shuddery breath, and then, with a grin, props herself into a sitting position.

"Your turn," she says.

My head rushes. If she means what I think she means— *damn*, does she really want to do that? I know a lot of girls don't like it, as Candace was fond of reminding me, though later I heard she once gave John a blow job under a table while I was playing *Call of Duty* in the other room, so who the hell knows what was true.

I don't want to think about that, don't want her here even as a specter of the pain she caused me. I'd assumed I was going to go down on Su-Lin and then we'd have sex, but I don't have a condom, after all. I pull Su-Lin toward me—whatever she wants to do, I need her close—and then her hands are all over my body, her mouth on mine. I lie back, enjoying the feel of her tongue against mine—

My mouth is moving from his lips to taste along his jaw, along his neck, and down his chest. I'm taking my time, partly because the way he's breathing now is super sexy and because I want to kiss every part of him—

And, okay, partly because I'm starting to panic now.

I said "your turn" with the saucy confidence of someone who

154

has any clue what the hell they are doing. I do not, and maybe the alcohol is wearing off, but the closer I get to his boxers, the more aware of that I'm becoming.

I'm kissing the muscles of his stomach—they are surprisingly taut, even though I don't think he works out regularly, so he must just be genetically blessed—when I finally muster the courage to reach into those boxers and feel another area in which I can tell he's also genetically blessed.

He makes a moaning sound as my fingers move over him, so I do more of that, more exploring and caressing. He seems to be into it, and god knows I am.

The hands part isn't what I'm most worried about, though. I've never handled the whole stick and berries, so to speak, but I think I'm pretty good with my hands.

I'm committed now, and even though I'm worried I'll suck at this—ha!—I'm also eager to try. Because it's Brendan, and because of how he makes me feel and how I want to make him feel.

'm gasping in heavy anticipation—is she really going to do this?—as her fingers stroke the outside of my boxers, her lips working over my stomach.

Then her fingers are underneath my boxers, and she's running them the length of me. My whole body is moaning as she slides off my underwear, and all I can think is that she loves me, god, she loves me. That she wants this, wants to do something so totally just for me—it's mind blowing. My eyes are closed, and my mouth is open, and my body is arching back—

lower my head and start. Several thoughts click through my brain, like dominoes toppling.

My first thought: OH MY GOD THERE IS A DICK IN MY MOUTH.

Second: OH MY GOD IT'S BRENDAN'S DICK. IN MY MOUTH.

Third: Does he have a name for it? If so, why don't I know this?

Fourth: I think I'm supposed to do something with it while it's in my mouth.

Fifth: Should I have Googled how to do this first? Should I take a break and Google it now?

But Brendan makes another moaning sound, and I think maybe I don't need to take a break to watch blow job tutorials. I move my mouth and my tongue, and I try to listen to the sounds he's making, try to do more of what brings out those gasping noises. Soon I'm barely doing much of the moving at all, because his hips are doing so much of that, and his hands are in my hair now, and I really hope he's enjoying this. Or maybe he's just trying to make me feel better, maybe it's not really working for him, but—

The sensation is overwhelming, and I'm afraid I'm going to finish the moment I'm in her mouth, but I hold my breath and her tongue runs up the sensitive part of the tip, and I reach for her shoulder and cry out.

I have no more thoughts, no more words, I can't breathe as the sweet pressure overwhelms me. My whole body burns as the pressure builds and builds, alight with the nearness of her, with the soft touch of her hands on my legs. And then the dam breaks, and I cry out her name.

Nope.

It worked for him.

I have this heartbeat that I worry I might gag, just out of surprise, but I don't. I just swallow it down. It doesn't taste bad—different, not what I expected, but not bad.

And more importantly, when he finished and his body shuddered, I heard him say my name in that gasp, and it makes me feel better than a million vid views, better than ten million.

I expect her to pull back, but she doesn't, she keeps going until my body relaxes, and as she crawls up next to me, she doesn't even seem like she minded. I guide her against me, my body still coming down, settling into a tired, satisfied weakness. I feel eerily floaty, like I'm dreaming, though I've dreamed this night a hundred times and never did it feel *this* wonderful, this pure and right and good.

I can't believe it's real. "Su-Lin *is* unpredictable," I whisper.

She snuggles close to me, like she's still enjoying the press of our skin. I definitely am. "Even to you?" she asks.

I smile, running my hand down her cheek. It's such a thrill just to touch her, even after all of that. "Especially to me."

His naked body presses against mine, our heads resting together on the pillow. And though we didn't have, like, actual intercourse, I feel so warm and utterly satisfied and still somehow tingly and perfectly drowsy. It feels good, so good, to know that even with as much as he knows me, better than anyone ever has or probably ever will, I can still surprise him sometimes. Because he can clearly still surprise me. God, I hope this surprise is something we can do over and over and over again.

She pulls the covers over us, wrapping me safely up in her, a physical extension of the haven she's been for me since we met. I don't know what magic this is, what other-worldly force has brought us together, allowed me this little slice of perfection.

All I know is, I never want it to end.

We fall asleep like that, together, and the last thought I have is that I'm pretty sure I've never been so happy in my life.

SIXTEEN

Brendan

I wake up feeling warm and safe. I know I've been dreaming, though the details are fading fast, and I keep my eyes closed, hoping to shift back into unconsciousness. I roll over—and my ankle brushes Su-Lin's under the covers.

My eyes pop open. She's here, her shiny black hair spilling over my pillow, the smooth curve of her bare shoulder visible even burrowed as she is beneath the comforter. It isn't a dream, though it feels like one.

Last night. The snap of her bra catch releasing, the smooth glide of her skin against my bare chest. Her body shuddering. Her mouth, warm and wet, and the delicious things she did with her tongue.

My body is reacting to the memory, and I long to curl up next to her, hold her while she wakes. Not just because I want more, though I do. I long to make love to her for real, but even if she wanted to, I don't have a condom, which feels like more of a problem than it did last night.

Still, here in the morning, with only the faintest bit of head-ache, I think about all the things I could do next. Hold her until she drifts awake, kiss her neck, tell her how very much I love her. Make sure she knows how safe I feel with her, how I trust her more than any other person, more than I ever thought I could trust again.

Su-Lin shifts in her sleep, her legs stretching out, and I almost take her in my arms. But the soft, dreamy quality of sleep is leaving me, and slowly, inevitably, my chest is seizing, my muscles squeezing in like an iron vise, pushing the air out of me. Things Candace told me are whispering to me like ghosts from the shadows; all the ways I failed her sexually, and her final, disgusted word on the subject: "Come on, Brendan. You didn't think I could be satisfied with just *you*." And yeah, I know Candace was cruel, and she was saying that to justify her cheating, but the way she so rarely really wanted me spoke to the truth underneath it. I'd always thought it was mismatched sex drives, but apparently she and John went at it like rabbits.

Last night, Su-Lin *wanted* me, and I can't bear to watch that desire fade into disinterest, or worse, disappointment and disgust. Not from her.

I'm not ready. I love Su-Lin more than anything, would do anything to protect her. But I know from past experience that if I allow myself to be that close to her, I'll love too much. She's beautiful and fun and the most deeply good person I know, but she could one day want different things. The idea of losing her makes my heart thump awkwardly, a tight cramp cutting through me from armpit to sternum.

I lie perfectly still. I'm just inches away, and I can feel her warmth on my sheets, inviting me to pull closer.

I want to.

I can't breathe; I can't move; I can't think. I can't be this in love with her, because I know exactly where that road leads. Candace made it very clear what a lousy husband I was. Our relationship was like the rock wall Su-Lin climbed yesterday, so steep and sheer that the many times I fell were inevitable. I almost didn't survive the final slip, where I fell all the way to the bottom, landing like Jason, with a sickening smack.

I can't go through that again.

160

With Su-Lin, it would be a million times worse.

When I'm sure I can stand without passing out, I slip out of bed, careful not to disturb her. I slide on my boxers, which I find tangled with her bra. I collect the rest of our clothes, arranging hers in a pile next to her on the bed so she won't have to search for them, and slip into the bathroom to put on mine. Then I grab some of the leftover bread from the party and pop in a few pieces of toast. Part of me wishes I had a bigger kitchenette and supplies to make her a real breakfast, but the other part is glad I don't. That would be too much. Too special.

We have to keep this casual. It's too much, too fast, and while most of me hates myself for that, the other part—the panicking part—is so vocal that it always gets its way, and I hate myself for that, too.

I sit in the chair beside the table, watching Su-Lin smile in her sleep. I want to be with her so bad it physically hurts. I want to wake up with her every morning.

But not like *this*. God, what was I thinking? We had a plan. We were going to ease into it. We were going to wait until I could give her more, give her all of me, if she still wants it by the time I unpack all my baggage.

I know what I was thinking. I was thinking that I've been fantasizing about her for four months, and there she was, touching me, wanting me, telling me that she was ready for this. Su-Lin has made it clear she's no saint, but I do know that sex means something to her. I know she's had boyfriends in the past who broke up with her for not being ready fast enough, so the fact that she wanted to do this with me—

I was right last night. It didn't feel casual, because it's not. My throat closes, and I hunch down in my chair and wish I could disappear, be someone else, someone who could function like a normal human being. A normal human being who just made love to his best friend who he's desperately in love with and should damn well be happy about it in the morning.

I squeeze my eyes shut. That's the problem. That's why I did this. It's because I thought I'd be okay in the morning. I thought the catharsis of finally being able to be with her would quiet the voices, would help me be ready for more.

Like so many people before me, I had a problem and I thought sex would fix it, only to realize in the morning it's made it worse.

I look at the door, think about leaving, but no, that would hurt her. I have to stay. I have to face this. I have to figure out what the hell I'm going to say to her to make this okay.

And then the toaster dings and the toast pops up and Su-Lin stirs and adrenaline rushes through me like someone has beaten down the door and come in with a gun. I turn on my phone and look for something—anything—to remark on while I figure out what else I'm going to say.

It's the coward's way, I know. But if I allow myself to fall into this, I know what will happen. I'll wrap my whole being up in us and never want to let go, not even if it's better for her.

I can't do that again. Not to her.

Su-Lin squints over at me, smiling as she sees the toast in the toaster. Then she seems to notice that I'm dressed, and finds her clothes next to her and stares at them.

I finish my Google search and wave my phone at her. "TubeDaily did a piece about our launch today. She called the original *Sockwives* 'pure brain-breaking crazy,' and she also says she peed herself, so I think that's a good thing."

Su-Lin's smile turns tentative. "This is what I live for. People fake laughter but not bladder failure."

I try to ignore the tightness in my chest, which is now throbbing with a dry, empty ache. But Su-Lin proceeds to put on her clothes under the covers, like we're friends at a sleepover.

Because our date is over. The last one this week. And now we have to go back to being casual, which is the last thing I want. But I also don't want to start sweating and crying uncontrollably, don't want her to face that kind of a mess the morning after we finally slept together.

So instead I butter the toast. I put some on a paper plate and hand it to Su-Lin. She sits down on the couch, and I take the chair, and we eat and talk about our nerves for the upcoming launch, as if nothing has happened. As if we didn't just have earth-shattering, transformative, mind-blowing sex that magnified my feelings for her a hundred times over.

Su-Lin smiles at me again and I try to smile convincingly back at her.

She's fine with this. Maybe it's even what she expected. I'm the one whose heart is shattering, blown apart by the force of my own expectations.

Stick to the plan, Brendan, I tell myself.

But mostly I wish I was somebody else.

SEVENTEEN

Su-Lin

When I fell asleep last night—sometime after Brendan did, his warm breath soft and even against my bare skin—I'd had this image of what it would be like waking up in bed with him. I'd roll over, and he'd be there, and I'd realize his arm was still around my waist, like he didn't want to let go. I'd scoot up against him as his eyes fluttered open, and he'd smile. And we'd tease each other about morning breath, but that wouldn't stop us from kissing and tangling up in each other all over again. Which would, of course, lead to incredible morning-after sex and possibly another round in a nice, steamy shower afterward. I've never had the experience of waking up with a guy after sex before, so maybe this image comes from too many movies.

There are a few seconds after I wake up, smelling toast and feeling the warmth of him in the sheets, that my heart swells with this sense of perfect happiness—and then I open my eyes and see him sitting hunched over in a chair across the room, staring at his phone. Fully dressed.

Another look around, and there are my clothes in a neat pile by the bed. Like he put them there in hopes I would get them on as soon as possible.

My heart deflates so fast it's painful.

Don't be paranoid, I tell myself. It was a polite gesture, setting my clothes there for me like that. A *nice* gesture.

But he barely looks up at me as he reads a comment about our launch today, or as I fumble with a halfway normal response.

That's when I really know. He doesn't want to talk about last night.

He wants to pretend it didn't happen.

I put on my clothes under the sheets, which still smell like him. They're yesterday's clothes, so I'm going to have change again, but he clearly doesn't want me walking around naked, even if it's just as far as to my suitcase and then the bathroom.

Everything in me feels sharp and jagged with uncertainty— my heart against my ribcage, my breath in and out of my lungs. I'm smiling, taking bites of buttered toast that tastes like cardboard, but it's like I'm made of delicate glass. Like I'm afraid to move too suddenly or I'll break.

So different from last night, which was all heat and solidity and smoothness and hope.

And love.

I'm in love with him. So crazy in love with him. I should have known it before, and probably on some level I did. But I couldn't look at it too closely, couldn't let myself think about how much I might be in love with him if he didn't—couldn't yet—feel that way about me. Like it was something we had to fall into together, at the same time.

When really I'd fallen a long time ago, all by myself.

Our conversation right now, our jokes—it all sounds so hollow, I can't stand it. I finish my toast and grab a random shirt and some underwear from my suitcase and take a shower. I stand there under the hot water, and I think about last night.

It felt so perfect. Him and me, together. Like he wanted that as much as I did; like he felt the same overwhelming bliss, the same longing and satisfaction and passion and love . . .

But if he did, why would he go out of his way not to acknowledge it happened?

I could understand if he was having a panic attack—I know any movement forward could trigger that. The whole plan was based on trying to avoid causing him to suffer as much as possible. But I've seen him have panic attacks, seen him struggle to breathe, to talk, his face tight with pain.

This didn't look anything like that. It looked like avoidance. Like dread.

I grab a thin white hotel towel and dry myself. Now that I'm out of the shower, I can't remember if I even bothered to shampoo my hair or do anything other than stand under the water.

I wipe the steam from the bathroom mirror and stare at myself. I try to see the Su-Lin I felt like last night, with him. The Su-Lin who was beautiful and sexy and womanly and wanted. Desperately. *Intensely.* Who didn't need perfect boobs like Jane Shaw or the perfect blond hair and full lips like Candace.

All I see is normal me. Cute, maybe. Little, definitely. But just me.

Who was I kidding, thinking I could measure up to his previous sexual experience? Candace was a heinous person, but after six years together—oh my god, how much sex must they have had over *six years?*—she would definitely know what she was doing. She would know exactly what he liked in bed and exactly how to make him want more.

That was the problem, wasn't it? He always wanted more from her. He always talks about that like it's a bad thing, and in most ways it probably was—her being the Queen Bitch of Bitchland and all.

But it seems like the opposite—not wanting more, *especially* when it comes to sex—could also be a pretty big problem in having a real relationship. And maybe in my stupid, impatient desperation to know if he could feel passion like that for me, all I did was prove to him that no, he doesn't.

I wonder how many mornings they had like the one I'd imagined. Smiling and laughing and making love. Even though she was screwing his best friend and probably several others, even though she was so selfish and stupid that she took him for granted at every turn and didn't realize how amazingly lucky she was to have a guy like Brendan.

I scowl at myself in the mirror; with this expression, I don't look like me at all.

For the moment, I like that.

I finally manage to stop making faces in the mirror and get dressed. I don't have the energy to dry my hair, so I put it into two braids. I put on the barest of makeup, just a little mascara and some lip gloss. I'm not sure I would have even done that, but we have the launch today.

That's what I need to focus on. That's what I need to direct my thoughts toward. Not the elation of last night; not the whatever-the-hell-this-is of this morning.

When I get out of the bathroom, Brendan is busy cleaning up the table—putting the unused bread back in the bag, sweeping crumbs off into his hand to drop in the garbage.

Not looking at me.

My deflated heart twists miserably.

I sit on the bed, the same bed we slept in last night, the same bed we—

No, stop. Don't think about it. He doesn't want to.

I tug on my chucks, though a mean little part of me wants to throw one of them at him, just to make him see me.

But even though he doesn't want to look at me, and he definitely doesn't want to talk about last night, he is aware of my presence, because he says, "So, is there anything else we need to get ready for the launch, you think?"

Just like the talking before I got in the shower, his tone is a weird, fake attempt at normal. Probably like mine, when I say, brightly, "I think we're good. We probably just need to check in with Kira, make sure there's nothing else she needs from us." Kira's our convention liaison, though I've only seen her once so far this week—we're far from her biggest priority. I hop to my feet. "Actually, I can go do that now. I was thinking I would run

167

down to the booth and check on Emily, too."

I wasn't thinking that. I actually have no idea what I would need to check on Emily for; the woman is way overqualified to be running a merch booth. But I need to get out of this room. I need to get away from him right now.

In four months, I've never felt like I needed to get away from Brendan before. It's always been the exact opposite.

But I'm so deeply in love with him, and he doesn't feel the same. He probably regrets everything we did last night, and I can't handle being face to face with how badly I screwed everything up.

He looks over at me now, but I can't read his expression. "That sounds like a good idea."

The thought that he wants me to go hurts almost as bad as all the reasons I want to.

"Great." I force a big smile. Do I normally smile this big? What is my normal smile even like? For all that I do it, I can't seem to remember now. "I'll text you if Kira says she needs anything. But I'm sure it'll be great. Yay launch day!" I sound like the world's most pathetic cheerleader.

I am an idiot. Brendan smiles, but he looks a little dazed. And confused. (Isn't that a movie? About people who are stoned? He doesn't look stoned. Just dazed and confused.)

Then I grab my messenger bag and all but run from the room.

I barely register my flight from the hotel to the convention center, or weaving through the early but already substantial crowds at the exhibition hall—except the several times I inadvertently smack someone with my bag and the one time I run into a display banner and nearly end up wrapped in PewDiePie's giant vinyl face.

Pull it together, Su-Lin.

Thankfully, there's not much action happening at our booth currently—not from the fans, anyway. Tate and Emily are there, chairs scooted so close together she might as well be in his lap. He's showing her something on his phone and she's laughing, and then he leans in to nibble on her earlobe, and I'm just standing there staring like I've never seen two young, attractive people be so into each other.

I wanted the two of them together. So why does seeing it make me feel scraped dry, like the last tiny remnants of freezer-burned ice cream?

Tate notices me first, and his happy expression drops. "Hey, Cuz. What's wrong?" His brows draw together. "Did my mom call you? Because I told her the last thing you need is to be reminded that your big launch day is on the fourth—"

Emily elbows him, cutting him off. Clearly guessing that a call from Aunt Alice is not my problem.

Though now maybe it is.

Shit. It *is* the fourth. I'm not superstitious, but four is a pretty bad number for Chinese people. The word in Mandarin sounds just like the word for death, and no one schedules weddings or any big events on that day.

Like a big launch for your new series. Or maybe sleeping for the first time with the best friend you're totally in love with.

No. A stupid number isn't to blame. I am.

"I'm great," I say, shaking my head. Maybe too much. "I'm . . . the launch is going to be great. Great."

Smooth. All it was lacking was a few more "great"s.

Something passes wordlessly between them, and Tate jumps to his feet. "I'll go get us some booth food. We'll need the sustenance to deal with the post-launch crowds dying for t-shirts." He slings an arm around me and plants a kiss on the top of my head. "You've got this, Cuz."

Then he takes off. Emily slides her chair toward me, raising her eyebrows. I sit down tentatively on the very edge of the chair. I still feel like I might break.

"So things are still going well with Tate?" I ask, even though I know my false cheer isn't fooling her for a second.

"Yeah," she says, still watching me carefully.

"Jason said you told him Tate wasn't your boyfriend." I don't know why I feel the need to say this like an accusation, and I feel bad when Emily flinches.

"He's not," she says, after a few seconds. "But this morning he said he wants to be."

"That's fantastic." I'm even able to churn up the slightest amount of genuine happiness. "That's really . . ."

"Great?" She gives me a look, and I sigh. "Okay, Su-Lin. What's happening? This isn't about the launch."

"No." I toy with one of my braids. "It's about me and Brendan. And what we did last night."

Her eyes widen. "Did you guys finally have sex?"

My cheeks burn. "Um. Sort of."

"Sort of? How do you 'sort of' have sex?"

I shrug. "We were staying in for the night, you know, and we had a little bit to drink and we . . ." I draw in a breath. I tell pretty explicit sex jokes all the time. I should have the words for this without dying of embarrassment. "He went down on me, and then I, well—returned the favor. So, yeah. Sort of."

She gapes. "That's—why do you look so miserable? That's what you wanted, right? He didn't pressure you into—"

"God, no! I mean, yes. That's what I wanted. If anything, I pressured him. I'm the one that—" Now my eyes are starting to burn. No, I am not going to cry. I am not going to—

"I'm in love with him," I blurt out.

Emily blinks. "Yeah, I know. I think the only one who didn't know was you."

She's probably right. God, even Brendan probably knew. And he cares about me. He loves me as a friend. He always has. Maybe all of this, even him wanting to date, was just for me, to make me happy.

Maybe he thought he would feel it if he put the effort in. He probably hoped he could be in love with me someday.

Is that what he didn't want to say to me this morning? That he knew now that without that passion he never would?

"Hey." Emily leans forward. "Hey, what's—sorry, we're closed right now," she says in a firm voice to a guy digging through the basket of finger puppets. The guy looks up, startled. She makes a shooing motion, and he walks away.

"You don't have to—" I start, but she shakes her head.

"You put me in charge of the merch. And right now we're not selling merch. We're talking. He'll deal with it."

Or he'll be a pissy ex-fan who will loudly hate on me on the internet, but right now I can't bring myself to care.

"I thought it would be this incredible thing, you know?" I say, already forgetting about the disgruntled fan, suddenly desperate to get the words out so they won't be pinging around in my head like a broken arcade game. "And it was for me. But I don't think it was for him. I think he . . . I think I wasn't, um, as good as he was expecting."

Now Emily's jaw has practically dropped to the floor. "Did he *say* that?"

"No, he didn't," I say quickly, because she sounds pissed enough to track him down and strangle him with one of our XXL *Starving with the Socks* t-shirts. "He didn't say anything. I mean, neither of us did." I frown. Maybe I should have. But it was so clear he didn't want to talk about it, didn't want to even think about it. "When I woke up, he was already dressed, and it was so awkward, and he just kept talking about the launch, and—I think he wishes it had never happened."

"No way," Emily says, after a moment of consternation. "There is no way in the world that boy wishes you hadn't given him a blow job. That goes against everything I know about both him and men in general. No."

"It's not like I don't think he wanted it at the time. But I don't know. Maybe it wasn't very good for him."

I'm trying to avoid Emily's increasingly confused expression, but she turns the chair so I have to face her. "Um," she says slowly, like she's talking to a very, very stupid person. Which I'm feeling more and more that I am. "It's kind of hard to miss whether a guy enjoyed a blow job."

I glare at her. "I'm not saying he didn't enjoy it at all. Yeah, he came, okay? But it's that whole sex as pizza thing—"

She groans, but I roll over any protests she's going to make, though she clearly already knows about the sex as pizza theory. "I know guys always like sex," I say. "Because it's like pizza. Even if it's bad pizza, it's still pizza, you know? But there's a world of difference between, like, crappy pizza and really good pizza, right?"

"And in this very scientifically sound metaphor, you think he just had some cheap freezer pizza?"

"Right. Or maybe mall food court. But the kind that gives you heartburn afterward. And regret." I slump down in the chair. Candace was probably like Chicago deep dish. Or maybe the perfect slice from the best pizzeria in New York.

Zing.

I'm scowling again now. Becoming un-Su-Lin.

"There is no way you are mall food court pizza," Emily says. "Not to him. Not to any straight guy with a working dick, but definitely not to him. Are you sure he didn't just panic?"

I shrug self-consciously. That wasn't a panic attack. It was something else, and I think I know what. "It's not like I have a *ton* of experience," I say. Or any, really. But Emily doesn't need to know that. Maybe no one does, ever. Maybe I'm just going to die a virgin, and no one ever needs to know. "And he had all this passion with his ex-wife—"

"His cheating bitch ex-wife."

"Yes. Definitely. But that doesn't mean she wasn't great in bed. Or that he can't help but compare me to her and—god, look at me!" I glare down at myself, at my frayed jean shorts, and my chucks, and my faded vintage-looking tank top with the Care Bears on it. "I'm wearing a Care Bears t-shirt! And braids! I'm not a grown woman. I'm a fucking cartoon character!" Tears are spilling over, and I wipe them away furiously. "There's no way he can feel that way about me. God, why did I think we'd do that and he would actually want me *more*? There's no—ow!"

I grab my head, wincing at the hard tug she just gave one of my aforementioned braids. "What did you do that for?"

"Because you were saying awful things about my friend Su-Lin and you need to stop," Emily says, her eyes narrowed. "You are fun and adorable and sexy and tons of guys wish in their wildest dreams they could bang you."

This is true about Emily, for sure—it always has been. She's gorgeous, with her shiny dark hair and her dark eyes and delicate features. In high school, she always seemed to care way more about whatever project she was working on than whether guys liked her or not. And actually, she's kind of like that as an adult, too—except now when she does want a guy's attention, she knows how to turn her focus to that and get it.

God, I envy her that. (Though not with Tate, because ew, my cousin.)

Is she right about me? Or is she just being a friend and saying what she thinks I need to hear?

The truth is, I don't care if there's a bunch of guys who want to sleep with me. I only want one particular guy, and for him to want me the way I want him. Always and forever, and over and over and over.

"Thanks," I say, because I know she's trying to help. But she can't change who I am or what Brendan feels (or doesn't) for me. "I need to get going, I've got to check with Kira on the launch and—"

"Su-Lin."

I stand up. "It's okay. I'm going to be fine. I'm Su-Lin. I'm just—I'm excited about the launch, and it's going to be great."

Peppy and happy and smiley. That's what I need to be. That's what I am.

And when Brendan finally gets the courage to tell me he doesn't want to do this anymore, if that's really what's going on here, then that's what I'll be then, too. I owe it to him. He's my friend, first and foremost, and it's not his fault if he doesn't feel the same for me. It's probably killing him, thinking of how to tell me. He doesn't need to add guilt to everything he already has to deal with.

I ignore Emily's concerned expression and straighten my shoulders. I can do this. I can be happy Su-Lin, for myself, and for our show, and especially for him.

EIGHTEEN

Brendan

’m afraid I’m going to have a series of panic attacks as we get ready for the launch, but instead I settle into ambient anxiety. I don’t want to burden Su-Lin with this while we’re getting ready for the launch, so I avoid her for most of the morning, which isn’t hard because we’re running around like crazy getting everything ready. Su-Lin seems even more Su-Lin-like than normal, spending most of her time talking to fans and organizers in sentences that could only be punctuated with exclamation points. It’s sort of like when she’s had two Big Gulps right in a row, but I’m pretty sure she’s been too busy to hit the 7-Eleven.

I know it’s my fault that we haven’t talked about last night, but it still stings that she hasn’t brought it up. I get that we’re doing the casual thing, but I told her last night it didn’t feel casual to me, and unless she was way more drunk than I thought, she should remember that.

It’s my fault. *I* could have brought it up. I still could, but even as the panic from this morning is wearing off, the knowledge that I’m about to be on stage in front of a thousand people is setting in. I’m not sure how I’m supposed to get up there and pretend that I belong, even though she’s the YouTube sensation, and nobody knows me from Adam. This, on top of this morning’s residual jitters, ensures that the last thing in the world I want to be doing is talking to anybody, so I mostly stick with my job.

Su-Lin is the people person. I handle the tech. The tech doesn't ask awkward questions. The tech doesn't get offended. The tech doesn't get its feelings hurt, except for the Apple computer that I try to connect to the generic projector, which insists that talking to such a plebeian device is beneath it. I eventually coax it into connecting anyway.

Before I'm ready, and just after I realized I haven't had anything to eat today besides a piece of Gudetama toast, we are up on stage and Su-Lin is working the crowd, smiling and waving and introducing me with such excitement that you'd think I was one of the Jonas Brothers.

I try to smile, but I'm afraid it comes out more as a grimace. Su-Lin arranged for her friend Perry to interview us, and soon we're answering questions about the differences in the reboot, the nuances of our partnership, and the return of iconic *Sockwives* characters Ruby and Terrence Clarence, as well as the imminent appearance of our new puppet Shuby.

"Rather than tell you about Shuby, why don't we show you?" Su-Lin says. Then our show is playing, starting with the opening bit by Ruby and Terrence Clarence, which is set up like an SNL host speech. Ruby and Terrence begin by debating about their favorite TV shows, with Terrence favoring the infamous *Socktor Who* and Ruby preferring the more high-brow *Socks and the City*. The audience laughs, and I grab Su-Lin's hand, glad that at least they aren't all sitting there in silence.

She doesn't look at me, but she does squeeze back. Touching her again quiets the anxiety, grounding me. I don't want to worry about whether or not it's casual right now—I just need to be touching her.

The Ruby and Terrence bit cuts directly into our first episode of *Sock and Order*, the only show that both Ruby and Terrence Clarence could agree on. In the background we have a sock behind a shoebox that we've taped together to resemble a judge's bench. Behind the prosecutor's desk—another shoe box—sits Reginald Watsonberg, rainmaking lawyer, sexy star, and Ruby's main reason to watch. The defendant is my invention, Barry Blowright, the welding glove who is on trial for sexual harassment after being too handsy with his employees.

This gets a laugh, and I grin. Anxiety aside, it's pretty awesome to be able to share this after four months of wondering if anyone could ever love it but us.

After *Sock and Order*, we cut back to Ruby and Terrence, who suddenly find themselves face to face with the real Socktor, who emerges from—of course—a shoe box that's bigger on the inside. I got to use my editing skills on that one, and I'm proud of the results. The Socktor brings along his companion—Shuby, a sock with a frizzy, crazy version of Ruby's hair, and her eyes positioned too close together. When Su-Lin first made her, I was the one who suggested she looked like she wanted to be Ruby, and we brainstormed late into the night, until we were both rolling on the floor from exhaustion and laughter.

Shuby immediately becomes enamored of Terrence Clarence, and decides to stay instead of leaving with the Socktor—and the Socktor is eager to be rid of her. And thus begins Ruby and Terrence's journey into being sucked inside all their favorite TV shows, giving us the creative freedom to tell lots of stories, and not just ones suitable to the original *Sockwives* concept.

When the episode ends, the crowd cheers. Su-Lin lets go of my hand and my head feels light. While she walks to the front of the stage to answer more questions, I take deep breaths and try to soak in the excitement of the crowd.

We did it. We debuted our first episode, and even if it doesn't end up taking off like Su-Lin's first series, the crowd didn't boo us off the stage or groan through the entire episode.

This, I feel, is success.

Su-Lin is bouncing up and down like someone slipped her some uppers—a fear of hers, as she's known a lot of people who desperately want to see how hilarious she would be while high—and cheerfully answering questions from the crowd about what made her decide to return to the *Sockwives*, and why she's branching out. On panels, she's usually bounced some questions back to me, but this time she's fielding them all herself, and I wonder if she's worried about overwhelming me.

Except she's not looking back at me, not appraising my mental state, like she does so often when we're out in public.

A stone settles in my gut.

Something's wrong.

I move closer to her on the stage, just as Su-Lin picks another audience member for a question. The con staff pass the woman a mic, and she looks right at me. "This question is for Brendan," she says, and a chill passes through me at realizing there are now thousands of people I've never met who all know my name. "What was it like working in the *Sockwives* world with Su-Lin?"

Su-Lin looks back at me, and I swear she looks a little scared. I shove aside my worries about her. We can't deal with those while we're up on stage, anyway. I take the mic from Su-Lin, and the crowd quiets.

"It's been an honor," I say. "I'd seen her work before, and when she asked me to be her business partner, I was flabbergasted. Just completely astounded that she'd trust me enough to bring me in to this thing that she built by herself, that she was so amazing at. And since we've been working together—I mean, I was working as a video editor. I liked my job. So that should put it in perspective when I say that I've never had so much fun working on any project in my life, and most of that's because of Su-Lin. She makes everything better."

A soft *awww* emanates from the crowd, and my cheeks grow hot. Su-Lin doesn't look particularly thrilled with me as she takes the mic back, which is completely fair. That wasn't a very casual thing to say, but it was the truth.

"Well, that's all the time we have," Su-Lin says. "This episode will be up today, and we'd love if you'd share it! We can't wait for you to see the rest of the run, so subscribe to our YouTube channel, mmmkay?"

The crowd claps and cheers and there's a scream of "Hell yeah!" and then the whole thing's over. Su-Lin and I sit down at the edge of the stage and sign t-shirts and cell phone cases and sock puppets and a few people's arms. The whole time I'm trying to catch Su-Lin's eye without making it obvious to the fans—we have fans! Who are now fans of both of us! My brain is not sure what to make of this.

When the whole thing is over, I unplug our laptop, and Su-Lin says thank you to Kira, our con liaison. Su-Lin walks toward me, looking utterly deflated.

"That went well, yeah?" I say.

"Yeah," she says. "I think so."

The anxious rush of the event is starting to wear off, and now that I'm not trying to avoid her, I can plainly see that the usually blinding Su-Lin light is running out of batteries. "Are you okay?"

"Yeah," she says, waving me off. "I'm just tired. I think I'm going to go lie down."

I could stand to get somewhere quiet myself, after all that. And it'll be better to talk in the hotel room than in the exhibition hall where we might be ambushed by fans at any moment. "I'll come with you."

"You don't have to," Su-Lin says, still not looking at me.

Yes, something is definitely very wrong. I've been so wrapped up in my own fears and failures today—how long has she been like this? Was it the launch, or the awkwardness this morning? I'd thought that was all about me and my issues, which I now think was pretty self-centered of me.

"Obviously," I say. "But I want to. I need some down time, too."

Su-Lin nods and heads back to the hotel. It takes all my self-control not to beg her to tell me what's going on in her head as we take the elevator up to our room, but a gaggle of teenagers in cat ears climb in with us, and I don't want to start this in front of them.

The door barely clicks shut behind us before I sit down on the end of her bed. "What's wrong?" I ask.

"Nothing," Su-Lin says, heading for the bathroom. "Just tired."

"Stop that. I know you when you're tired. This isn't it. What's wrong? Is this about the launch? Or last night?"

She freezes in the doorway and slowly turns around. When she looks up at me, I see fear in her eyes.

It is about last night. I walk over to her, putting my hands on her arms. "Hey," I say. "I freaked out. I'm sorry. Can we talk about it?"

"You didn't seem like you freaked out. You seemed like you just didn't want it to have happened."

Oh, *god*. Is that what she thought?

"No," I say. "I really wanted that to happen."

Su-Lin rolls her eyes. "Yeah, last night. But you clearly regret it today."

I wrap my arms around her, relieved that she lets me. She feels so small in my arms, like she's shrinking in on herself from worrying about this.

I am an asshole.

"I'm scared today," I say. "And angry with myself. But that was the best night of my life, and I don't think I could bring myself to regret it."

Su-Lin's eyes widen. "Really?"

I brush a strand of her hair that has fallen out of its braid back out of her face. "Yeah, really," I say. "If I regret anything, it's that I let it happen before I could be the person you deserve me to be."

Su-Lin squeezes me tight, and I hold her back, still wishing I could pour my heart out, tell her that I want her to be my girlfriend and marry me and be with me forever and ever.

The words catch in my throat, and my whole body goes weak at just the thought of that one word.

Marriage.

My throat closes.

That's what I really want, isn't it? But I can't. I can't fail her, can't see the look on her face when she realizes that I'm not who she thought I was, who she needs me to be.

"Thanks," she says quietly. She wriggles out of my arms and climbs into bed, bunching her blankets up around her like a big Su-Lin cocoon. I want to curl up right there in the blankets with her, but we aren't having a date tonight, and even if we were, I have no right to go to bed with her again until I can guarantee I won't hurt her like that. I lie down on my own bed, though I can still smell her on the sheets, and my whole body aches to be closer to her. She might as well be miles away, but I still hear her voice, emerging softly from her blanket pile.

"So, what we did last night," she says, "you liked it?"

I pause for a moment, confused. She can't mean the sex, can she? Could she not *tell*?

"Um, yeah I liked it," I say. "You clearly know what you're doing."

Su-Lin is silent and still, but there's no way she fell asleep that fast.

Did *she* not like it? I mean, I'm pretty sure she had a good time when I was going down on her, but . . .

I can hear Candace's voice in my head. *Come on, Brendan. Do you think anyone really wants a dick in their mouth?* Su-Lin hadn't seemed like she minded, but now I can't remember if I actually said that I didn't expect it, actually told her that she didn't owe me anything. I've heard a lot of girls can't finish in regular intercourse, so it just seems smart to start there—and god, did I want to start there, tasting every bit of her—but I didn't mean for her to feel like she had to reciprocate.

Tears prick my eyes as the memory of last night floods with shame.

I hurt her. I made her feel obligated. And what I read as something amazing was actually causing her pain.

"Su-Lin," I say.

"Yeah?" Her voice is pitched higher than normal, like she's really nervous about something.

"I'm so sorry if you didn't want to do that. I should have been more clear that I didn't expect it. You don't ever need to feel like you need to do that for me again."

I squeeze my eyes shut and bury my face in the pillow. Not that I think she *would* do it again, because I've clearly ruined everything, and we're clearly never going to—

"I really liked it, actually," she says.

I look over at her, but her face is turned away from me, so all I can see is the ends of her braids poking out of the top of her cocoon.

"But it's okay if it wasn't the best thing ever for you," she says.

I sit up. "*What?* Are you kidding?"

Su-Lin rolls over and there's this unaccountably vulnerable expression on her face. She's actually worried about this.

"It was fantastic for me," I say. "Truly fantastic. I've been wanting to be with you like that more or less since we met, and never in all of my fantasies was it that good."

Now she looks skeptical. Blood drains from my face. I thought I'd been okay at expressing how much I wanted that last night, but I know from experience with Candace that sometimes what I think is good is really just mediocre from the other side.

"Really?" she says.

"Yeah. I'm sorry if it wasn't as good as you expected."

"Oh!" Su-Lin says, her eyes widening again. "God, no, that's not it at all."

I feel as if we're having two totally different conversations, but I'm not sure what hers is about. "Then what is it? Did I do something wrong?"

She shakes her head and burrows further into her covers.

"Come on," I say. "Talk to me."

There's a pause. "Ummmm," she starts. "I suppose you could say that I'm a . . . I mean technically, *very* technically—"

I have a glimmer of where this conversation is going, but I don't believe it. Su-Lin has talked lots of times about the guys she's been with, and—

"No way," I say, sitting up. "You're not a virgin."

She lets out a low pitched whine and buries her face under a pillow. "Very technically," she says, muffled.

Huh. I guess the stuff she said could still be true. It's not like she's ever opened a conversation about sex with *so this one time, while I had a guy's penis in my vagina* . . .

"Okay," I say. "But you've done other stuff, right? Like, the stuff we did last night."

Su-Lin is silent, and my stomach drops like a brick.

"No," I say. "No, no, no. No. That was your—"

"Don't say it!" Su-Lin shouts, and she throws her pillow at me. It hits me in the face. I get up and sit on the edge of her bed.

This can't be right. I can't have done that to her. That was her first time, and I just ignored her in the morning like nothing happened?

"I'm a douche," I say. "I'm a complete asshole. I'm so sorry that I—"

"Shut up!" she says, grabbing my arm and shaking me. "You didn't know, because I never told you. And I was there last night, too, you know. I wanted to do it."

I bite my lip. "You did, right? I mean, I thought we were both on board with—"

"Yeah, I was, okay? I put my hand on your dick. I made myself very clear." She yanks her covers out from underneath me and burrows down into them again. "But I didn't really know what I was doing, so you don't have to lie to me and tell me it was great for you if it wasn't. I'm sure you and Candace had a lot of phenomenal sex, and it's not like I think I could compare."

"That's not true," I say. "But I made you feel that way. I'm such an asshole."

She shakes her head. "It's fine! We're fine and I'm fine and everything's fine."

"Are you mad at me?" I ask. "You should be mad at me."

"No," she says. "Not at all." This, unlike the over-enthusiastic declarations of being fine, sounds true. "You really liked it?"

I finally understand what she's asking.

"Yes. You did everything just right. I clearly didn't know that you didn't have experience. I just hate that I wasn't paying attention, you know? I would have made sure you were really okay with that, helped you through it." I smile. "Not that you needed the help, apparently."

She cuddles closer to me, and I hope in some small way I'm repairing a bit of the damage I've done.

"Why were you scared?" she asks, her voice soft. "This morning, I mean."

"I'm not sure that I can explain that entirely," I say. "I just—I want to be with you, and I want to be ready for that and I'm mad as hell at myself that I'm not." I shake my head. "You deserve better, you know? And I think some stupid part of me might have thought that being together like that would help, and I'm mad at myself for thinking that, when obviously it didn't."

Su-Lin looks crestfallen, which is exhibit A of exactly what I was afraid of this morning.

She's tired of waiting for me. *I'm* tired of waiting for me, but I'm stuck with myself, and it's only a matter of time before she realizes she's not.

"I'm aware that we're basically just telling each other this over and over," I say. "But if I did do anything that made you uncomfortable, or that you didn't like, it's okay for you to tell me. I know I can be too aggressive, or too into certain things, and you need to tell me when I do that."

Su-Lin looks confused. "Too into things? I don't even know what that—" She pauses, her face hardening. "This is a Candace thing, isn't it?"

My face flushes. "Yeah, I mean, I know I'm not super great at this stuff. From experience."

"Experience with Candace," Su-Lin says flatly. "Who made you think you weren't good with . . . what now?"

I really don't want to go into detail about this, but I suppose she got all up close and personal with the details last night. "I guess I'm just sometimes . . . too enthusiastic."

I'm only confusing her further and I know it, but it's so hard to say the words.

"Too enthusiastic about . . ." Su-Lin says.

"Breasts!" Now I'm the one burying my head in a pillow. Oh my god, I sound like an idiot. "I'm kind of into breasts."

There's a long pause.

"Okaaaay," Su-Lin says. "This is not exactly a shocking revelation coming from a straight guy."

"No," I say, rolling my head to the side so I can see her. I almost turn right into her breasts, which is really unfortunate timing, and I sit up again. "I mean, like, *too* into them."

Su-Lin blinks at me. She looks pretty annoyed, but I'm hoping that's aimed at Candace. "How can you be *too* into a girl's breasts? Like, did you never want to do anything else?"

"No, not like that," I say.

She shakes her head at me. "Because what you did with my breasts last night was *hot*. Was it that kind of stuff that she was mad at you for?"

It was, actually. I mean, we were together for six years, so I definitely spent much more time with Candace's breasts than I have with Su-Lin's. "You'd probably get sick of it after a while."

Su-Lin presses her lips together. "What exactly did she say to you about this?"

I really do not want to repeat this, but I'm the one who brought this whole thing up.

"I don't know," I say, even though I damn well do. "When I'd do things like that, a lot of times she'd be like, 'God, Brendan, you're such a pig,' stuff like that."

Su-Lin flinches like this physically stings. "She actually said that to you."

"Yeah," I say. And worse. "But I probably deserved it, right? Because I'm—"

"Would you say something like that to me?" she asks.

I pause. "No."

She nods. "Even if I was too into something, and it made you uncomfortable, would you say that to me?"

I shake my head. "No, of course I wouldn't."

"No," she says. "You'd find a way to talk about it that was respectful and kind, because you're a decent human being."

Logically, I can see that she's right. It's just such a far reach from how I feel about all of it that I have a hard time believing it.

"So you were okay with it," I say.

Su-Lin looks at me like I'm an idiot. "Um, yeah. I was way more than okay with it. I was totally into that."

That, at least, is a relief, though I'm still not a hundred percent convinced she wouldn't eventually figure out what Candace meant, and no matter how polite she is when she tries to explain it to me, I still know it's going to be awful when she figures out I'm not what she hoped that I'd be.

"Well," I say, "I think after the idiot I've been about this, you've earned a free pass if you ever do anything you're worried I'll be upset about."

She bites her lip. "Really?"

I give her a half-smile. "Yeah. Though I doubt you'll ever be able to rise to my level of douchery."

She reaches out and puts her hand on my arm. Her touch is gentle, and my eyes flick briefly closed. I hope she doesn't notice.

"Wellll," she says, squinting.

I look down at her. "What?"

"There might be something I should have told you about."

I sink down on my elbow, lying next to her on the bed. "Yeah?" My pulse is racing, and my mind along with it. I know there's no way she could have betrayed me like Candace—she doesn't owe me anything, or at least not much. But—

"After that conversation we had the other day, about your dad? I might have Googled him."

For a second I'm confused about why this is a problem.

"I found your dad's court records, and . . ."

I close my eyes.

"I know what your dad was incarcerated for," she says.

I'm struck by how relieved I am that she knows about this. I've never wanted to bring it up—to anyone, really. Saying it out loud makes my throat close up, and it's humiliating to admit how much it affects me.

But if she already knows . . .

"Are you mad?" she asks. "I realized after you left to go back to the room that it didn't really make sense that he was still in jail twenty years later for just domestic abuse, and—"

"No," I say softly. "I'm not mad. I just . . . you could have told me you knew."

"Yeah." She wrinkles her nose. "I guess I should have told you a lot of things."

"No, it's okay—I would have talked to you about it. Or, I guess, I will now. If you want."

"You don't have to," she says. "You never seemed to want to before."

"It's hard for me to say out loud. I don't like to tell people, because it's weird to bring up."

"I get that. I just figured you didn't want me to know." Her fingers gently brush my arm. I'm struck by how much the opposite is true.

"No, I'm glad," I say. "And I really am okay to talk about it."

"Yeah?" she says. And I realize that, even still, neither of us has said the words. It's easier for me, somehow, now that I don't have to worry about what her reaction will be. Like getting to see the answer key before the test.

"Yeah," I say. "My dad molested me, and my mom caught him. Turned out he did it to a bunch of other kids, too. That's what he went away for, but I usually just say it was abuse, and people assume that he hit me. Maybe because I'm a guy."

Su-Lin makes this sad noise, and then throws the comforter over me and wraps her arms around my neck. She hugs me tight, and I squeeze her back. "I'm so sorry that happened to you," she says.

187

"Me too. And I hate that it messes me up. I don't even remember it, you know? I mean, I remember feeling scared, and this other emotion that's hard to describe, like a weird mix of arousal and deep, deep shame. And I remember a lot of yelling. I remember a man's voice, and there was never a man's voice in my house, so that had to be him. But I was three years old. It's all really unclear. So I don't feel like it should affect me at all. But it does."

She holds me closer, pressing her forehead against my jaw. If I thought my longing for her was strong from across the room, it's nothing compared to what I feel now.

"Thanks for telling me you knew," I say.

She squeezes me tighter. "I should have said something before."

"I'll make you a deal. I'll try not to feel terrible about treating your first time like it was nothing, and you try not to worry about this. You didn't do anything wrong."

She leans back, and the free tendril of hair falls across her face again. I reach up and brush it behind her ear.

"Neither did you," she says.

While I don't believe that, I'm grateful for it anyway. "Do you still want to be doing this? The Plan?"

Su-Lin is quiet for a minute. "Do you think it's working at all?"

It sucks, the whole arrangement. But I can't deny that I'm clearly more comfortable with a lot of things than I was at Mei-Ling's wedding.

"Yes," I say. "Slowly, but yes."

Su-Lin nods. "Then I definitely do."

I bury my face in her neck, grateful that no matter how badly I've messed this up, she's not ready to give up on me yet.

NINETEEN

Su-Lin

Okay, maybe Brendan hasn't totally ruled out the possibility of someday feeling the "I'm so in love with you and please be my girlfriend" thing for me. He wants to keep trying the Plan, which means he hasn't totally given up. Which is hope, right?

I squeeze the steering wheel of Brendan's beat-up compact car as I drive, trying not to examine how good of an idea it is to want to be with someone who has to try so hard to feel that way about me.

Because I don't just want to be with someone. I want to be with Brendan.

And besides, he said he really liked the sex, that I clearly knew what I was doing (even if I did not, other than in theory). He said it was "fantastic," actually, which is definitely how I viewed it at the time—though I would add a bunch more words to that, like "life-changing" and "amazing" and "holy shit, that was incredible." I draw a deep breath. Fantastic. That's definitely better than mall food court pizza. Nobody calls mall pizza fantastic. Someone might call Dominos or Pizza Hut fantastic if they hadn't had pizza in years, which is probably more realistic. But I can handle that. I can get better, right? Learn how to toss the dough, add more spices to the sauce . . . okay, this metaphor is getting away from me. But he liked it. He said that.

I'm not sure how much I believe him about it being the best night of his life—though god, I wish it really had been—but given the kinds of things Candace apparently said to him about his own performance, not having someone be a total bitch after sex probably meant the night as a whole felt a lot better. That doesn't mean the sex itself was actually as good as he was used to. Or that he feels the level of passion for me, that high he used to feel with her—despite all the horrible ways she treated him.

God, I want to punch Candace. (Though not as much as I want to punch Brendan's dad. That monster.) How could she say that kind of stuff to him? How could she even think it?

There's a tight lump in my throat, and I pull into my driveway. Dad's car is gone, which is rare—he must have taken Lan somewhere. This is good. I'd rather not have to answer questions.

I told Brendan I needed to run home to pick up my dress for the masquerade, which is totally true but implies it was because I forgot to bring a dress, which is not true. I had a dress in my suitcase already, another fun, fluffy number like I wore to prom.

But at some point in our conversation—or maybe even when I was with Emily and whining about my Care Bears t-shirt—I realized I needed something more for tonight.

I need to wear The Dress.

I know I'm not going to be on a date with Brendan tonight. But more and more, I'm starting to feel like the Casual Dating Plan—and more importantly, the desired results of said plan—is hanging by a very thin thread, though I'm not even totally sure why I feel that way. He did say that he thought it was working, if slowly, and it's unrealistic of me to think that a single con's worth of pseudo-dating other people would get him over some very real and long-standing relationship-panic issues.

Unrealistic, but still what I was hoping for.

He's definitely not ready to be with me yet, though, even after what we did, and I worry that every moment is a step closer to him realizing he may never be. That I'm his best friend and a great person to have " back in the saddle" sex with—he did say fantastic, after all—and he feels safe trying this out with me, but that there's still something missing that he needs.

What if the problem now isn't actually his issues, but just that I'm not the girl who can get him past them? The girl he can fall in love with?

He should get to be with that girl, even if it's not me. No matter how much it breaks my heart.

But if there's even the shred of a chance that I can be that girl for him . . .

Desperation. This is what I am, personified. I am just a ball of tiny Asian desperation.

And this dress is my Hail Mary.

I run upstairs and dig it out from the back of my closet, hoping it's everything I remember it being.

I think it is. It's a long gown, with this gorgeous, sheer, flowing fabric that's the blue of the sky just before total dark. And speckled across it are tiny silver beads that shimmer like stars. The moment I first saw it, it reminded me of our beach house, of that fantasy of us lying in bed and staring up at the stars, of hearing the ocean lapping the shore just outside our big picture window.

Then I tried it on, in the dressing room of the bridal shop while Mei-Ling was out looking at veils, and I felt like a whole new person. A Su-Lin who wasn't just cutesy and silly and fun, but as beautiful as the sky full of stars. The top of this gown basically has no back and not a ton on the front—enough to cover my breasts and hook into a delicate halter around my neck, but with a deep V in between. I was a sexy, confident Su-Lin who knew she could make someone feel more than friendship for her.

A Su-Lin who probably doesn't exist. But in this dress, maybe she could, for the night.

I try not to think about how a relationship needs way more than a sexy dress. Because this is what I have now. This is what I can do.

When I get back to the hotel, it's already almost time for the dance. I text Brendan that I'm here, and to meet me outside the ballroom. I'm shaking from nerves, and I can't handle walking all the way to the hotel room and from there to the dance. I check myself one last time in the little mirror in the driver's sunshade. My makeup looks good, and the advantage of having wet hair in braids all day is that the part of my hair I didn't pin up has this natural wave to it, falling over one shoulder. I can't see the dress in this tiny mirror, but I'm committed now.

I get out of the car and make my way to the big exhibition hall—the same one where the prom was held—and I wait. I shift from foot to foot. I consider the fact that I am half-naked in public. I think about whether the effect will be spoiled if I go back to Brendan's car and grab that ratty old blanket from the backseat to use as a kind of hobo-chic shawl.

Probably I shouldn't.

Besides, I'm still way more dressed than many of the other girls I see going in, who have basically put on a mask and a nightie. Maybe I should have done that. Maybe—

"Su-Lin?"

I freeze. It's Brendan. I turn and see him there, in that suit—the same one from the wedding (and his wedding) and the prom. Looking so unbelievably handsome and breath-taking.

His blue eyes are wide and his mouth parted. My cheeks flush. He's clearly checking me out. Is it too much to hope that maybe he's having a little trouble breathing, too?

I smile at him. "Hey," is all I manage to say.

He blinks, several times. "Hey," he says back. Sounding a little hoarse.

My heartbeat speeds up, which I didn't think was a possibility given how fast it was already going.

"You look . . ." He trails off, and the idea of how he might finish that thought kills me.

What? I look *what*? Beautiful? Sexy? Like the kind of girl

192

he could feel intense passion for? The kind of girl he could fall in love with?

"You look like the night sky through a skylight," he says softly.

I melt completely. He's thinking of the beach house too, and the stars, and maybe, maybe he wants that as much as I do.

"Really?" I say, wishing that I could hold the way he's looking at me right now like it was a physical thing.

"Really," he says.

There's a moment where we're just staring at each other, until I can't take it anymore. I have to look away or I'm going to jump him right here on our not-date, in the middle of a crowd of people making their way past us to get into the dance.

"Well, I learned one lesson from Mei-Ling's wedding," I say, and hike up the skirt of the dress just enough to show that underneath this elegant gown, I'm still wearing my sneakers. "No heels ever again. Chucks forever."

He laughs, this kind of startlingly light sound after the heavy feeling of moments ago. "They're perfect," he says. And we stand there for another long beat, just smiling at each other.

I don't want this to end, and I really don't want to date anyone else, and I really really don't want to pick out girls for him to date. But we can't stand out here forever, so I gesture to the dance. "Come on," I say, and he follows me in.

The masquerade is in most ways the same as the prom. Same packed, loud exhibition hall with the same thumping music and strobe lights and bars serving those bright, non-alcoholic drinks. No bubbles this time, sadly, and the theme seems to be veering toward a Mardi Gras atmosphere, with cheap plastic bead necklaces around every neck—there are people handing them out at the doors, though I imagine that unlike actual Mardi Gras, flashing for beads is neither required nor encouraged. The big screens around the hall are showing clips from various YouTube shows, and on the stage behind the DJ, there is a group of acrobats dangling and swinging from long silks.

I usually love a good party, but I don't want to be here at all. The beat of the music makes my heart feel out of sync, the twisting, jumping press of people makes my nerves feel frayed at the ends.

I want to be back in our hotel room. Even if we can't date or do anything more than just hold each other like we did earlier today. Brendan is looking around the room with about the same level of enthusiasm I feel, his hands jammed in his pockets. But he's always uncomfortable in a situation like this. That's normal.

What's *my* problem?

We stand there awkwardly for several minutes, both of us declining beads offered by a passing convention employee. Not talking to each other, sort of vaguely moving to the beat like we care about the music. He's probably waiting for me to pick out a girl for him to dance with—that's what we're here for, after all. I reluctantly start scanning the room—there's lots of cute girls here, and not *all* of them are dressed like they just stepped out of the changing room at Victoria's Secret, so I'm sure I can find one that—

"Hey, guys!"

It's Jane Shaw, standing right next to us, smiling her big, gorgeous smile. In the world's sexiest Queen of Hearts cosplay, complete with short skirt made of playing cards over red fishnet stockings, and a tight corset adorned with red lace and vintage Valentine hearts. Her long legs look even longer in tall leather boots in the same cherry red as her full lips.

I want to sink into the floor. Any sexiness I might have felt in The Dress seems ridiculous now, like a game I tried to play to which I never knew the rules. She might be the one in costume, but I'm the one playing dress-up.

"Hey, Jane," Brendan says, and I realize I should probably respond too, so I give a pathetic little smile and wave.

"Wow, Su-Lin," Jane says, looking me over. "That dress is gorgeous. You look incredible." She sounds like she means it, too, which she probably does. She's always seemed legitimately nice, not one of those fake-sincere girls, dishing out compliments and then being bitchy behind your back.

"Thanks," I manage. "You too." And I certainly mean that, though I wish I could do so with the same level of generosity she did.

Jane grins. "Thanks! And congratulations on your launch. I had a signing then, but I heard it was amazing. I wish I could have been there."

I try not to notice how this seems directed squarely at Brendan.

"It did go really well," Brendan says, smiling back at her. "Though I'm pretty glad it's over. One less thing to stress about."

"God, I know how that is," Jane says sympathetically. She edges closer to him.

Brendan's eyes flick over to me for a moment and then back to her. "Hey," he says. "Would you like to dance?"

My heart stops.

Jane beams at him. "Absolutely," she says, then grabs his arm and pulls him onto the dance floor. And then they're dancing, moving to the fast beat, so close together.

I think my blood has pooled somewhere in my feet. He asked *her* to dance, and not because she was some girl I picked out for him and he approved.

He asked her because she's *Jane Shaw* and he really wants to dance with her.

Can I blame him for that, even a little bit?

I can't, but it doesn't mean I can keep my lungs from squeezing in at the thought.

It takes me a long minute before I realize I can't just stand here and stare at them. I should find someone to dance with myself. I don't want to, but that's the Plan, even though I feel like that thin thread is fraying more and more with every beat of the music.

I'm about to ask the next guy I see, but the next guy I see is Jason, who is wearing the fluffy feathered red coat of Naked

Mole Rat from the *Hemlock* movies. He's headed this way. Looking super pissed.

Uh-oh.

"Jason!" I say, when he gets closer to me. "How is your head? I'm so sorry about what happened on the wall. I mean, I know I apologized before the med staff took you away, but you were kind of out of it then, so I just want to say I'm so—"

"What the hell, Su-Lin?" he yells at me over the thumping music, and I flinch back. "You were the one who told Emily I was a player?"

I cringe. "I . . . I may have—"

"I thought she just got that impression, but no. I talked to her earlier today, and she said you *told her* I was." His brows are drawn together. Even his spiky hair somehow manages to look extra angry.

Guilt floods through me. "Okay, yeah, I did. But I thought maybe you were. I thought—"

"But you didn't even bother to ask me first, did you?" he says, getting right up in my face, and I shrink back. "*I* thought we were friends! *I* thought—"

"Hey, back off," yells another voice, startling me, and suddenly Warren steps in between us, looking pretty pissed himself, and I have this moment of *oh god, did I do something to him too*?

But he's glaring at Jason.

"Who the hell are you?" Jason yells back.

Warren stands his ground and folds his arms. "Just leave her alone, man."

I'm pretty sure that if it came to a fight, Jason could kill Warren in two seconds with his freakish upper body strength, but thankfully Jason's not really a fighter or a total asshole, so he steps back. He glares at me and shakes his head, and more than anger there, I see hurt.

Then he storms off, back into the crowd.

I want to call him back, to really apologize—that *was* awful of me to just assume he was a player and then tell Emily like

196

it was fact. But he's long gone, and my gaze lands on Jane and Brendan dancing even closer than before, and I'm starting to feel woozy.

"I'm sorry," Warren says. "I know that was none of my business. But I saw him yelling at you, and you looked kind of scared, and—"

"No, it's fine," I say, shaking my head. "He wouldn't have hurt me or anything. He was just mad." For good reason. "But thanks for looking out for me."

Warren smiles. "Of course. Are you okay?"

No, I'm really not. I haven't been for a while now. But even though Warren seems like a great guy, I don't really know him, and I don't want to go into all the details.

"Yeah," I say, letting out a breath. Forcing a smile. "Yeah, I'm great."

Peppy, happy Su-Lin.

"Good," he says, apparently buying it. "By the way, you look stunning."

It's a super nice compliment, and I don't hate hearing it, but all I can think of is Brendan.

You look like the night sky through a skylight.

My heart aches. Is that enough? Especially when compared to a girl—a woman, a sexy goddess of a woman—like Jane Shaw?

I can't think of that. I can't, or I'll look over there again.

"You look pretty great yourself," I return with a smile, although I hadn't really noticed what he was wearing until this moment. He's dressed up a bit more than at the prom, in a nice, slim-cut suit, but he's got the same fedora on, his shaggy blond hair hanging down from underneath. The whole look works for him.

The music has changed, and a slow song is playing, and now I can't help but look.

Brendan and Jane are still dancing. She's pressed up against him, and they're swaying to the music.

Smiley, happy Su-Lin.

"Do you want to dance?" I ask, with far more enthusiasm than I feel.

"I thought you'd never ask," he says with a wink. He starts to make the hand motions like he's going to do the chicken dance, but I grab his hand and step in close. My hand at his shoulder, just like Brendan taught me.

He blinks in surprise, but he recovers quickly and puts his arm around my waist, and we start to dance.

The song playing, I realize, is "So Close," that one from the ballroom scene in the movie *Enchanted*, which is one of my favorites. It's beautiful and haunting, and over Warren's shoulder, I can see Brendan and Jane dancing, their arms around each other, and all I want in the world right now is to be her in this moment, dancing to this perfect song with him.

I force myself to look away again. To smile at Warren, a cute, really nice guy who likes me. Who wants to be with *me*. His hand is warm against the bare skin of my back, but it feels wrong that it's not Brendan's hand there. That it's not Brendan's blue eyes looking into mine, or Brendan's breath whispering against my cheek.

It feels wrong, but I keep dancing anyway. Because we're still following the Plan, and I'm scared, and I don't know what else I can do.

TWENTY

BRENDAN

Dancing with Jane is fun and all—she's a good dancer, and has an upbeat energy about her that puts me at ease, which is more than I can say about most people. I intend to dance a couple songs with her and then go back to Su-Lin, having done my casual-dating duty for the first part of the evening. The first song ends, and Jane and I begin dancing to the next song, a slow one where she's closer to me than before and her arms are around me and mine are at her waist, but I'm not paying much attention to how the transition happened.

Because as I turn, I spot Su-Lin talking to that guy again. *Warren.* He's standing close to her and leaning in as if he's saying something confidential. She smiles and says something, and he grins, and seconds later, she's in his arms.

Dancing to a song I've heard dozens of times before, because the *Enchanted* soundtrack gets a lot of play when we work in the studio. Su-Lin always gets this dreamy look on her face when this song comes on, and I imagine I always have a similar expression, just watching her.

My stomach sinks, and I force myself to look away. To smile at Jane, to seem like I'm enjoying myself and not dying inside.

"Hey," Jane says. "Do you want to find someplace to sit down?"

"Yeah," I say, realizing seconds later that she meant *with her* and not, like, that it's so obvious that I need to recover from the sight of the girl I'm in love with looking even more fantastically gorgeous than usual—which is a feat—and dancing in the arms of another man.

Really close. In a top that hardly covers more than her bra, which I'm assuming she *isn't* wearing, given the backless nature of the dress. Unless they make those without backs? I do not understand the physics of that.

Jane takes me by the hand and leads me over by the bar, where there are a bunch of egg-shaped chairs just large enough for two people to sit, all sheltered from the noise and the lights. She sits and pulls me down beside her, and I'm feeling weak in the knees, so I let her. "I'll grab us some sodas," Jane says, and she bounces up again so quick that her card-skirt flaps open on her way over, revealing most of her ass and the strings of the red thong she's wearing underneath.

A lot of the room is blocked, by the chair and the side of the stage, but I can still see Su-Lin and Warren dancing, her head resting on his shoulder.

My body flushes, remembering the feeling of her head resting on *my* shoulder, my mind wandering over all the wonderful sensations of last night—her bare skin against mine, her lips on my abdomen, my hands in her hair.

"Raspberry or orange?" Jane asks, thrusting a pair of sodas at my face.

"Um, orange." I take one of them, and Jane sits down almost on top of me. This chair is tight, but it's not that tight, and I struggle not to turn to stare at Su-Lin again.

I am hopeless. There's a girl in a barely-there skirt and thong practically sitting on my lap.

And I don't care.

All I want is the girl across the room who looks like she's literally wearing the sky I've always imagined above us as we lie in bed together beneath our beach house skylight. I want to stalk over there and punch Warren in the face and tell him he can't have her because she's mine.

I hate myself for this. It's my fault she's not with me. She deserves better—she deserves a guy who will dance with her the way Warren is now, with his hand resting on the bare skin of her back.

She obviously likes him. It's not just coincidence that *every* time she has to find someone to spend time with, she finds him. And there he is, dancing with her like I would be if I wasn't so caught up in myself and my issues. Now I'm imagining us actually getting two houses on the beach, installing two big picture windows and two skylights, and she's living in one house with Warren, and I'm alone in the other.

"Are you always this quiet?" Jane asks.

I shrug. "Yeah. Parties aren't really my scene." Usually that's it, but tonight it's that I can't think of anything to say that isn't wallowing in a pit of self-pity.

I don't want to be here anymore. I want to call my mom.

"Hmm," Jane says, scooting up close to me. Her breasts are about an eighth of an inch away from a wardrobe malfunction, and she leans into me so they're right under my chin. "Well, you could have fooled me."

The song ends. Su-Lin looks over at me, and I hope she's going to come over here and finally introduce me to Warren, so I can at least size up whether he's a decent person who would be good to her. Or maybe she'll see me with Jane and want to break *that* up. Not that I want to have done anything to hurt her, but I wouldn't hate it if she was a little bit jealous.

Instead, Su-Lin and Warren move off the floor and out of my eyeline. I want to follow her, but I'm not going to be the jerk that breaks that up tonight. I turn toward Jane, who I'm supposed to be trying to date. She seems like a nice enough girl—someone I might have been able to casually date if I wasn't in love with Su-Lin, and if I was a person who was capable of that kind of social exertion.

"So, tell me about yourself, Brendan," Jane says. She shrugs her shoulders forward so that her breasts pop out another sixteenth of an inch.

I look up at her eyes, and from the playful curve of her smile, she knows where I've been looking.

I should be into this. I should be happy that a gorgeous, fun girl wants to spend time with me while Su-Lin is off obviously having a good time on her own.

For once, I remember to say something about myself that doesn't have anything to do with Su-Lin. "I'm in film editing, obviously," I say. "I got into it in high school because some of my friends wanted to be YouTubers, but they couldn't figure out the software. I used to take their stuff and mash it up in the school computer labs, and I kind of got a reputation for it."

Jane smiles like this is fascinating, though she does keep looking at my lips.

I fight the urge to pull away. I've been failing at the Plan all week. Tonight, I'm going to make myself do this if it kills me.

"Do you do the editing on your show?" I ask.

Jane shakes her head. "Nah. I was one of those wannabes who sucked at it. My friend Quinn does all my editing now. They're awesome."

"Yeah, totally," I say, before realizing that she's using the plural pronoun for her friend Quinn, not for Quinn's editing. I'm guessing Quinn is non-binary, but I never know how to ask about things like that, or if I even should.

"Though sometimes they get behind," Jane says. "If I ever need someone in a pinch, I'll remember you. If you're still taking freelance stuff."

I take a drink of my orange cream soda. "Yeah. When I have the time."

Jane smiles like this makes her happy, and I wonder if she means it. I was starting to get the sense that she's looking for a one-night stand—which I'm obviously not available for, and thank god. They say panic attacks can't kill you—something I repeat to myself often enough—but I think trying to have sex with someone who is basically a stranger might be an exception to that rule.

Jane leans against me, her hand brushing my knee, and I remember what it felt like when Su-Lin did the same, the current that ran through my body when she moved that hand elsewhere. It wasn't just that it physically felt good—although it did—but what it *meant*, that my best friend, the most beautiful person I've ever known, the woman I long for and who knows me better than anyone in the entire world, wanted *me*.

And I don't hate sitting here with Jane, but she's just a girl I'm here with and nothing else.

I look back over at the dance floor, but if Su-Lin and Warren are still dancing, they're lost somewhere in the crowd.

"You seem distracted," Jane says. "Is everything okay?"

"Yeah," I say, looking back at her. "I'm fine."

"Is it the social anxiety thing? Like at the party, when you had to leave?"

I blink. It makes sense that she noticed that. I guess probably a lot of people did, but I hadn't thought much about anyone but Su-Lin.

"I asked Emily if you were okay," she says quickly. "She wasn't talking behind your back or anything."

"No, it's fine. I mean, it's not a secret."

Jane smiles. "So what does it mean, exactly? You don't like crowds?"

I open my mouth, then close it again. Having this conversation is always awkward; I really don't keep my anxiety a secret—how could I?—but it's still weird to have to explain to new people how it works when it doesn't even make sense in my head. "Yeah, that's part of it. I'm really more of a one-on-one person."

I instantly regret this wording, but Jane grins. "Really?" she says. "That doesn't sound like a bad thing."

She sets down her soda and leans into me, her eyes flicking

toward my lips again.

I want to say that I have a seizure, or sudden full-body paralysis. But really what I'm picturing is Su-Lin dancing across the room with Warren's hand on her back, on her skin right where mine were last night as her mouth moved down my body.

I choked this morning. I hurt her and ruined everything. If I'd just been able to hold her while she woke like I wanted to, she wouldn't have spent the day feeling betrayed. She gave me her first real sexual experience and then I dissolved into selfishness and threw it back in her face.

Now, my beautiful best friend, the girl I love more than anyone else on the planet, is wearing a dress that is at once sexy as hell and also symbolic of everything I want for our future.

And she wants to be in someone else's arms.

My whole body feels hollow, like a cheap chocolate Easter bunny. Su-Lin has always been too good for me, and I should let her go, but this desperate part of me wants to hold on to her, whatever the cost, which is exactly what I did when I was with Candace, and I hate myself for it.

That's why, when Jane rocks up and puts her mouth on mine, I let it happen.

TWENTY-ONE

Su-Lin

Warren is talking to me—congratulating me on the launch, telling me it wasn't really my fault Jason fell off that wall (because he assumes that's why Jason is mad at me, and I'm not about to go into the real reason). I'm managing to respond in these little sound bites that approximate normal conversation, but I can't pay attention because I've lost sight of Brendan and Jane.

My heart stutters. Did they just move further into the crowd? Did they decide to get out of here, go somewhere more private?

"I'm glad he's okay, though," Warren is saying.

Yeah, Brendan's okay. He wanted to dance with her, he was *eager* to dance with her, and they're dancing with her incredible, perfect body pressed up against him—they're still dancing, right?— so he's probably more than okay.

"Even if I hate that he's being such a dick to you about it," Warren continues, and my gaze jerks back to him quickly. Defensively.

"He's not being a dick," I snap at him, pulling back. "He's *supposed* to be dancing with other . . ." Oh. I trail off with sudden realization as I see Warren's confused expression.

He was still talking about Jason.

I flush. I am the world's biggest idiot, for so many reasons.

"I mean, uh, Jason's supposed to still be resting," I say, in the most neutral tone I can manage. "Head injuries, you know? And he's not really acting like himself right now. I think he was just embarrassed."

I am babbling, and Warren gets this look on his face that is no longer confused.

In fact, he looks like maybe he's starting to understand way more than I'm letting on.

"Yeah, that makes sense," he says, a little sadly.

I'm pretty sure it doesn't, but I don't know what to say or do to fix that. The guilt is gnawing at me again—should I even be dancing with Warren? He's a good guy, and he likes me, and I am *so* not available for anything more than a super-distracted dance. I'm taken already, crazy in love with my best friend. My heart is Brendan's and has been pretty much from the day we met—even though Brendan may not end up wanting me, even though right now he may be realizing he can have someone he wants even more.

I still don't know what to do, and I can't keep swiveling my head around looking for Brendan. So I just lean my head against Warren's shoulder and neither of us says anything for the rest of the song.

The song ends, and Warren looks at me, chewing on his lower lip like he's deciding something. "Thanks for the dance, Su-Lin," he says after a moment.

"You too," I say, and I'm sad because I know he likes me and he has to know I'm not returning the feelings. But I can't keep leading him on like this. It's not fair.

As we turn to walk off the dance floor, I finally see Brendan and Jane. They're sitting in one of those chairs shaped like a big egg. She's pressed up tight against his side, all but on his lap, and they're just sitting there, each holding a soda, but her breasts are just inches away from his face, and her long legs crossed over his, and I think I'm going to cry, right here and now.

He sees me see him; my heart thuds painfully.

I look away, blinking too much, willing the tears to stay put, even as I give a small smile to Warren, and we walk away from the crowd, his hands in his pockets.

They're just talking, I tell myself. *That's all it is. Casual.*

Casual. Like Brendan and me.

I think I'm going to be sick.

"Well," Warren says, when we're back near the doors. "I should probably . . ." He gestures vaguely behind him, like he wants to leave, and I just smile and nod and try to breathe. Try not to think about Brendan and Jane doing *any* of the things Brendan and I have done.

"Okay," I say. And I'm about to say I'm sorry, because I definitely owe him an apology, but then I see Emily charging toward me, looking as pissed as Jason was before, only she's got mascara smudged down her cheeks, and I have a horrible feeling that's not the makeup look she was going for.

"Emily!" I say, "What happened?"

"Your *cousin* happened!" she shrieks. "Your idiotic plan happened!"

"I—I . . ." I have no idea how to respond, but my insides are churning with dread. Warren backs away, his hands in his pockets. Clearly he doesn't feel the need to defend me from Emily—an angry, crying girl in a sheer nightie—though honestly, a furious Emily is a bigger threat to my safety than Jason any day.

"I went up to my room—*our* room, because like an idiot I've been letting him stay with me so he didn't have to drive all the way home—and he was sleeping with some other girl!"

I gape. "But . . . didn't he ask you to be his girlfriend?"

This is clearly not the right thing to say, because Emily gives me a death glare, made scarier by the raccoon eyes.

"Yes, in fact, he did. And I agreed. But he clearly has a different definition of 'girlfriend,' because he's screwing the very woman I introduced him to as a job contact!"

Oh my god. My mind is reeling. I'm trying to picture my

cousin doing this. (Well, not, you know, doing *that*, but being the type of guy who would.) He's a bit full of himself, yeah. But he's the kind of guy who made sure to dance with my grandma at the wedding. He's the kind of guy who sends me and my sisters funny cards—in the actual mail!—on our birthdays. The kind of guy who got perfect grades and plays, like, four instruments and is—

Apparently a total dick when it comes to dating.

"Emily, I'm so sorry," I say, reaching for her arm, which she pulls back. "I didn't know. I would never have set you up with him if I'd—"

"*I* knew!" She yells. "Deep down, I knew he was a snake, and that's why he bailed the first time. But I didn't trust myself. I trusted *you* instead, because *I am an idiot* and I believed in your stupid plans to meddle in my life. And I let myself get played, and I pushed away a guy I actually really like."

"I'm so, so sorry," I say, the tears I'd been holding back welling up, but she turns away, shaking her head at the ceiling like the strobe lights are the problem here.

Your stupid plans.

My stupid plans that just mess everything up.

"Emily," I say again, pleading for her to hear me, but she swipes at her eyes and wobbles off on really high heels that normally she wouldn't have any problem in. She doesn't look back, even as I call after her.

I stand there for a few moments, my arms wrapped around myself, trying to hold myself together.

I hurt Jason. I hurt Emily. I probably hurt Warren, who has walked away toward the bar. I've messed everything up, and everyone hates me. And Brendan's with Jane, on their *date*, and—

And I don't care that he's on a date. I need my best friend. I need Brendan to tell me everything's going to be okay, and maybe I'll believe him, if just for tonight.

I need my Brendan.

I push through the crowd, back toward that egg chair, and

I can't stop hearing the fury in Emily's voice—my fault—or seeing the betrayed hurt on Jason's angry face—also my fault—and my eyes are burning and I'm probably going to embarrass myself by crying in front of Jane, but if I can just feel Brendan's arms around me—

I see them and jerk to a stop, like I hit an invisible wall.

An invisible wall through which I can see Jane and Brendan. Kissing.

She's pressed right up into him, her hands in his hair. Their lips moving together.

That tiny thread of hope snaps apart, and that snap reverberates through my whole body.

I can't breathe, and yet somehow I make a sound like a whimper, like a dog who's just been kicked, maybe because I feel like I've been punched in the gut and I hurt and hurt and hurt.

I turn away, gasping. The room, the crowd, the lights—all of it is swimming around me and blurring together.

He's kissing Jane.

He wants her; of course he does.

Stupid Su-Lin. I knew this. I knew he could never really want me. I was a friend, a silly, stupid friend, and he tried, just to make me happy, but I always knew I wasn't enough for him.

God, he even told me he was a *breast man*! So why would he want me? Why, when he could have *her*?

And now he does. He has this girl who's beautiful and sexy and is a better version of Candace, because she's all those things and she's actually nice. She'll treat him well and I should be happy for him. I should be happy because he's my best friend and I *want* him to be with someone he can fall in love with and feel intense passion for, someone good and not a cheating bitch.

I should be happy, but I have never in my life been so far from happy.

I push back through the crowd, trembling, my head dizzy with the hurt, with the confusion of it all—the sight of Jane's fingers in his hair clashes like a stumbling drunk against the memory of my fingers in those pink curls when he went down on me.

Best night of his life, my ass.

I shouldn't be mad. People who are casually dating kiss other people all the time, right? We didn't have rules against kissing anyone else; it didn't occur to me, in all my stupid naivety, that we'd need them. I never thought he would do something like that without telling me first. I knew my chances with him were slim and getting worse every day, but I thought he'd tell me first that this thing with us wasn't working, that he wanted to kiss Jane and be with her instead, and it would hurt—god, it would hurt—but not worse than this.

Or maybe it would always hurt like this. Maybe it *will* always hurt like this.

The tears are spilling out now, hot trails down my cheeks, and whether or not I should be, I'm mad. I feel used and tossed aside and so, so ashamed. The anger and the hurt wrap all around each other, and there's none of peppy, smiley Su-Lin left.

Through blurry tears, I see Warren there, at the edge of a group. He's got a drink in his hand, but he's not dancing with anyone in particular. And I know even as I'm heading toward him that this is a terrible idea, but I don't care. I'm hurt and I'm desperate to feel, just for a moment, that someone wants *me*.

I barely think to scrub away the tears before I grab his arm. "Warren," I say, and there's nothing natural about my voice at all.

He looks at me startled, and his eyes widen. "Su-Lin. Oh my god, are you okay?"

Apparently wiping away the tears didn't help. I can feel more bubbling up anyway.

I'm not okay. I'm in love with a guy who will never be in love with me and I'm not okay.

"Dance with me," I say—no, I *plead*, pulling him away from the group.

"Yeah, okay, but—" he starts, but I press myself up against him, and he cuts off, swallowing hard.

I move against him to the music, and he's got one hand on me and the other still holding his drink and he looks so confused and it's all so awkward, and I should run now, because "sexy seductress" is way outside my skill set (unless we're talking about my Samantha-based *Socks and the City* character). But I can't, because I need to feel this, need to feel wanted, and part of me stupidly thinks that maybe it would somehow hurt Brendan the way he hurt me.

Which is ridiculous. Brendan doesn't want me, so why would he care?

I wrap my arms around his neck, hoping Warren can't feel how much my hands are shaking. "Kiss me," I say.

His eyes widen even further, but he doesn't lean in. "Su-Lin, I don't think this is a good idea."

"You like me, don't you?" I say, and the way his gaze cuts away confirms it. "So kiss me."

I hate that there's a pleading note in this, too. Jane would never plead; she'd never have to.

Warren stops even pretending to dance—not that he was doing much of that to begin with, mostly just standing there while I swayed against him. He pulls one of my hands down from around his neck, taking a step back from me, and the tears spill over again, my already cracked and broken heart thudding painfully against my chest.

"I'm sorry," I say, my breath hitching in my throat. "I thought you liked me. I thought you'd want to kiss me." I can't look at him anymore.

"I do like you," he says, holding my hand. "But you're obviously in love with your friend Brendan."

At the sound of Brendan's name, a sob escapes me.

I tug my hand out of Warren's. "I shouldn't have—I shouldn't be here," I choke through tears. "I'm so sorry, for this, for everything."

"Su-Lin," he says, and his expression is full of concern and all it does is make me feel more guilty and awful, both for trying to use him and because I failed so spectacularly at it. "Do you want to go somewhere and talk? You can tell me what's going on—Su-Lin!"

I barely hear him, because I've started running. I can't do this anymore. Sobs are racking my whole body, and the only person I've ever really wanted to talk to, or been able to talk to, when I hurt like this—well, when I hurt at all, since I've never hurt like *this*—is Brendan, and that's gone. How can we even be best friends anymore, when I'm so in love with him and every time I see him will be a reminder of how much he isn't in love with me?

Why couldn't he just be in love with me?

I run from the ballroom in my elaborate ball gown like Cinderella, only I've got well-laced footwear, so I'm not leaving any shoes behind for my prince to find, and it's not like he's looking anyway, since he's got his tongue down some other princess's throat.

I run, gasping and shaking, into the hallway, where the brighter lights hurt my eyes. People are looking and I should go back to our hotel room, but my legs are so weak and I'm trembling so hard I don't think I can make it. So I find a big pillar I can hide behind and slide down it until I'm sitting in a puddle of dark blue fabric and beads like stars, and I pull my knees up to my chest and let myself cry.

TWENTY-TWO

BRENDAN

The moment Jane's lips hit mine, my brain cramps.

This is wrong. Wrong wrong wrong.

Her lips are too soft and too firm all at once, too . . . *wrong* against mine. She's pretty and she's fun, and it's not like she doesn't know how to kiss.

But she's not Su-Lin, and I never want to kiss another girl who is not Su-Lin for the rest of my life.

I break away, leaning as far from her as I can get in the egg chair.

"Are you okay?" Jane asks. "Are you having a panic attack?"

Apparently Emily told her a lot of things. "No, I just, I need to go."

Jane's eyes widen. "I'm sorry! I thought we were on the same page."

"Yeah, no," I say, rubbing my eyes and shaking my head. "It's not you, it's just—" The words fall out of my mouth before I consider whether I should be saying them to Jane. "I'm in love with Su-Lin."

Jane looks stunned, and then she smiles. "Really? You guys would be so cute together! But I thought you were just friends. Oh my god, did she reject you?"

I blink at her, my brain so muddled that I can't keep up with her. "No," I say. "No, we're . . ." I need to go find her. I need to go find her and tell her that I'm in love with her and I want to be with her every day—every *minute*—for the rest of my life. "I have to go."

Jane's smile softens. "Go get her, Tiger," she says, and takes a long swig of her soda.

Okay, Jane is awesome. She's not Su-Lin, but she's awesome.

"Sorry," I say. "It's been a really confusing week." I squeeze her arm gently and fully extricate myself.

Jane settles back in her chair like she's enjoying taking a back seat to this drama, and I get up and canvas the room, looking for Su-Lin.

I don't find her, but I do find Warren. He's sitting by himself in one of the egg chairs on the other side of the room, looking down at his drink like it's offended him.

I don't want to talk to the guy, but I'm betting he knows where Su-Lin is. "Hey," I say. "Have you seen—"

"She went that way." Warren points to one of the doors out into the convention center. "Tell her I'm sorry. I feel like shit, but I doubt she cares to hear it from me."

My mouth falls open. "What—" I say, but then I shake my head. Whatever happened, I don't want to hear it from Warren.

I need to find Su-Lin.

I tear out of the ballroom, growing more certain with each step. I can't do this anymore. I can't. Su-Lin is the most important thing in the world to me, but I haven't been treating her that way. I've been giving in to my fear, living my life small, as my therapist would put it.

I'm done now.

I need her.

I have to find her and lay it all out for her, no more holding back. And if I have a panic attack in the middle of it, well. Fuck it. It wouldn't be the first time.

I move through the halls of the convention center, past the couples making out in the hallway, past a group of teenagers

214

sitting around and playing *Mario Kart* with each other on their handhelds. In the lobby, there are people draped all over the couches, some of them drinking out of plain containers that I assume from the loudness of their voices contain alcohol.

I scan the room, but Su-Lin isn't there. I'm about to head toward the hotel, assuming she went back to our room, when I see a tuft of gauzy, blue fabric sticking out from behind one of the decorative pillars on the far side of the room.

I walk over slowly, and as I get closer, I can hear her crying.

My heart breaks open, and a chill runs through me.

Warren said he was sorry. God, what did he do to her?

I step around the pillar and drop to my knees beside Su-Lin. She's crunched up on the marble floor, her dress puffing up around her. Her makeup's running and her face is stained with tears.

"Hey." I reach out to take her hand. "What's wrong?"

Su-Lin sobs again—god, I've never seen her cry like this. I want to scoop her into my arms and tell her that everything is going to be okay, but I'm too uncertain that it will be.

"Warren said to tell you he's sorry," I say. "He says he feels like shit."

"Is that why you're here?" Su-Lin asks between sobs. "Because Warren found you?"

I want to tell her. I've just resolved to tell her. But I don't want to make this moment worse for her, and what I have to say can wait.

"What *happened*?" I ask.

Su-Lin bends over, putting her face in her hands. Her body shakes with sobs, and I can't help it. I sit down beside her and put my arm around her, still holding her hand in mine.

"I tried to kiss him," she chokes out. "But he rejected me."

My whole body goes cold. My hand is numb and can no longer feel hers.

I was right that she's really into Warren, but he's not into her. My heart breaks right down the middle, for me and for her. I pull her close and press my lips against her temple.

No, this is definitely not my moment. In fact, I'm becoming increasingly sure that I missed that moment altogether, maybe back at her sister's wedding or on our first date.

"I'm sorry," I say, and Su-Lin just cries harder.

I knock my head back against the pillar. It was true, what I thought before. I don't deserve her. She'll be happier, not with Warren, probably, but with somebody else.

I close my eyes.

The fantasy about the beach house is nothing more than a fantasy. I'm not good for her, and I've never been good for her. I'm poison in a relationship. Candace tried to break up with me so many times, and I always went after her. It was like a compulsion. Within minutes I'd be calling her phone a hundred times, leaving sobbing messages, driving by her house, our friends' houses, making desperate threats against my own safety.

My heart is bleeding out in my chest, but I take a deep breath—to my stomach, like my therapist taught me—and I make a decision.

No matter how much pain I feel, no matter how many tears I cry alone later, no matter how this breaks me—I'm not going to do that this time.

Su-Lin will be happier without me, and I'm going to let her go.

"You really like him, huh?" I hate myself for the way my voice breaks. I hate that it's so obvious how jealous I am.

But I still don't see this coming.

Su-Lin pulls away from me and shoves me hard with both hands. I fall out from behind the pillar and roll onto the marble, getting my feet under me. She's up on her knee now, glaring at me with a ferocity I've only seen from her on TV, in that moment when Chad Montgomery admitted it was him who fucked her puppet.

"*No!*" she screams at me. "I do not *really like* Warren, Brendan! Because I'm in love with *you!*"

My mouth falls open, but no sound comes out. Meanwhile, my heart is doing a crazy dance like it's just been brought back from the dead.

She loves me.

She loves me.

She loves me.

I must have hardcore misread this situation, because she's saying that she loves me.

All the tipsy people on the couches are turning as one to look at us, but she just keeps going.

"But you *kissed* her! I hate that you did that, and I know that's wrong, because it technically wasn't against the rules. But it sucks that you wanted to. And it sucks that you did that. And I'm mad at you, even though I shouldn't be."

"Hey," I say softly, like I'm trying to reduce her hysteria by being extra calm, even though I feel anything but. Because oh god, she saw me kissing Jane and *she* has misread *that* situation and, um, I guess that was my moment, after all.

Su-Lin continues to shout over me. "And why did it have to be *Jane*, of all people? I mean, fine, yeah, she has a *nice rack* and I could never be sexy like her or make you feel *intense passion* like Candace. So that's fine. That's just *fine*. I hope you two will be very happy."

"Su-Lin," I say, "that's not—"

"I don't want to hear it! I don't want to hear about how you can't bring yourself to want me. The Plan was supposed for be for *us*, but you only ever wanted me because you felt safe with me, and you used me and that sucks and I hate you for it."

With that, she gathers up her skirts and runs out of the conference center in her sneakers, leaving me staring after her, her words echoing in my mind, and all the drunk people still watching me. I'm pretty sure a couple of them have their phones out. One guy on the couch nearest to me mutters, "*Damn.*"

I have some stronger words I'd like to use at that moment, but instead, I burst into tears.

TWENTY-THREE

Su-Lin

I'm a total mess. I just shoved my best friend and screamed—very publicly—about how I love him and how he kissed Jane and also how I hate him for it, and (surprise!) this somehow didn't make me feel any better. If anything, I feel worse.

Worse, because I'm pathetic, and I threw myself in this horribly embarrassing way at Warren, and that's the only reason Brendan came out to see me, because Warren probably told him I'm having a nervous breakdown. Which I am, like some table-flipping Real Housewife, and now Brendan had to see that, too, when he wanted to be making out with Jane Shaw, and things will never be normal between us again.

I'm running out of the conference center and across the street and into the lobby of our hotel, but really I'm running from Brendan and from the shambles I've made of everything—not only Brendan and me, but Jason and Emily and—

Tate.

I pull up short just as Tate emerges from the elevator into the hotel lobby. He's not dressed for the masquerade, just wearing a tight t-shirt and fashionably ripped jeans, and he's got a duffel bag slung over his shoulder. Probably full of his stuff, since I'm guessing Emily kicked him out of her hotel room.

My anger flares again at seeing my cousin. Who I *trusted*, and who hurt my friend.

"How could you?" I yell at him. I have lost all capacity for preamble. Did I ever have this to begin with?

Tate startles. "Su-Lin, hey, I—" He stops, looks me over, taking in the fancy dress and the blotchy face and ruined makeup. "You look like hell."

I storm right over to him until I'm only a few feet away. "Well, *you* look like a cheating asshole!"

Tate cringes and looks around. I'm obviously creating another scene—this seems to be what I'm doing tonight.

Whatever.

"I guess Emily talked to you," he says sheepishly. He runs a hand through that long swath of hair that hangs over one eye, brushing it back. It flops back in place immediately.

"You had just asked her to be your girlfriend! And then you sleep with some—"

"Keep it down, okay?" He narrows his eyes. "It's not like it's your business, anyway."

My rage burns even hotter. "The hell it's not! Emily is my friend, and I set you two up because I thought you liked her."

Tate shrugs. "I did. I do." He fiddles with the buckle on the strap of his duffel bag. "I'm just not really a one-woman kind of guy."

I want to kill him. He may be my cousin and I may have lots of happy family memories with him, but right now I just want to kill him on behalf of all women everywhere.

"Why did you ask her to be your girlfriend, then?" I seethe, my hands balled into fists at my sides. "Why did you even act like you wanted to be with her at all? You *know* Emily hates . . ." I trail off, seeing the way he looks uncomfortably off to the side.

And suddenly it all fits together—him talking about Emily so fondly in the very same conversation where I'd brought up the possible networking opportunities at YouCon, all the connections that both Emily and I have, him sleeping with one of the contacts

Emily introduced him to . . .

"You used us *both*," I say, taking a step back, my mouth dropping open. God, does my stupidity have any limit? Apparently not. It is a bottomless well that I draw from over and over again. "You used me to get you here and set you up with Emily, and you were using her for all her contacts."

He rolls his eyes, but his shifting stance tells me it's true. "It wasn't like some criminal master plan, Su-Lin. Emily and I had fun. She's a big girl. She knew what she was getting into."

"How could she, when you *lied* to her? When you said you wanted her to be your girlfriend?" Tears are stinging my eyes again, and my chest is tightening. "When you made her think you liked her, and you wanted something more, and then you *used* her?" My mind flashes back to Jane and Brendan, all wrapped up in each other.

It's not the same thing. It's not the same thing, and Brendan would never have meant to use me, but god, it hurts and hurts . . .

Tate narrows his eyes. "Do you even hear yourself? Geez, it's like we're in middle school or something. Emily and I are adults, and it's more complicated than that."

"More complicated?" Than you having sex with someone who is *not* your girlfriend?"

"God, just grow up, Su-Lin!" He yells, and I freeze. He shakes his head. "My mom is right about you. You're like this immature little kid with a puppet show and no idea of how the world works, and you seriously need to *grow up*." His voice drips with the same contempt I hear all too often from Aunt Alice.

The same contempt I would hear from my mom, usually aimed at my dad, but sometimes at me. Because we're so alike, and just too much for her. Too much for everyone.

Too much and yet somehow also not enough.

I stand there, all at once too cold and too flushed, my mouth working silently.

Just grow up, Su-Lin. It echoes and echoes.

I'm not sure if I would have figured out what to say, but Tate looks over my shoulder and groans, just as I hear Emily's voice coming up from behind me.

"Really, Tate?" she says icily. "You're telling *her* to grow up?"

I look behind me, and there's Emily, her face scrubbed clean of all that running mascara, her arms folded. She's glaring in a downright badass way, despite still wearing a nightie. Standing next to her is Jason, also glaring.

For this moment, at least, neither of them are glaring at me.

Tate rolls his eyes but doesn't say anything.

Emily keeps on going, picking him apart word by word. "*She* doesn't know the way the world works? Your cousin made enough money from her 'puppet show' to buy and sell your sorry ass a hundred times over. Because she's talented and smart and people love her. *And* she manages to be a good person, and not a selfish, lying prick. So I fail to see how she's the one in your family who should do any changing."

Tears swim in my eyes, and I want to hug her. Emily may be mad at me, and I may have hurt her, but she's still my friend.

Maybe this means I haven't ruined absolutely everything good in my life—though if I've lost Brendan, I can't help but feel that I have.

Tate's eyes cut back and forth between Emily and Jason, totally ignoring Emily's defensive rant. "What, so you're with him already? I knew there was something going on there. Good job holding on to that moral high ground."

"Don't even try to play the victim here," Emily seethes, but Tate brushes her off with a dismissive wave of his hand, then looks directly at Jason. Tate's lip curls into a sneer.

"She's all yours, bro. Hope you like your piece of ass with a side of overbearing bitch, because that's what you're getting."

What did he call my friend?

All that anger explodes out of me, and I growl and lunge for him. His eyes widen and he stumbles back just as a pair of freakishly strong arms grab me around the waist and haul me back. The same arms that stopped me from attacking Chad

Montgomery in a blind rage back on *Starving with the Stars*.

"Not worth it, Hobbit," Jason says, as I kick and claw the air futilely.

Tate just gapes, and the way his face has paled is pretty satisfying on its own. "Whatever, I'm leaving," he says, hefting his duffel bag dramatically before stalking out of the hotel.

I slump down, all the fight drained out of me, and Jason lets me go. "Is this my entire role in your life?" he asks wryly. "Keeping you from very public assault charges? Not that both those pieces of shit didn't deserve your tiny-but-vicious Hulk rage."

I shake my head, tears spilling over my cheeks. Again. "I'm so sorry. To both of you. I should never have said you were a player, Jason. I assumed shallow things about you the same way people always do to me, and I should have known better. And Emily, god, I had no idea Tate is such an ass. He's always so *nice* with the family, and—"

"I know. It's okay, apology accepted," Emily says, and she's the one pulling me into a hug, and I weep against her shoulder and hope her nightie isn't super expensive, because now it's probably got my snot all over the thin shoulder strap. "It was Tate I was really mad at, and at myself for overlooking my instinct that he's a total snake."

"He is," I mumble. I pull away from Emily just in time to see her give Jason a pointed look.

He clears his throat. "Yeah, we're all good, Hobbit," he says. "I'm never going climbing with you again, but other than that . . ."

Emily elbows him playfully, and they grin at each other, and a tiny bit of my cracked-open heart feels lighter. They do seem to be really into each other. And maybe I was wrong. Maybe they would be great together.

I appear to have been wrong about a *lot* of things.

"I am, however, taking Emily climbing," Jason says proudly. "We're going to scale the convention center, legality be damned."

"Jason assures me illegal urban climbing is the best way to

get over cheating assholes." Emily winks at me, and I know very well that the climbing isn't the way she's most looking forward to getting over Tate. Which, good for her. "But I do need to change into some more appropriate climbing clothes first."

Jason shrugs. "Suit yourself. I did warn you, though, that I celebrate climbing a new building by getting naked at the top."

Emily's cheeks flush, and she looks like she's about to say something flirtatious back, but then she seems to really see me huddled there, brushing away tears.

"Hey," she says. "Are you that upset about what I said to you? Because I really didn't mean to scream at you like that. I shouldn't have—"

"No," I say quickly, sniffling. "I mean, yeah, I felt really bad about doing that to you, but . . ." I look down at my feet, scuffing my sneakers on the hotel carpet.

Emily looks around as if she's just realized something. "Where's Brendan? Is everything okay?"

I didn't think my heart could keep breaking over and over again, but it seems to be able to. "I don't think so," I say, thinking of Jane's lips on his. Of me shoving him and screaming at him that I hate him, when I don't hate him at all.

I just hate that I'm not who he really wants. And I hate that I let myself believe I could be.

Emily looks over at Jason. "I think I should take a rain check on convention center climbing and stay with her," she says, but I shake my head.

"No, please," I say, trying to make my voice sound as normal as possible. "I've ruined your life enough. Go have fun." Emily looks dubious, but I squeeze her hand. "I'll be fine. I just want to be alone right now, anyway."

"Okay," she says after a moment. "But remember, it's you and Brendan. You guys can work anything out, and you will. Right?"

I nod, but it's just to make her feel better.

She and Jason head off to change or climb or have sex (or

most likely a combination of those three), and I go to Brendan's and my room, alone, to fall apart even more—at least this time where no one can see me.

TWENTY-FOUR

BRENDAN

I sob all the way out to the hotel parking garage, where I climb into my car. It smells like Su-Lin's perfume, Clinique Happy, which I'm a little startled that I know. She doesn't wear it often but when she does . . .

I pound the steering wheel with the heel of my palms, then pull out my phone and call my mother.

It takes her four rings to pick up.

"Hey, Brendan," Mom says.

"Hey." I sound like I'm crying, which is a sound Mom is all too used to hearing, and it shows.

"Are you okay?" she asks.

"No. I fucked everything up."

"Honey," Mom says. "What happened?"

I appreciate that she doesn't tell me she knows I didn't fuck up. She had a front-row seat to my entire relationship with Candace. She knows exactly what a screw-up I am. "I messed things up with Su-Lin. Like, irrevocably."

"Okay. How?"

"Well," I say, not really sure where to start. "I slept with her."

Mom is quiet for a moment. "And . . . that was a bad thing?"

"Not for me," I say. "It was fucking revelation. It was so good

I can't even tell you."

"And please don't," Mom says. "But she's not happy about it."

"I panicked this morning. And I got up and pretended nothing happened."

Mom's tone drops. "Oh, Brendan."

"I know," I say. "But that's not even the half of it. Turns out, she was a virgin."

"What?" Mom says, sounding surprised. She's seen the *Real Sockwives*, and knows well Su-Lin's brand of innuendo-based humor. "She was?"

"Is, technically. Because we didn't actually have, like, intercourse. We went down on each other. Which was amazing."

"No details!" Mom says. "Damn it, I am your mother. You really need to find some friends."

"Anyway, we talked about that, and I apologized, and I asked if she wanted to keep dating other people and she said yes—"

"*Really*," Mom says.

"Yeah, but then we went to this dance tonight, and I figured I'd show her that I'm really trying, you know? So I asked this friend of ours to dance, and then Su-Lin was dancing with this guy who she'd been hanging out with a lot, and I thought she liked him, so I let this girl kiss me—"

"Oh god, Brendan," Mom says.

"I *know*. And then I found Su-Lin crying and I thought it was because that other guy rejected her, but it turns out that she saw me kissing Jane, and then she screamed at me about how she has no right to be mad at me for that because it wasn't against the rules but that she is and she hates me for it anyway." The words just rush out and I'm getting all choked up. I take a deep breath, then realize I forgot the most important part. "She also screamed that she's in love with me."

"Please tell me you told her you're in love with her, too."

"I tried," I say. "But she kept yelling at me and ran away."

Mom is quiet for a minute, and I know she can hear me crying into the phone.

I fucked this up. Of all the things I never wanted to fuck up, my relationship with Su-Lin was it.

"Okay, Brendan, listen," Mom says.

I lean back, feeling tears trickle down under the collar of my stripper shirt. "Listening."

"You're in love with Su-Lin, right?"

"Yeah," I say. "Hopelessly."

"And she's just told you she's in love with you."

"Yes. But she also said—"

"And you've clearly done some things you need to apologize for, right?"

I'm quiet for a second. "Yeah. And I will. But I don't think I can fix it."

"It sounds like an apology would go a long way. And a long talk about how you both really feel."

I know she's right, but I still— "I don't think I should tell her how I feel. What would be the point? She'd be happier without me."

"How can you say that?"

The tears are coming in full force, and I can barely get the words out. "I'm a mess, Mom. It sucks, because I know you've spent years trying to help me, but I'm still fucked up. When things went bad with Candace, I chased after her and wouldn't stop. I was awful to her. I clung so hard and I wouldn't let her go, and it wasn't until after I knew she'd been fucking my friends for six years that I finally let her walk out on me. I'm not going to do that to Su-Lin. I'm not."

Mom hesitates. "No," she says. "You're not."

"Exactly."

"I mean right now. You're not doing that. You're not calling her or chasing after her or begging her to take you back."

I nod. "So that means I'll apologize, and then I'm done. That's the right thing to do. Spare her my messed up brain and my messed up life."

Mom is quiet. I know she thinks that's the wrong answer,

227

but I don't know what else to do.

"Or," Mom says, "you could apologize, be honest with her, tell her exactly how you feel, and see if you guys can work something out."

I sniff. My nose is running like hell, and I don't have anything to wipe it with. "I thought we just said chasing after her would be the wrong thing to do."

"Don't chase her, not in the way you did with Candace," Mom says. "But honey, Su-Lin loves you. And don't you think she knew about your issues before this week? I think she understands."

I shake my head. "But I'm different in relationships. It's my attachment issues, you know? They turn me into a terrible person."

"Brendan," she says. "You've only had one relationship, and I'm going to tell you this right now—she's the one who was fucked up and awful. You made some mistakes, but you did the best you could. You have the best heart of anyone I've ever known, and when you give it to someone, you give it all the way. Any girl would be lucky to have you, but I have never seen you as happy as you are with Su-Lin. Not once in your whole life. So you need to go talk to her and tell her how you feel. If she doesn't want to be with you, you can let her go, but think about it. You don't want to let her go if there's any way you could prevent it."

She's right. I don't. But this terrified part of me is sure it's hopeless, and that's the part that wants to run away from all of it, to never see her again.

That would mean no more show. No more job. No more hours on end spent laughing with the most incredible girl in the whole world.

I can't. I can't lose her knowing there was more I could have done.

"I'm such a fucking coward," I say.

"No," Mom says. "You're the bravest person I've ever met. You've spent years facing down demons that scare the pants off of me, but you just keep getting up and facing them all over again, no matter how many times they beat you down. That's courage. And now it's time to step up and do it again."

My eyes fill with tears all over again. My mom is the person who knows me the best, after Su-Lin. I've always felt like I've failed her, like she's given me every advantage to overcome the shit my father did to us and the hell that was my relationship with Candace, and I just can't rise above it.

To hear that this is the opposite of what she feels . . .

"Thanks, Mom," I say.

"I know it doesn't mean anything coming from me, because I'm your mother. But—"

"No, it does," I say. "It means everything, actually."

Mom is quiet. I know she feels like she's been trying to talk sense at me for years and I never listen, but it isn't true. I listen. It just doesn't make the problems go away. "I'm glad," she says finally.

My brain is still running in circles, trying to find a way to get out of facing Su-Lin, of handing her my heart to do with as she pleases.

"She doesn't want to talk to me," I say feebly.

My mom sees right through it. "Honey, she's upset. And you're upset. But unless you're planning to hide from her forever and give up your friendship and your job, you need to talk to her."

I take a deep breath.

"Those aren't really options," Mom says. "You have to talk to her."

I laugh, in spite of myself. "Yeah, I got that."

"If I were you, I'd lead with the apology. And follow it shortly after with how much you love her. And then another apology."

"Okay, okay! I know how to talk to Su-Lin."

"Do you?" Mom asks. "Because—"

"Thanks!" I say into the phone, cutting her off. "Thanks a lot, Mom. I'm going to go do that now."

"I love you. I'm here for you, no matter what."

"I know," I say, more sincerely this time. "Thank you."

I hang up and climb out of my car, continuing to take deep breaths. The panic is there, starting in my chest and bleeding outward.

She's going to reject me. She's finally, once and for all, had enough of me, and I'm going to lose her forever.

But if I don't get off my ass, I'm going to lose her anyway, and I love her so much that I have to tell her how I feel. It's necessary, for her and for me.

I stalk across the parking lot, and then I have an idea. It's crazy, and stupid, and something Su-Lin would love, if she wasn't too mad at me to love anything.

So I get back in my car, start the engine, and head off to buy some supplies.

TWENTY-FIVE

Su-Lin

When I get into our room, I try not to see all the reminders of Brendan and me, but it's impossible to escape. The Gudetama toaster next to a bag with only the butt-ends of the bread loaf left. Twister, set on top of a few boxes of left-over merch that Emily had brought up earlier in the day when the dealers room closed. Shot glasses from last night, which the maids apparently rinsed out, stacked inside each other.

I've only known him for four months, but my whole life is a reminder of us.

I wanted it that way; I wanted more, in fact. A whole life that *was* us, together in every way. I still long for that—for *him*—more than anything in the world, even though I know now it was just a fantasy, like our beach house. Just a dream that won't ever come true.

I don't know how I'll ever stop wanting it.

I strip off The Dress with far less reverence than I put it on, back when I thought it was some holy relic to put all my desperate faith in. The dress drops to the floor and I leave it there, on top of the sneakers I kick off. I grab the first shirt I can see in my suitcase—Cookie Monster, a long-time fave—and some comfy pajama shorts with bright polka dots on them.

231

Just grow up, Su-Lin, I hear again and again.

But the truth is, even as I complained to Emily about my Care Bears t-shirt and braids, I like the way I dress. I like fun clothes that make me smile, with bright colors and goofy jokes on them. I like bubble machines and cartoon eggs having existential crises on toast. And I love making a living—and a damn good one!—with a puppet show that makes people laugh.

I don't know how to be anyone else, and I don't think I could be happy trying.

I wish it was enough for Brendan. Not that he doesn't love me as I am—I know he does. He's my best friend. But enough for him to be *in* love with. He wanted to be, I really do believe that, despite my angry accusations. He wasn't using me. He really tried.

He should get to be happy, to find that person he can truly love. I know I want that for him, even through my hurt.

But right now, there's nothing making it through that hurt but more of the same.

I wash my face, only looking in the mirror enough to see that I got all the makeup off. No faces at myself this time; I already know I'm way too sad to look like Su-Lin. I pull the pins out of my hair, dropping them each with a little plink on the ceramic. Then, even though the room lights are still on—for some reason I can't handle the thought of being in the dark right now, though that's not usually a fear I have—I crawl into my bed and squish my little person-shaped pillow up against me. Tears leak out onto the puffy clouds on the fabric, a kind of upside-down rain, but at least I'm not sobbing anymore. Mostly, I'm starting to feel numb. Like my body is trying to shut out the pain.

I appreciate the effort, but I know it won't work for long. It's not really working now.

I don't know how long it is I lie like this, crying intermittently, trying so hard not to think or feel, before I hear the sound of the key-card in the door.

My body stiffens; I can't talk to him right now. I can't.

I'll apologize tomorrow for screaming at him, for saying that I hated him. Maybe even for saying that I love him, so he can feel better about not loving me back.

But I can't handle hearing him tell me that right now. Or about Jane. Or any of it.

I squeeze my eyes shut, though I know he won't believe I'm sleeping. I'm just hoping he'll pretend along with me. There's the muffled sound of his steps in the room, which grow closer, then a shuffling sound right beside my bed. I feel something dropped on top of me—so light I probably wouldn't have noticed it had I actually been sleeping.

I almost open my eyes right then, out of sheer curiosity, but stubbornness keeps them tightly closed.

"Hey," his voice says, but there's something a little off about it and it takes me until his words to figure out what it is. "Pssst. Yo, Ruby!"

Brendan's doing his Terrence Clarence voice—it's the one most similar to his usual speaking voice, but with a hint of California dudebro tossed in.

I open my eyes, rolling over just enough to see Terrence peeking up over the edge of the bed. He's a neon yellow sock with spiky hair made with a bunch of bright blue pipe cleaners.

"Ruby, babe. You there?"

He leans over and nudges my side, and I see my Ruby Van Raspberry puppet lying on top of me.

I hesitate; I'm not sure I have it in me to play along. Ultimately, though, my curiosity is too great.

Besides, Ruby would never be able to ignore Terrence—she's pretty crazy about him.

I slip on the familiar hot pink sock with the long strands of feathery, baby-pink hair. "Hey there, handsome," I say, my voice way too thick with emotion to actually be Ruby's. But at least I manage her southern drawl.

"So I was talking with my boy Brendan," Terrence says. "Apparently that dumb fuck let some other girl kiss him—this girl who wasn't Su-Lin. He feels awful about it."

I swallow past the thick lump in my throat and have Ruby make a miffed sound. She would definitely not approve—she can be a little judgmental sometimes, that Ruby. "Well, he should feel awful," she says archly. "Su-Lin told me all about it. In my opinion—and you *know* I don't just go around sharing my opinion all unsolicited-like—"

"So true, babe," he cuts in. It's a bit they do.

"—He should have told Su-Lin first that he wanted to be with Miss Shaw." I manage to keep her voice firm, but my heart feels like it's breaking all over again.

He should have told me. But the truth is, I lose him either way.

"That's the thing, though," Terrence says. "Brendan doesn't want to be with that Jane chick. He never did."

My heart thuds uncertainly, and I sit up a tiny bit more. I have Ruby raise an eyebrow. "I find that hard to believe."

"It's true." Terrence looks back and forth like he's making sure no one else is listening, and then leans in toward Ruby. "Brendan told me that he is totally in love with Su-Lin. He has been for months."

Now I can barely breathe around the pounding in my chest.

He's in love with me.

Has been for months.

Can that really be true?

"Is that so," Ruby says, but it comes out as little more than a whisper. Like the sudden flare of hope in me is too much to actually give voice to.

Terrence nods. "Better believe it, babe. Not only that, he really wants her to be his girlfriend."

Tears spring to my eyes again, and a little noise like a whimper escapes me.

Terrence looks down, like he's the one abashed. "Do you think she might still want that?" he asks, and I can hear Brendan's Terrence accent slipping, until it's just Brendan. "Do you think she could forgive him?"

I swipe away the tears and set Ruby down, then lean over the side of the bed to where I can see Brendan lying on the floor. His eyes are red and puffy like he's done his own share of crying, and he gives me a sad smile.

God, I love him so much.

"Yes," I say to him. "Yes to both."

He lets out a shaky breath, his smile wider. Hopeful. "Really?"

I bite my lower lip. "Did you mean all that?"

"Every word, including the part about me being a dumb fuck." He takes the Terrance puppet off his hand, and his face grows serious, his blue eyes shiny with tears. "I'm so in love with you, Su-Lin."

I wonder for a crazy heartbeat if I'm dreaming all this, and my heart stings, like I've been out in the cold and suddenly stepped into a hot shower. Tears are back to spilling onto my cheeks, and I don't bother trying to hide them anymore. "I'm so in love with you too, Brendan. Though I guess you already knew that from me screaming it at you."

He laughs, and it comes out a little choked.

"Come up here," I say, scooting over to give him room next to me in the bed. "Unless you really like the floor—what are you wearing?"

I hadn't noticed until he stood up that he's wearing that faded, old jacket that's always in the backseat of his car, even though he probably hasn't worn it in, like, ten years. Or at least that's how long since it might have been in fashion.

"Well," he says, his cheeks getting pinker. "I thought, just in case you needed some extra convincing . . ." Then he unzips the jacket.

He's not wearing his suit coat or even that sleeveless stripper shirt underneath.

Just a plastic, novelty coconut bra.

I sit straight up and let out a surprised squeal that immediately becomes a fit of giggles. "Oh my god. That is amazing."

He gets on the bed next to me, and we're both lying down on

our sides facing each other. With his big plastic coconut boobs in the way. "According to the girl at Walmart who gave me a five minute lecture, it is also cultural appropriation and super not cool for me to buy. Or wear."

"Well, I like it."

"I knew you would." His eyes crinkle at the sides as he smiles. "Though I still don't know if it's because you actually think this is hot, or because you think it's hilarious."

I shrug the shoulder that isn't pressed into the mattress. "Maybe I think it's both. Especially on you."

We're staring at each other, and I feel like I could just fall into that gaze. But we're still not touching, like there's some residual hurt there we haven't yet broken through.

He feels it, too, because he says, quietly, "I'm so sorry."

And I need to ask, even though Terrence seemed pretty sure of himself. "You really don't want to be with Jane?" I shift, closing my eyes briefly. "I would get it if you do."

Brendan shakes his head. "No, I don't. I didn't ever want to be with her or anyone else. And god, I knew the minute she kissed me, I never want to kiss anyone else but you again, ever."

My heart flutters happily.

"The only reason I even let her kiss me . . ." He sighs. "It was stupid, I know. But I saw you with Warren, and I just thought, after everything this week, after you chicken dancing with him and not inviting him to lunch, and then at the masquerade—I thought you wanted him. And I just got so jealous and hurt, and—"

"You thought I wanted Warren?" My mouth falls open, as the memories of the week reform in my head, trying to piece together how it must have looked to Brendan. I can see it, now, how all those things I was doing could have been taken in a totally different way—dancing all goofy with Warren at prom because I couldn't stand to really dance with anyone but Brendan, not inviting him to lunch because I didn't want to give Warren false hope and then not telling Brendan why. "No," I say firmly. "Warren's a nice guy and all, but no. I never wanted to be with him."

"Are you sure? Because the way you smiled at him . . ." He looks down at the bedding. "It was the same way you smile at me."

My chest squeezes at the sadness in his voice, and I reach out and take his hand, lacing my fingers through his. "You must have been too far away to see clearly. Because *no one* makes me smile the way you do. I seriously never wanted to be with Warren. I promise. I actually kind of felt bad for him because I could tell he was into me, and I knew I'd never feel the same. Because, you know, I've been super in love with my best friend for a long time now."

"Yeah," Brendan says. "I don't think Jane was even that into me. I blurted out that I'm in love with you right after she kissed me, and she thought that was adorable."

I arch an eyebrow at him. "Seriously?"

Brendan smiles. "I know. I thought it was generous of her, since I was kind of a dick to her, too."

I cuddle into his side, and his body is warm and inviting against mine. I'm so, so glad he's here, and yet . . . there's still something bothering me, tugging at my mind. "Do you think," I start, steeling myself, "do you think you can really be happy with me, even if you never feel that intense passion that you felt for Candace?"

Brendan looks confused. "What?"

"Like, I know I'm not that sexy," I say. "I mean, I'm cute, sure, but I'm not, like, overtly sexual like Candace or Jane. Do you think that—"

"*What?*" Brendan's whole face scrunches in disbelief. "Who told you that?"

"No one. But I have eyes."

He gives me a long look, like he's horrified we're having this conversation, and my cheeks burn, and I try to think of something to say to change the subject, because really, what do I expect him to say?

"Um," he says. "You're sexy. You're so incredibly sexy. These last four months have been an intense trial of my self-control." His eyes widen. "And we had sex last night. Did you feel like I didn't want you? Like I wasn't into you? I mean, I know you were worried because you felt inexperienced, and I know I'm not always the greatest at—"

"No!" I say. "No, I definitely felt like you wanted me then. And later, you did say it was fantastic, which—"

"Which if anything, was a major understatement," he says, staring at me. "Okay. So you felt like I wanted you, and you must have noticed my persistent need to hide the evidence of how much you turn me on, like, ever since we started spending time together."

My cheeks continue to flush. "I may have noticed something a time or two. But you hadn't had sex in three years, and—"

"A *time* or *two*?" Brendan rolls over and looks down at me, propping himself up on his elbows on either side of my shoulders, and my whole body heats up. "I have had a constant case of blue balls ever since I met you, and that wasn't true for the three years before that."

I giggle. "That shouldn't make me as happy as it does."

He shakes his head at me, mock annoyance on his face. "Go ahead. Laugh at my pain. My literal pain, because I want you so bad and I haven't been able to express it."

I can't help but feel a little doubtful, even though I can tell that he means it. "But when I asked you how things were with Candace, you talked about this intense thing you guys had. And then I asked you if you could ever feel that for me, and you said no."

Brendan closes his eyes, and he's quiet for a minute. "What I meant," he says finally, "is that I don't want the kind of sick relationship with you that I had with Candace. I don't ever want to treat you the way I did her. If you need space, if you need to be away from me, I want to just give it to you. I don't ever want to be in a situation like that again, where things are so bad most of the time. I'm not going to do that to you. I can't, and I won't."

I run a hand up his neck, and he shivers. "I know you won't," I tell him. "I'm not worried about that at all." I can't take it anymore, having even these few inches between us. I lean in, and he leans in, and our lips find each other. It starts out gentle, soft, but as heat flares through me, our kisses quickly become all need and longing and fire, his hands in my hair, and mine at his neck, down his bare back, my body pressing against his—

Plastic coconuts. I make a little sound of surprise, because I'd totally—somehow—forgotten he was wearing big plastic coconuts. I burst out giggling, and he starts laughing, and we're just holding each other and laughing and so, so happy.

"As amazing as these are," I say, when my giggles have calmed down. "I think they're getting in the way."

"You didn't factor *that* into your fantasies, did you?"

"Rookie mistake." I trail my hands down along his side, feeling the muscles of his abdomen. I'm aching all over, but not in that sharp, painful, horrible way. "You know," I say, in between tiny kisses, our lips lighting against each other again and again. "I'm still technically a virgin. Care to help me with that?"

His breath catches, and he pulls back just enough to look in my eyes. "Do you really want to?" he asks. "Because I'd understand if you need more time, or—"

"I want to," I say, pressing my forehead to his. "Sooooo much."

He chuckles. "Yeah, me too."

I bite my lip. "Ugh, but we still don't have condoms."

His cheeks go pink. "Well . . ." He runs a hand through his hair. "I may have picked some up at the store. You know, just in case."

I laugh. "Had a lot of faith in the effect that coconut bra would have on me, huh?"

"Maybe I just really hoped that I hadn't totally screwed everything up with you, and that maybe I'd get the chance to be with you like this again."

I smile against his lips. "I think you should definitely take that chance now."

He clearly doesn't need to be talked into it; he draws me closer toward him, his lips against mine again. I may have kissed him before, so many times now—even just moments ago—but the fire of it, the longing, floods through my body just as hot, just as all-consuming as the first time, maybe even more so.

Because OH MY GOD I'M GOING TO HAVE SEX WITH BRENDAN.

Again and for the first time, all at once. I'm all giddiness and flame, and his warm skin under my fingers, his lips moving against mine—

It's only the beginning and already it's everything.

TWENTY-SIX

Su-Lin and Brendan

Brendan's hand cradles my face as we kiss, the other still propping himself up, and I sit up more so he can wrap both arms around me and put his hands on my body, because god knows my hands are going to be all over his.

He pulls back just enough, his hands tugging up my Cookie Monster shirt and tossing it to the side. And while I might have been embarrassed not long ago to be wearing Cookie Monster pajamas for this, might have worried it wasn't sexy enough, now I just want to laugh—happily, so happily—at how sexy it all is.

Me wearing ridiculous muppet character pajamas and him in a plastic coconut bra and somewhere on the floor is Ruby and Terrence, and it's like we're made for each other, Brendan and me. Like we belong together and always have. Like we belong to each other and always will.

The boy with the pink hair and the girl with the sock puppets.

I want to giggle with that swell of pure happiness, but his mouth presses against the tops of my breasts, and I let out a little moaning gasp as I sink back into the bed with him above me. He kisses a blazing trail along my breasts and down to my nipple, tugging it gently between his lips and tongue, and my breath catches. My body is light and sensation.

241

"So perfect," I hear him murmur against my skin, and maybe he's talking about my boobs, which suddenly do feel perfect, or maybe he's talking about us together, which definitely is.

I need to feel more of him against me, and that damn coconut bra—much as I love it—is in the way.

I reach for the strings, hoping to pull them apart with one confident, sexy tug, but the knot only winds tighter. I groan and he laughs, which makes me giggle again as I fumble to undo the strings.

Finally, the thing unties and the coconuts are tossed aside in the same direction as my shirt. His chest is pressed to me, his forehead against mine, his breath light against my cheek as he whispers over and over again how much he loves me. I whisper it back, again and again, like those words have been pent up so long, we can't get enough of saying them.

My hands can't stop roaming him, feeling along the lean muscles of his back and his abs, and oh, yes, it's definitely time to get those pants into the cast-off pile. I unbutton them and he slips out of them and now my fingers move down under his boxers. His whole body shivers and his breath catches as I stroke along the hard length of his dick.

Which I still don't know if he has a name for.

Should I ask right now? Or is this something that should wait until after—

His hands move back to my face, and my breath is stolen all over again as he kisses and kisses me, and my head feels swirly, and yeah. I can wait on the dick-related Q & A.

But Brendan's got his own Q.

can't believe I'm here with Su-Lin in my arms and her hands dipping down into my boxers, shivers running the length of my body. I can't believe she's forgiven me, and all I want is to make up to her all the pain I've caused her, to heal the cracks from all my stupid mistakes. The coconut bra didn't last long, but the perfection of Su-Lin's miraculous giggle as she pulled it off makes me feel like everything good in the world has settled right here. I can't get close enough.

She's never done this before, with anyone, and I'm getting a second chance to make up for being so inconsiderate last time. I take her face in my hands and kiss her and kiss her, and then, breathless, I whisper against her mouth. "Do you know what you'd like to do first?" I ask. "Or should I try some things, and you can tell me if you like them?"

Su-Lin lets out a little whimper, like she's remembering the things I've done to her before. "I just want to be with you."

"Yeah, okay," I say, slipping my hand down to the waistband of her shorts and pulling them off along with her underwear. "If you don't like this, or it makes you uncomfortable, tell me right away, okay? This is all for you, so there's no point in you suffering through it if it's not what you want."

Su-Lin bites her lip. "I want you to enjoy this, too."

I grin at her. "Oh, trust me, I am, and I will." I start by running my hands up the inside of her thighs, gently stroking her lips and exploring further. Su-Lin lays her head on my chest, gasping and panting as I slide my fingers inside her, shifting my palm up to rub her right where it makes her cry out. I work her gently, rolling her over so she's lying on her back on top of me. I move one hand up to her breast, massaging her gently both inside and out, jolts of pleasure moving through me as she writhes against me and gasps, and I'm so, so hard from the feel of her soft skin, the desperate way she's moaning. Su-Lin's legs spread apart and her cries grow more urgent.

She likes that. Which means there's no way I'm going to stop.

The transcript of my brain now would be something like this: My Brain, as Brendan gently rolls me over so I'm lying on my back on top of him, letting out a moan at feeling him so hard against me: BRENDAN.

My Brain, as he continues massaging my nipple and between my legs: BRENDAN.

My Brain, as my heels dig into the mattress, as I arch my hips up against the current building and building and building: OH GOD, BRENDAN BRENDAN.

That part wasn't just in my brain. I cry it out as each one of my nerves becomes a Fourth of July sparkler, my thoughts looping over and over. I spasm, coming completely, gloriously undone.

I shudder with the delicious aftershocks, feeling his heart slam against my back, murmurs escaping my lips that I'm not even sure are supposed to be words.

"I guess that worked," he says, and he's a little breathless too, and I think maybe some of those moans were his. I let out a shaky laugh and roll over to face him, my body still pressed against his.

"Yeah," I say, and I can't stop grinning, and I see that he can't, either. "That definitely worked."

Then I reach down and stroke along that hardness again. I'm definitely starting to feel like I'm getting pretty damn good at handling the hardware, so to speak, by the way his eyelids flutter closed and he groans deep in his throat. I would keep going, but he draws me close and kisses me again. He rubs against me right there—oh god, right there—but not inside yet.

I so desperately want him inside.

As one, we roll so he's on top of me.

"Are you ready for this?" he asks quietly.

"Yes. Please, yes."

He kisses me softly again, and then reaches over the side of the bed for the box of condoms, getting one out and opening the wrapper with way more skill than I managed with the coconut bra (seriously, did he take some Boy Scout knot-tying class?)

I stare at him, marvel at him. At the slight curve of his eyelashes, at the shape of his lips. At the line of his jaw and the blue of his eyes. At the light in those eyes, the intelligence and hilarity and bravery and sweetness behind them.

All things I had thought I'd memorized, for all the time I spent trying not to openly stare at him and probably failing. But I know now that he loves me and he wants me and it's like seeing it new, all over again.

He rolls the condom on and is back on top of me again, where I think he should always, always be.

He grins and I grin, and there's this moment where we're just looking into each other's eyes, and everything around us has disappeared and all I can see is him. All I ever want to see is him, looking at me like this, forever.

There's this long, brilliant, moment of anticipation, of love and need like I've never thought I'd know—and THIS IS IT THIS IS IT I'M HAVING SEX WITH BRENDAN—and then he's inside me and it's pure light and perfection and *us*.

I guide myself into her, and my whole body shudders with pleasure. I'm seeing stars, and I can't find my breath, and then we're moving together and crying out together and my mouth finds hers and we're connected, she and I, locked in sync in a way I've never felt in my life. I'm with Su-Lin, and that's exactly how things are supposed to be, how they were always supposed to be. We whisper and moan each other's names, and promises of love and desire and need that I never imagined she could feel for me the way I do for her. My whole body ripples with waves of ecstasy, and Su-Lin urges me faster, harder, pulling me deeper, and everything drops away that isn't me and her, and this incredible thing building between us.

"I love you," I whisper. "I love you, I love you."

"Brendan," she responds.

Then we're coming together, her frantic cries echoing mine as my vision explodes in a flash of bright light. We collapse together, and Su-Lin giggles the most miraculous of giggles, one I'm not sure I've ever heard before this moment. I wonder how many other variants of her laugh there might be. I want to spend the rest of my life discovering them all.

TWENTY-SEVEN

BRENDAN

"Mmmm," Su-Lin says against my chest. "Yeah, okay. That was intense passion."

"Right?" I ask. I tickle her side, and she squeals and holds me tighter, our bodies pressed together as we both come down from the rush of being together. "That was everything I imagined it would be and more."

Su-Lin sighs softly, and I kiss the top of her head. We breathe for a few more moments, and then she speaks so quietly I almost don't hear her. "Do you think you'll panic in the morning again? Need to pretend this didn't happen?"

I dig my fingers through her hair, combing out the tangles. "No," I say. "You're my girlfriend, and I'm not going to pretend otherwise ever again."

Su-Lin makes a happy whimpering sound. "You can say that word now."

"I can," I say. "Took me long enough."

"And not, like, a 'casual' girlfriend, right? Because I really hate that word now."

I grin. That feeling is mutual. "You are definitely not my casual girlfriend. You are my very serious girlfriend." A tremor runs through me, a tiny slice of fear that cuts through the glow of lying here, holding the woman I love. "I still might have panic attacks about it—I mean, I probably will, because it's me and I have panic attacks about everything." I take a deep breath. "I've put you through hell, and I'm sorry. But do you think that's something you can put up with?"

Su-Lin shifts on my chest to squint up at me. "Put up with?"

She says this in the same tone that I used when she suggested I might not feel *passion* for her, which was thoroughly ridiculous. But this isn't: "I'm always going to have these problems, you know? I'm always going to have an anxiety disorder. And the truth is, they can't kill me, no matter what they feel like. And they don't change that I want this, I want to be your boyfriend and be with you, but I know it's a lot to ask of you. My life isn't something I would want to live with, but I'm stuck with it and you're not and—"

"*Brendan*," Su-Lin says. She drags herself up so that her face is even with mine. "I don't *put up* with you. I *love* you."

"Yeah, okay," I say. "But you don't love it when I freak out and hurt you."

"No," she says slowly. "But I don't want you thinking that I'm wishing that your problems would all go away so that my life could somehow be easier."

I think that over, but it doesn't make sense. "Why not? I do."

She lays her head on my shoulder, her lips brushing my jaw. "I love you. Not some version of you that I hope will be all fixed some day. The more I'm with you, the more I experience what your life is like—I love you *more*, not less. And I don't want you to be in pain, so yeah, I hope things get better. But not for me. I'm happy with you, just as you are."

My whole body goes weak. I don't know how to believe what she's saying, but I believe she means it. And that, in itself, is a miracle. "Thank you," I say. "Thank you for waiting for me to be ready."

She smiles. "Of course." Then she giggles again. It's one of my favorite giggles—the one that means she has a secret that she's about to burst open and share.

"What?" I ask.

"So one of the things I was thinking last night, when I was . . ."

Oh, god. She could have been thinking any number of things, at any number of moments. I wonder if this is about the toaster and the random ding. "When you were what?"

There's a long pause. "When I had your dick in my mouth." More giggles.

I join in. "Okay. Do tell. What were you thinking?"

"First, I thought, oh my god, there's a dick in my mouth."

I close my eyes, groaning both from embarrassment and from the memory of what *I* was thinking at that moment. Or, more accurately, the way all my thoughts turned to mush, and all I could think about was how loved she made me feel.

"*Then* I was like, oh my god, it's Brendan's dick! In my mouth."

I laugh. "You really didn't have to do that—"

"I wanted to! But, um, I might have been overconfident, because I definitely didn't know what I was doing, or if it would even work, so I thought maybe I should stop right then and Google a tutorial—"

We're both laughing so hard now the bed is shaking. "I'm kind of glad you didn't," I say. "Though that would have been hilarious."

"And *then*—" she continues, and I am not sure how many thoughts a person can have while giving a blow job, "—I wondered if you had a name for it."

"Like, maybe I should have introduced you properly before you got up close and personal?"

"Maybe!" Su-Lin says, grinning. "So do you?"

"Ha," I say. "I do not. Candace did, but you really don't want to know what it was, because you will hate it."

She cringes. "Is it awful?"

I sigh. I obviously have to tell her now. "She called it the leash. Like, it's what I'm led around by."

249

Su-Lin wrinkles her nose at me. "I do hate that."

I love that she does.

"Was she really a bitch to you about sex?" she asks. "I mean, not just the breast thing, but other stuff, too."

"Yeah." I want to pull away from her. She knows a lot about the things Candace said to me, but this stuff embarrasses me more than most because I imagine some of it was deserved.

"Really?" Su-Lin says. "Because I don't have any complaints."

I smile, because god, I love to hear that. But what I'm about to tell her still fills me with so much shame. "Did I ever tell you the thing she said to me when I confronted her about sleeping with John?"

Su-Lin shakes her head, and she holds me tighter. Her body is basically glued to mine, and I'd be happy if she never let go.

I close my eyes. "She says to me, 'God, Brendan. Did you really think I could ever be satisfied with just *you?*'"

"Seriously?" Su-Lin says, a horrified look on her face.

"Yeah. But, I mean, she probably had a point. She shouldn't have cheated on me, but it's not totally her fault if I couldn't—"

"Stop," Su-Lin says firmly, her dark eyes locked on mine. She takes a deep breath. "Okay, I'm going to say something, and I hope you're not mad at me for it, but I need to say it anyway."

"Is it something bad about Candace? Because I can't imagine being mad at you for that."

Su-Lin props herself up. "I think Candace was abusive to you."

I shake my head. "No. I mean, it was bad, but—"

"I think," she says, biting her lip, "I think it was bad because it was emotional abuse. She was keeping you right where she wanted you, desperate and lonely. And yeah, maybe you didn't always handle that well, but it's because you were being deprived of basic things. Love. Security. Safety."

My mouth goes dry. That doesn't sound wrong, and now that I think about it— "My therapist said something like that, once. But I told her it wasn't true."

Su-Lin presses her forehead to mine. "I believe you when you

250

say you'll never be like that with me. Not like you were with her. It's partly because I think you're a different person now, but it's partly because I'm never going to do that to you. So whatever Candace said about who you are, it doesn't apply with me, okay? You are good and strong and amazing and I love you. I can't imagine *not* being satisfied by you. Okay?"

My eyes are stinging, and I lean up and kiss her. "Okay," I say when we stop, and I let out a sigh. "I told you that I wasn't sure that I'd been in love with Candace. And I don't know, maybe I was. But even if so, it was a sick, toxic love. And what I feel for you . . . it's different. I know it is because if you had really been into Warren, I would have let you go. It would have completely broken my heart, but what I really want is for you to be happy."

Su-Lin snuggles up against me again. "I am happy. The most happy I've ever been."

I believe her, because I feel the same way. But there's still this whisper in the back of my mind that she might not always be. I can say the word "girlfriend," but there are other words. "I know someday you're going to want more. More than being my girlfriend, I mean."

She reaches for my hand and squeezes. "You don't have to—"

I do. I need her to know. "I want that. I want all of that with you. I don't know when—or god, even *if* I'll be able to do that, for sure. But you need to know that when it comes to you and me, I'm in this for the rest of my life. I want to be with you, for always."

Su-Lin squeezes me so tight I can't breathe, but right now breathing feels highly overrated. "That's all I've wanted pretty much since the day I met you," she says.

"Me too."

Su-Lin giggles again. "I think I have a name for it."

Oh, god. "Okaaaaaaay."

"Big Gulp." She dissolves, and I laugh along with her. I'm not going to argue with that.

TWENTY-EIGHT

Su-Lin

We ended up deciding to book an extra night in the hotel. Partly because we slept in right up to check-out time, but mainly because neither of us had any inclination to leave that bed. There wasn't any panic, any pretending—just us tangled up together and happy and ordering room service for breakfast and then having more sex.

So maybe the movies didn't totally mislead me, after all.

We did manage to get some actual work done. Following the official launch, the views on the first eps were huge and just keep trending up. We picked through the advertisers practically shoving fistfuls of cash at us, approved some awesome social media ideas Emily had come up with and emailed at four AM (apparently from Jason's hotel room, her creativity stoked by all kinds of climbing, the email implied—so I guess *that* went well). People love the show. They love us. Everything is brighter and better than we could have imagined.

We celebrated with more sex—having Brendan as my boyfriend is *awesome*—and finally made it down to the convention hall to help Emily pack up the booth in the late afternoon. Jason and his guys were busy dismantling his climbing wall, but I was happy to see him stop by long enough to circle his arms around Emily's waist and give her a kiss with enough heat to challenge

Brendan and me for hottest couple on the con cleanup floor.

I'm pretty sure we won that award in the end, though.

But there's still another slight hurdle. And now, as I'm back home, standing in the kitchen and seeing Brendan's car pull up in the driveway, I feel that itch of nervousness under my skin. It's nothing compared to what he's feeling, I'm sure.

Today we're telling my dad about us. Yikes. Brendan dropped me off at home a few hours ago, ostensibly so he could run some errands for his mom and so I could spend some time with my dad before we drop this bomb on him. Really, I think Brendan needed some time to mentally prepare himself.

Brendan opens the front door and walks in, like usual. Since our studio is upstairs, he's over here so much we gave up the formality of him knocking by, like, week two. He had his own key by the end of the first month—given to him by my dad, actually, after Dad had to get out of his armchair to unlock the door the one time I wasn't home yet.

Dad *likes* Brendan. And Dad isn't exactly a scary guy. So it'll be okay, right?

I finish rinsing off my plate from lunch and hurry over to the entryway. Brendan's face is pale, and he's shifting nervously.

"Hey," I say, putting my arms around him. He relaxes against me just enough. "You're sure you're ready to do this?"

His fingers stroke along my back. "Yeah. Yes. I don't want to sneak around, and I definitely don't want to spend a night away from you." He gives me a nervous smile. "Pretty much ever again."

"Me neither," I agree. Which means we have to tell my dad. Whether we're spending the night here or at Brendan's place, he'll figure it out soon enough, and I think it would really hurt him that we felt we had to keep it a secret.

I'm convinced that would be worse in his eyes than me dating a very white non-Chinese guy. I just hope I'm right about that. But it's not like Dad could do anything about it even if he hates it. I'm an adult, for one, and I paid off the house and still pretty much support him and Lan with my *Sockwives* money, for another.

But his disapproval would hurt me, and worse, I know it would hurt Brendan, who is convinced no dad could ever like him dating their daughter, and has the tendency to think they would be right.

"He's in a good mood, at least," I say, though that's not saying a ton. My dad's usually in a pretty good mood. "He actually made—from scratch—these amazing pork dumplings with chili sauce. He said it was to celebrate our launch, but he and Lan had already eaten theirs by the time I got here and told him about it, so who knows."

"Your dad can cook?" Brendan looks skeptical, which is fair. Mei-Ling and I have been taking turns doing the cooking at home for as long as he's known me.

"Really well, actually. He just acts like it'll kill him to do so," I say with a grin. "I think he got sick of ordering from that sub shop down the street the whole time I've been gone."

Brendan's eyes keep drifting toward the living room where we can hear the sound of the TV, and he looks like he's about to do battle with a giant troll instead of talking to a small Chinese man in a beat-up old armchair.

"It's going to be okay," I assure him, though I realize it's a lot easier from where I'm standing. His mom was so excited when we called her from the hotel to tell her we were officially together, I half-expect a parade when I see her next. Okay, maybe not an actual parade. (Though how awesome would that be? Maybe I can convince her to toss some candy at us.) It made me feel so good, hearing her tell me how happy she was, and how much she loves me and wants to do a girls' lunch next week.

My own mom may not want anything to do with me, but Brendan's mom is incredible and wants me in her and her son's life. I just really hope my dad can help Brendan feel the same, at least someday.

Brendan nods and squeezes my hand. "Yeah. Right? Yeah." He lets out a breath, and we walk hand-in-hand into the living room.

My dad doesn't look up as we walk in, his attention squarely focused on the TV, where *Matlock* is speaking in front of a jury in his white suit. Lan is sprawled across the couch, tapping away at her phone, and doesn't look up either.

"Hey, Daddy," I say. "Do you have a minute?"

"For one of my beautiful girls? Of course." Dad says, still staring at the screen, reaching to the empty plate on the tray at his side. His fingers not finding a dumpling there manages to tear his attention away from Andy Griffith. Which is when he looks over at me and Brendan, a smile stretched across his face.

His gaze lands on our joined hands, and that smile slowly starts to drop.

My heart constricts on Brendan's behalf. I grip his hand tighter, so he knows I'm not letting go. No matter how my dad reacts.

"Daddy," I start, "we wanted to let you know that we're not just friends anymore. We're dating. Brendan and me," I add lamely after a long moment in which my dad doesn't react.

Dad just blinks at me.

"Brendan's my boyfriend!" I blurt out with a little too much enthusiasm. (Well, not too much for how I actually feel about this fact. But maybe too much for *Dad*.)

"It's about time," Lan says without looking up from her phone.

"I see," my dad says.

Brendan clears his throat. "Mr. Liu," he says, and I can feel his palm sweating against mine. "I know I wouldn't be your first choice for Su-Lin, or even close. But I love your daughter more than anything. And I promise I'll do everything I can to make her happy. Always."

Always. Hearing him say that still takes my breath away. I look up at him, feeling those happy tears prick at my eyes again.

Dad eyes us for another long moment, his brows drawn together. "So there's no Chinese in your ancestry at all? Not a single Wu or Chen?"

I start to glare at Dad, then see the amusement in his eyes.

Brendan must see it, too, because he lets out a relieved chuckle.

"No, Mr. Liu, I'm pretty sure not."

"Well, I suppose no one's perfect." Dad smiles at us knowingly, and I have the feeling he isn't exactly surprised by our big announcement. "There's some dumplings for you in the fridge, Brendan. And call me Arthur." He turns back to the TV.

"Thanks, Mr . . . Arthur," Brendan stumbles over the name, but he's clearly happy. Wes didn't get the "call me Arthur" until about a month before the wedding.

It's not exactly the thrilled reaction Brendan's mom had for the news, but for my dad, this is a pretty great outcome.

"Oh," Dad says, as we start to head out of the room, "So I know I'm not a creative genius like you two, but I have the perfect idea for a character for your show—*Matsock*." He points the remote at the TV, grinning. "Get it?"

Lan and I both groan, and Brendan laughs. "*Matsock*. I like it."

Dad winks at me. "He's a keeper, Su-Lin."

Don't I know it.

"That went surprisingly well," Brendan says quietly as we get back into the kitchen. He gives a confused look back toward the living room, like he's wondering if my dad was involved in some alien body-snatching incident while we were gone.

"I told you he loves you, Chinese or not." I wrap my arms around him. "Speaking of surprises, I've got one for you. Give me, like, ten minutes—have some of those dumplings!—then meet me up in the studio."

He raises his eyebrows, and I give him a quick kiss and then dart up the stairs.

I don't have too much left to prepare—I got most of it done as soon as Brendan dropped me off earlier today. But I strip down and get myself back into The Dress (complete with sneakers underneath). I pin up my hair sort of like it was the night of the masquerade, though I add some bright pink butterfly clips, just for fun.

Then I do a check of the studio. This room is where Brendan

and I spend the bulk of our time. Against the wall is a shelf crammed full of craft supplies, above which hangs the unicorn piñata I bought on a whim and which Brendan named Artistic Integrity, making her something of our mascot. There's a big comfy futon where we would usually be found draped over each other—probably way more than "just friends" ever should, looking back on it—working on scripts and editing. We do our filming in the basement, since there's less ambient noise down there. Brendan trapped the civilization of rats that were living down there when we first started working together—I like to imagine them building a barricade and one lone rat singing "Empty Chairs at Empty Tables" before they finally succumbed—and fitted the room with some foam that helps with the acoustics. All the prep work, though, we do up here. This is where the magic happens.

I'm hoping for a whole different kind of magic today. The studio is always a fun, happy workspace. Now, though, it looks totally transformed. I take in all my work.

Twister mat: spread out on the floor.

Strings of outdoor lights: hanging across the room.

Disco ball borrowed from Lan's room: lit up and spinning on the ceiling.

Bubble machine (because of course I have one): whirring away, churning out bubbles.

iPod: docked and ready to go.

I smile and turn off the overhead light. Perfect.

"Can I come in yet?" Brendan calls from outside the door.

"Yes!" I shout, bouncing on the balls of my feet and hitting play on my iPod.

He opens the door and stands there, stunned, his mouth dropping open as he sees the room, lit with strings of lights, sparkling in reflections off the spinning disco ball and glistening bubbles floating through the air. And me, in a dress of stars that I now know he really, really loves (both me and The Dress!)

"I thought we should get to have the prom and masquerade

we really wanted," I say, grinning at him. "No other dates. Just us." I gesture to the craft table, which now has a small stack of freshly-made Gudetama toast and full bottles of cherry vodka and 7-Up I grabbed from the liquor store next to Fong's. "And alcohol," I add.

Brendan laughs, a huge smile spreading across his own face. "This is incredible. I feel a little underdressed, though." He looks down at his *Sock and Order* t-shirt and slouchy shorts.

I grab his hand and pull him into the room onto the Twister mat/dance floor. "Aww, you look perfect."

He shakes his head and looks down at me with this expression that makes my heart beat harder and my whole body feel all warm and tingly. "No, that word is definitely meant to describe *you*."

I tug my lower lip between my teeth. "Care to dance?"

Just as he's about to take me into his arms, I start chicken dancing, and he grins and joins me, and we chicken dance to that Jonathan Coulton zombie song he loves. And then we fast dance to Kylie Minogue and Cardi B and LMFAO, doing every goofy, super uncool dance move we can think of to make each other laugh. We eat toast and we drink and we make a game of popping bubbles. And when that "So Close" song comes on, we dance again, together, his hand on the bare skin of my back and my head resting against his chest, where I can hear his heartbeat.

"This is exactly what I wanted at both those dances," he says, pressing his lips to the top of my head.

I pull back to look at him. "Sorry my stupid plan kept us from that."

"Hey, it worked, didn't it?" He smiles, then pauses. "Though that probably had a lot less to do with dating other people and lot more to do with dating *you*."

I raise an eyebrow. "So you're saying my plan worked despite itself."

"Maybe that's the true secret to *all* your plans," he says and laughs when I jab him in the side.

"Ah, maybe you're right." I lean back into him. "And I don't care, as long as it got us here."

He lets out a contented sigh that says he agrees, and we sway together a few beats more, and then he says. "So as much as I love the idea of transient living between my place and yours, with our families just outside the bedroom door, what do you think about looking for a place of our own?"

My heart skips about a half-dozen beats. "Really? You would be ready for that?"

He blinks, looking away. "Yeah. But I mean, if you're not, I totally understand—"

"Are you kidding? I would love that!" I jump up with a squeal and plant a big kiss right on him.

He chuckles, and his shy smile grows wider. "It might take a little while to find the perfect one, but given the initial success of the show, I think we might even be able to manage a down-payment on a little beach house. Something older, with character."

"A fixer-upper," I agree, beaming. "Where we can have a big window that faces the ocean."

"And a skylight under the night sky." He presses his forehead to mine.

I put on a mock-serious expression. "But we could probably only afford *one* beach house. We'd have to share. Think that would be okay?"

He looks into my eyes, and that smile of his turns my knees to jelly. "In my mind, there's only ever been one."

I can't stop grinning. I'm just so happy, thinking of our future. Part of me is dying to run to my computer and start looking at beachfront properties, but there will be time for that later, maybe after the song. Because right now I'm dancing in the arms of my best friend, my DIP, my boyfriend. The man who loves me and who I love, always always always.

And this is exactly where I want to be.

ACKNOWLEDGMENTS

There are so many people we'd like to thank for helping make this book a reality. First, our families, especially our incredibly supportive husbands Glen and Drew, and our amazing kids. Thanks also to our writing group, Accidental Erotica, for all the feedback.

Thanks to Michelle of Melissa Williams Design for the fabulous cover. Thanks to Dantzel Cherry for being a proofreading goddess, and thanks to everyone who read and gave us notes throughout the many drafts of this project—your feedback was so greatly appreciated.

And a very special thanks to you, our readers. We hope you love these characters as much as we do.

Janci Patterson got her start writing contemporary and science fiction young adult novels, and couldn't be happier to now be writing adult romance. She has an MA in creative writing, and lives in Utah with her husband and two adorable kids. When she's not writing she can be found surrounded by dolls, games, and her border collie. She has written collaborative novels with several partners, and is honored to be working on this series with Megan.

Megan Walker lives in Utah with her husband, two kids, and two dogs—all of whom are incredibly supportive of the time she spends writing about romance and crazy Hollywood hijinks. She loves making Barbie dioramas and reading trashy gossip magazines (and, okay, lots of other books and magazines, as well.) She's so excited to be collaborating on this series with Janci. Megan has also written several published fantasy and science-fiction stories under the name Megan Grey.

Find Megan and Janci at www.extraseriesbooks.com

The Extra Series

The Extra
The Girlfriend Stage
Everything We Are
The Jenna Rollins Real Love Tour
Starving with the Stars
My Faire Lady
You are the Story
How Not to Date a Rock Star
Beauty and the Bassist
Su-Lin's Super-Awesome Casual Dating Plan
Ex on the Beach
The Real Not-Wives of Red Rock Canyon
Chasing Prince Charming
Ready to Rumba
Save Me (For Later)

Other Books in The Extra Series

When We Fell
Everything We Might Have Been

Made in the USA
Coppell, TX
01 April 2022

75871156R00152